Margaret gard

GW00457083

CARREGAN'S CATCH

PIONEERS BOOK 2

PETER RIMMER

ABOUT PETER RIMMER

Peter Rimmer was born in London, England, and grew up in the south of the city where he went to school. After the Second World War, aged eighteen, he joined the Royal Air Force, reaching the rank of Pilot Officer before he was nineteen. At the end of his National Service, he sailed for Africa to grow tobacco in what was then Rhodesia, now Zimbabwe.

The years went by and Peter found himself in Johannesburg where he established an insurance brokering company. Over 2% of the companies listed on the Johannesburg Stock Exchange were clients of Rimmer Associates. He opened branches in the United States of America, Australia and Hong Kong and travelled extensively between them.

Having lived a reclusive life on his beloved smallholding in Knysna, South Africa, for over 25 years, Peter passed away in July 2018. He has left an enormous legacy of unpublished work for his family to release over the coming years, and not only they but also his readers from around the world will sorely miss him. Peter Rimmer was 81 years old.

ALSO BY PETER RIMMER

First published in Great Britain in November 2020 by

KAMBA PUBLISHING, United Kingdom

10 9 8 7 6 5 4 3 2 1

PROLOGUE

1896 — SOUTHERN AFRICA

*I*n 1890, the Pioneer Column, with Rhys Morgan, James Carregan and Willie von Brand as scouts, had marched into Mashonaland and proclaimed the territory under British rule. Three years later, war had erupted between the British and the native Matabele, and Rhys Morgan had died in an ambush on the ill-fated Shangani Patrol. Lobengula, the king of the Matabele, had died soon afterwards, and the strength of his kingdom had fizzled out in the damp mopane forests. Rhodes had come to power in the new country, which spread from the Limpopo to the Zambezi River.

With the war over, James Carregan and Willie von Brand had returned to their farm, Morgandale, twenty miles north-east of Salisbury. The original partnership of James, von Brand, Rhys Morgan, Michael Fentan and Captain Carregan, James's grandfather, was down to three. Fentan had died of dysentery in the Hartley Hills in 1891, searching for the gold that very few of the pioneers were to find. Three years later, James had gone to England to search out Rhys's natural son, Gavin, and Gavin's mother, who he found had since married and had two further children. She had woven her way back into the aristocracy where her father had thought she belonged, and had chosen, then, to ignore her natural son. To her, he had little value.

The Jameson Raid of 1895, which had seen 1,600 English filibusters trying to wrest the Witwatersrand gold from Paul Kruger's Transvaal Republic, had only just come to an ignominious end. Jameson had denuded Rhodesia of police and, shortly after, the Mashona, and then the Matabele, had rebelled. James and von Brand had gone with the Mashonaland Horse to Bulawayo to help suppress the Matabele rising. Unbeknown to them, Gavin Morgan, in company with Phillip Lagrange, had chosen that particular time to seek out his father's inheritance.

Gavin was as impatient as James was solid. As young as von Brand was old at fifty-five. He was then, and always was to be, a man in a formidable hurry. He had been born with everything wrong except an acute and mature brain, mature from circumstances far beyond his age, and a driving force that made him tear at life, tear it apart for himself and make it what he wanted, when he wanted and how he wanted. He had charm, too, which he used only when necessary. Used too often, he had found that it slowed him down. His passions were power and, even at the age of eighteen, women.

Like James seven years previously, he had sailed on the *Dolphin* from England with Captain Carregan and, during the six-week voyage on the clipper, had formulated the ideas that would force him through to what he wanted. His tutor at the public school he had been sent to with his father's money had seen the potential in Gavin's brain and had shown him, when Gavin was sixteen, the teachings of Socrates. Gavin had then learnt the need to know what was wanted before a purpose could be formulated and a progression made towards that ultimate goal. He used philosophy in a headlong, material pursuit which would have pleased neither Socrates nor Plato. He had been too young to understand the real meaning in what he had read. But, unwittingly, he had learnt the key to success.

James Carregan had not studied philosophy, a subject which he would have clearly understood. He had left England, and a rich father who wished to buy him everything, and fallen happily into the simple, rough life of a pioneer farmer. A degree in history had shown him too many of the wrongs of men. He was the very opposite of that which his father had wished to be above everything else. A snob. He was far more like his grandfather, a rough, basic, but very shrewd sea captain who was now nearing his seventy-eighth year.

Von Brand was a man of strength, physical strength. A German with two passions – a fight and a bottle. A big man, as big as his heart, he had hunted the highveld for more than twenty years with Selous and Hartley, and by himself, in fact in any way that would let him wander free and earn a living when it was needed. He had married, quickly and not very well, in Hamburg. He had forgotten what his wife looked like many years before.

And then there was Sonny Fentan, seven years younger than James, with a father and brother dead when he'd first met her in his search for Michael Fentan's heir in '93. Then her mother had died and there was only Sonny, free to choose her own husband and her own religion. By then she was older, her medical studies discarded, independent from the proceeds of her late brother's share in Morgandale, and she wished to do a little living.

PART I

1

Having been shot at twice on the road back, Phillip Lagrange, English of French extraction, was no longer sure of his liking for the country. Lagrange was a thin, indecisive man who could have been either a man or a woman. He was pretty rather than good looking and fell completely under the shadow of Gavin Morgan. He looked at Gavin, riding beside him, the amused expression still turning the corners of his mouth, and wondered if his friend felt emotions. It was unusual for him to think, and he smiled.

"That's better, Phil. Things are never as bad as they might be. You could have all this and be unaware of your female parentage."

"I don't think they'll have much time to worry about legitimacy," said Phil as he looked sharply at Gavin. Maybe the man had more sense of feeling than he thought. Maybe he could read minds.

"Another hour and we'll be in Salisbury," said Gavin. "Apart from a couple of stray shots they've all gone to ground. I'll bet the action's in Bulawayo. Luck is not ours, Phil, me lad. Not ours, it isn't. We'll be back in the Fort as raw as when we left it and not a mark to show for our troubles."

"Some would say our luck was good."

"Yes. Depends on how you look at it. Never mind, after Doctor

Jameson's raid we may yet have a full scale war."

"You're never satisfied."

"I have a feeling that to be satisfied is the worst thing in life."

FOR FOUR MONTHS Gavin Morgan had looked for a fight. It was in his nature to be aggressive. Lagrange followed and hoped that nothing would materialise. He thought he had kept his cowardice well away from Gavin's eyes and this was the only satisfaction that he had derived from the six hundred mile ride to Bulawayo and back. By the time they had arrived, the rebellion was over. Rhodes had parleyed with the rebel chiefs high up in the Matopos Hills and as usual Rhodes had succeeded. There are some people who always succeed even when it is clearly indicated that they should not. In Bulawayo they had found von Brand and James and with them had returned to what was left of Morgandale.

"WE'LL BUILD AGAIN," said James Carregan as he surveyed the remnants of his house. He was a lean man of twenty-eight, five feet ten inches tall and with clear cut features, brown hair and gentle, steel-blue eyes.

"This time we'll use rock and mukwa. Another year and the white ants would have crashed the place. Sundowners, Gavin, were accompanied by the falling dust of well-chewed roof timber. The real problem is to find out if we have any labour. The pleasures of Africa, but neither Willie nor I would wish for anything else."

"I could have done with sheets on a bed after four months campaigning," said von Brand. Von Brand was six feet two inches, bearded, with hair that had once been black but now showed traces of grey.

"Bring out the stores, Phil, and we'll drink to a new house. We'll camp on that flat piece of ground James once had the humour to call a lawn."

Gavin pulled at the head of the lead oxen. The wagon wheels

went slowly round and the two oxen, with covered wagon behind, began to move towards the level ground. Phil pulled at the second pair and the plodding pace was taken up in unison. The sun was down low, just high enough to see over the hills and the slopes that were covered with msasa trees.

"I don't think we'll rebuild on this site," said James, "so you may make your fire on my lawn."

"Very good of you," said von Brand as he eased his bulk into an oversize camp chair that he had taken from the lead wagon. "Wars and rebellions never have any respect for age. I said the war in '93 was enough for me."

"You enjoyed it," said James. "You don't look a day older than fifty-five."

"But I am fifty-five."

"So! You look your age. What better than to be what you are."

"Get the brandy, Gavin. He's becoming a bore. And to think that I've put up with him for seven years. Pity your father didn't live. Rhys Morgan was the only one who could keep him in his place, and, of course, that girl in Cape Town, but she's too far away for effective control. When are you going to convince her that marriage is the right thing, Jamie? Nothing like a marriage to weaken a man. Nothing like a little woman to keep him under control. What do you say, Gavin?"

"I prefer to keep them under control."

"Eighteen and he knows what to do with women. Oh, well, the tables had to be turned by a new generation. What do you do, Gavin, use the whip?"

"No. I just make certain that the one of the moment never means more than the one to come."

"You're hard," said Lagrange with a chuckle.

"That's what women say but they don't mean it."

"We've been in the bush too long, James," said von Brand. "The world is changing. Never mind, at twenty-eight you are young enough to change yourself. Hurt a good man and maybe he changes his attitudes towards women."

"I think we'll build the new house over there," said James, changing the subject and pointing to the side of a slope that looked out over the whole valley and the Morgandale Estate that they owned as far as they could see to the hills.

"That's a good site," agreed von Brand. "If we cut mukwa now it will be seasoned in a year and by then we'll have the house built and be ready for the panelling and mantlepieces. We'll need skins for the floors."

"Yes, and there isn't much game around here."

"Ah. But I have it," said von Brand getting up. "I know a place where the tsetse's still thick. There are elephant and every kind of big game. Selous and I have talked about it. Rhys knew it well. Last time I was there, the year before I came up with the column in '89, the hunting was how it used to be when I first came to Africa. That'll be it, Jamie. We'll show the boys the real Africa at the same time. There'll be good skins enough when we come back, and ivory. Skins on the floor and walls to tell of the last great hunt of Willie von Brand. A fine place for your grandchildren, James."

"I haven't found a wife yet, so I am not certain about the grandchildren."

"Give him a brandy, Gavin. He's talking like an old man. Granted he's been through the march, a war and now a rebellion, but I'll wager this is only the beginning of his destructive life. Say to yourself every night that you are but a fledgling and after sufficient time you'll begin to believe it, James."

James looked at him and said nothing.

"When do we start the hunt?" asked Gavin, handing around the brandy bottle.

"As soon as possible," said James. "In a week, hopefully, when we've found labour for ploughing. The ploughing will take a month and then we'll be back in time to plant the maize. They'll have cleared this rubble and prepared the new site over there. Do you like hard work, Gavin?"

"If it is profitable," he answered.

2

"Over there," said von Brand, pointing from where he sat on his horse, "is Mount Darwin. It is a sacred place to the Mashona. They say that the old kings of Monomatapa held court in the caves that burrow into the mountain. No one has ever found the caves but the legend persists. Selous gave it its new name. Incongruous, but a name. Some fifty miles further in that direction," he pointed to their right, "is the great escarpment that leads down to the Zambezi River. Here we are farthest from all the traders' routes and it is sparsely populated by the Shona. It is the last great hunting ground. Come, we'll take the horses a way up the mountain and I'll show you the game. From up there the grass will not obscure our view. There is great beauty to be seen. Oh, yes, James, this is the real Africa. I had almost forgotten what it was like."

For ten minutes they climbed up the slopes of Mount Darwin and they turned and looked back over the rolling grasslands and the forested hills, unbroken, virgin land that had never been tilled; herds of buck, impala, kudu and roan antelope grazed peacefully in the valley. Von Brand pointed out for them the buffalo, hidden among the msasa trees away from the sun.

"They will begin to move towards the waterholes when the sun goes down," said von Brand. "Then we'll hunt and afterwards eat. No, I was right. The game has not left Mount Darwin. It is sights like this that we saw every day. There are memories to be found for me in all that game. Maybe I am getting old. Nostalgia and getting old go together. No matter. I would not have changed it. We'll make a good camp and begin hunting tomorrow. If we keep a fire burning the lions and hyenas will keep away. It is like a holiday, James, after hunting Lobengula and then the rebellion. Why cannot men live peacefully among each other?"

"Because they like to fight," said Gavin. "Life becomes boring without something to fight about."

"I used to think the same. Maybe I still do."

"You will see his instincts for the gentle pleasures of life tomorrow," laughed James. "If the Boers fight the British he will fight and it won't worry him which side he fights upon."

"Humph," said von Brand and urged his horse down the slope.

The small troop of horsemen made their way into the valley of long grass and among the flat-topped foliage of the msasa trees. Small, multi-coloured birds, some with black tails as long as a man's arm, clung to the wands of flowing elephant grass and bobbed in the gentle breeze. James saw this but Gavin looked for game.

"THERE IS MORE comfort to be had from a camp fire in the bush than all the logs piled upon a family hearth," said von Brand expansively. "It enables one to belong to a very particular place and to ignore the surrounding darkness. The dangers are elsewhere for the moment."

They sat in silence.

"Now tell me, Phil," said Gavin softly, "where did your courage go today?"

"I lost my nerve for a moment," snapped Lagrange. "Is that a crime?"

"Leave him alone," said James.

"Courage is a strange thing. It only comes to some when they need it. You really surprised me, Phil."

"Just because you have no emotions or imagination."

"I don't see what my emotions or my imagination have to do with you dropping your rifle and then, with fear crawling up your backside, climbing up a tree. If James had swung round a moment later that buffalo would have had him and you didn't even warn him of the danger."

"I told you, I lost my nerve."

"Maybe tomorrow we should put you to a test to conquer this snapping of your nerve. To me this does not seem to be a good country for such behaviour. I have it you don't lose your nerve many times before you lose everything."

"A little fear is a good thing," said von Brand. "It teaches people to be careful. There are more reckless dead hunters than those who have climbed trees."

"And what about the hunters who did not have time to climb trees?"

"Every man must defend himself. And, anyway, the first time a wounded buffalo charges you is not the easiest time to show bravery. No one was hurt, so forget it. Turn the spit, James. Those steaks are burning underneath. After another three days' hunting, we'll have enough ivory and skins. By then our salt will have run out and we'll be unable to cure the hides."

The silence was heavy.

"Tell me about my father," said Gavin, sensing that he had taken the previous subject too far. He'd only wished to goad Lagrange into being the companion that he needed to carry out his plans.

No one answered him. James got up from his haunches and took the meat from the spit. He put it all into a billy can and offered them the buffalo steaks. They took them in their fingers and began to chew. It was rich and tough. James crouched down again and the flames reflected clearly in the steel-blue clarity of his eyes.

"There's no short answer to your question," he said, and went on chewing his meat. A log fell back into the fire and sent a shower of sparks up into the night. The cold settled on James and he shivered. His mind went back to the Shangani River and the battlefield.

"I met him in a tavern," said James. "Or rather I accosted him in one. I knew nothing of Africa and needed a sponsor to help me join the pioneer column that would take us up into the new country. Willie and Rhys took me in. You can say that we were never separated until Rhys was killed with Alan Wilson in '93. With our fourth partner, Michael Fentan, we put all our energies together and from this we established Morgandale, named after your father as the Fentan gold mine had been after Michael. We've prospered in wealth and spirit and we've lost two friends, but they'll remain alive in our memories for as long as we live. Maybe that is a good span of life if we live on after death in our friends.

'He was a good man, a good hunter and a good friend. If he had known you, he would have been a good father, too, as he wished to be a good husband to your mother. It is certain that your mother was the only woman in his life. You know this from when I came to England. You inherited one fifth of Morgandale. There are forty-eight thousand acres that will produce for all of us a good life, but I have the feeling we will have to fight for it many more times. We have already fought twice and that in four years. Those that have will always be subject to those that wish to take away. There is no permanent stability, no government that remains forever with perfect justice supporting the same man of property. If you are strong, you will hold what you have, but if you are weak then it will be taken away from you. This law has not changed."

"You have never told me the name of my mother," said Gavin very softly.

"No, and that I can never do. It is for her to tell you and for me to keep my word to both of them. She has another family and to merely sate your curiosity would unnecessarily hurt people."

"What type of person was she?"

"At the time she met Rhys they were both young and neither of them understood the responsibilities of life. Young love is a beautiful thing but it does not last except in the product of the origin. In retrospect, I do not believe that your parents could have made each other happy. Their origins were too different. There must be a similarity of backgrounds to make for a lasting compatibility. Rhys died holding a memory. That is enough. He left you educated and with something to start from. There are many with less than you have now. Enjoy it, as he hoped that you would."

"That I will," said Gavin and smiled to himself, and von Brand slapped him on the back to relieve the sentiment.

"Now, tell us how you two joined up together," von Brand said.

"Oh, Phil and I have grown up together. My foster parents were not well off and with me being sent to a different school to the other children in the street I made no friends at home. I met Phil at prep school. We went on to public school together, left together and come out here together. You can say that we have grown up used to each other. He has a progressive father to let him come to Africa, which is more than can be said for his mother. She is convinced that Phil will come to nothing. The two of us are after disproving the old wind bag, with no disrespect to you, Phil. 'Tea, Phillip,'" he mimicked, "'is something that one takes at four o'clock.' Enough to convince any level-headed son to go to Africa. She moves at a permanently adjusted pace and knows exactly what she will be doing at a quarter to three on any Thursday afternoon."

"Father gets away to his club," put in Lagrange, and this summed up his family.

"Do you have any brothers or sisters?" asked James.

"Two sisters. Both younger than me. They twitter and get along very well with Mother. In later years I am sure they will live to the same exacting order."

"Unless someone disturbs their equilibrium," said Gavin and the firelight showed up the amusement that sprang into his eyes. Von Brand saw this and raised an eyebrow.

"They are pretty enough and Louise at seventeen might even be classed as beautiful," went on Phil.

'You're right there,' thought Gavin, who had known the other side of Louise Lagrange for most of his life. A twinge of excitement, spiced with memory, surged through his body and immediately he wanted a woman.

"Maybe we should drink the last bottle of brandy," he said. After sufficient alcohol, the physical urge was deadened though the mental need sprung to greater life. He preferred the latter when he was away from women.

"Good idea," said von Brand, "Get the bottle, Phil."

Gavin knew why men drunk too much away from female company. It was the only escape they knew from the most powerful urge in man, the sex force, the power that drives men to greatness or to hell. He had taken his first woman at fifteen and since then it had become the dominating need in his life. It was this power that had convinced him that he must live near civilisation. Morgandale was good, as it was the foundation of his great idea, the one that had been sewn into his mind on the voyage out on board the *Dolphin*.

Gavin thought for some time in the stillness by the fireside and there concluded that it was necessary to put the second phase of, as he called it, his 'great operation', into motion. Over the six months of travelling, farming and hunting he had been able to think and write down in exacting detail all that was necessary to succeed in his plan. Captain Carregan had been convinced of the plan's viability and had backed up his talk with money, but it had taken Gavin six months of careful thought, planning, thinking ahead, seeing in his mind's eye the tasks, and the routes these tasks would take. And he had to be certain that James and von Brand would fit into the close-knit pattern of his 'great operation'. Having made up his mind, he leant forward.

"If war came," he said to James, "there would be a great need for shipping. There will be troops, stores, horses and all the paraphernalia of war. Ship owners will be able to charge what they like. In war, money is of no consequence."

"True. What do have you in mind?"

"Your grandfather. He has wealth and knowledge of the sea but no longer the youth to use them. He became a partner in Morgandale. Even with its great size there would not be enough room for you and I to run the same estate. Let us use our resources to the best for everyone. I have in mind a shipping company running out of Cape Town, with your grandfather providing the advice and experience. I'll provide the legwork and co-ordinate the operation. I may be young but I have grown up fast on my own. The new steamships must be bought. We must set up trading posts in Rhodesia and the other producing ports of the continent. We'll buy at source, use our own ships, and sell our own merchandise in England. If we buy without the use of middlemen traders and transport the goods ourselves we must always be cheaper than our competitors. And then, if war comes, we'll become rich. I say that the three of us here and your grandfather put our shares in Morgandale into a joint company. The *Dolphin* shall be put in as a fifth share and money borrowed against these assets to pay for the new ships. With your knowledge of the interior and where to buy, your grandfather's money and seamanship, and my energy, we can only make wealth. We have the proper ingredients for a partnership. Each man has his use in the scheme – he is worth something to the other."

"What about Sonny Fentan?" said James. "She's also a shareholder in Morgandale."

"What has she to offer the partnership?"

"Nothing. Nothing material."

"Well, then this is when we learn our first lesson in being hard in business. No person can expect something for nothing. You must prove a worth to receive a reward."

"What can I offer?" asked von Brand.

"Experience of Africa. You know the exact worth of these skins and ivory. You know whether they have been cured properly. You know what the farmers and miners will pay good prices for when we import goods on the return leg."

"And how do we sell in England?"

"I think your grandfather will know who will do that properly."

"Yes, he probably will," said James, smiling to himself. He was beginning to see something of Rhys Morgan in Gavin. He was also realising that some of Gavin's suggestions were concrete facts.

"I'll ask him to suggest a number of names and then visit them myself. If the person is watched carefully and then makes mistakes he can be discharged until we find exactly what we want. It is a question of organisation."

"It may sound simple when you talk about it," said James, "but there is a mountain of work, and organisations don't always run smoothly. In point of fact, they usually tangle themselves in knots, hey Willie?"

"Yes, you're right."

"Well then," said Gavin, "the most successful organisation, business or empire must be the one in which there are the least tangles. This is what we will strive for. We will think carefully before we embark upon any course. We will complete any task not only with perfection in mind, but with the will to be a little better than perfect. Not tolerate mistakes in ourselves or in others. We will not suffer fools, for their sakes as well as ours. A foolish man can change with dedication. We will define carefully our spheres of responsibility to ensure there is no overlap or gaps in our system. Above all, we'll study every task with a mind to finding a shorter route to its achievement, one that is less costly and always more profitable. And having made our money we'll use it in the pursuit of life. Not words of my own, but of my tutor, but they still say what I think is true of life and what I want from it in the ultimate. He told me that it was always necessary to have a definite goal. I have since tried to see my targets before I bring them under attack. Plato had the same philosophy, but he was in pursuit of goodness and I am at present in pursuit of wealth. Maybe, if one has sufficient wealth, one can afford to be good."

"Humph," said von Brand, clearing his throat. "And I was expecting to relax for the rest of my life."

"You would have grown bored," said Gavin quickly as he sensed agreement.

"What do you say to the idea?" said von Brand to James.

"I don't think it is up to us. The key is my grandfather. Have you spoken to him, Gavin?" James knew the answer as well as he knew his grandfather.

"It was his idea," said Gavin softly and with a smile. "We talked about it for six weeks on the *Dolphin*. He doesn't like the idea of retiring but knows that to compete he must go into steamships. He has the ideas but not the energy to put these operations into practice. That's where we come in."

"You're both right," said James getting up. "To solely rely upon the weather and this farm is dangerous. Having built it to what it is, we must use it to go forward again. We mined gold first, then we developed this farm and the cattle ranch outside of Bulawayo. The mine is finished and the cattle dormant for five years after the Rinderpest. And following Jameson's raid on Johannesburg, war with the Boers is inevitable, as is the outcome of such a war. Your only problem, Gavin, is that the war will be over so rapidly that you may not have sufficient time to reap the rewards. We may also have to fight. Have you thought of that?"

"If the shipping and trading operation has been set up correctly the fact that we may have to fight will not matter. The British base would be in Cape Town. The shipping line would require one of us to be there as much as possible. We will still make our profits, in or out of uniform."

"Do you mind if I have another piece of steak?" said von Brand. "I've become hungry. Come on, Phil, stop nursing the brandy bottle. This sounds like the beginning of an interesting evening."

"I presume my grandfather is talking to ship builders and banks at the moment?" asked James.

"I heard it rumoured that he was even talking to your father's insurance company. Three keels should have been laid some time ago. They will be launched in four months' time."

"You don't think one at a time?" asked von Brand.

"No. There is not sufficient time. Six months after the first launching there will be three more. We will have to work hard in peacetime to fill the holds of six ships. If we are all in agreement, it will be necessary to immediately commence the accumulation of non-perishable stocks in Rhodesia and the Transvaal. We must make contact with buyers and find out what they want and what they are prepared to pay. We'll need teams of oxen to move the goods to and from the railheads. We must always deliver on time and at the agreed price. If we are reliable, we'll be the only traders of our kind in the hinterland. Ultimately, we'll set up and man our own trading posts. The profit, right through from the manufacturer to the time it is retailed, will remain in our company."

"I presume you are now going to suggest that this particular hunt be terminated?" said von Brand.

"If we are all in agreement, then there is a great deal to be done. I would suggest that Willie stays in Rhodesia and begins taking options on raw hides, skins, ivory and the new tobacco they are growing near Salisbury. It would be good for you to make a list of any other commodity that is available. This information can be relayed to me in Cape Town by the telegraph. We will then look for English markets before we buy. Tomorrow, myself and James should set out for Cape Town with James going on to England to help raise the money for the ships. I'll set up the headquarters in Cape Town and arrange for docking, stevedoring, warehousing, repairs and, most important, crews. Our success will be in direct proportion to our ability to choose and motivate the people who will work for us. By the time the first steamship arrives I'll have set up a full chandelling operation. We will be self-sufficient. No middle men will make money out of our shipping line. Your grandfather, James, has set up a small line of credit with the Standard Bank in Cape Town. The operation will need finance for twelve months before we begin to see a flow of cash. After that, it will be a question of moving at a correct pace in relation to the trading opportunities."

"You have given this a lot of thought," said James. "I am surprised you did not mention it before."

"I wished to be certain that each of us could supply their part of the partnership."

"Yes, I see. A sensible precaution."

"Willie will be able to see to the crops and the new house. As Phil will not have to prove his courage immediately, I suggest he stays at Morgandale for a while and learns the farming and purchasing sides of our life. I am sure that Willie is a hard task master. When I've set everything up in Cape Town I'll need you there, Phil. James will be able to see Sonny Fentan as well. I don't believe she can control you, James, so this I must see. When we return to Morgandale, I would like us all to sit down and go through every detail of what I've written down. You hold a wealth of information that I need to know. Oh, and with James's permission as well, we thought of calling it Carregan Shipping. In time, of course, it will be the largest shipping line into Southern Africa, so it is essential to begin with a good name."

He smiled at them in turn and then they laughed.

"This reminds me of you, James," said von Brand. "To begin with, Rhys and I taught you what you wished to know and you followed behind, but not for very long. Looks to me as though we are now about to follow Gavin."

"It was a good idea, Willie. As to who is going to follow who depends on which one of us can run the fastest, hey, Gavin?"

"Carregan Shipping is going to make money," replied Gavin with genuine satisfaction.

"It may make money," said James, "but let us see whether it can make any happiness."

3

1898

"Ladies and Gentlemen," said Gavin Morgan as he raised his glass of champagne towards the calm sea and the three ships moving in line towards the harbour, where the quay had been set up with food and drink by the staff of the Cape Heritage Hotel. "I give you Carregan Shipping."

The two hundred people gathered to welcome the latest addition to the fleet raised their glasses and drank. Three of the younger women watched the Managing Director of Carregan Shipping in preference to the three ships which were at the end of their maiden voyages from England. Among them was Sonny Fentan. Watching Sonny watching Gavin Morgan was James Carregan. He was cold with jealousy. During three years of life in Cape Town he had never thought of this possibility and now that it was so obvious to him that his stomach began to twist, and with the movement, at thirty-one years of age, he saw the average woman for what she was, closing his heart once and for all to the utopia he had imagined existed between a good man and a good woman. Now he saw it all clearly. Women wished to be hunted, they wished to be stripped of their superior shell, they wished to be forced to the lowest level and made to enjoy the depths of their wildest imaginations. They were instinctively drawn towards the male who would let them be what they were and Gavin Morgan had no inhibitions.

Gavin Morgan liked women and as many of them as possible and preferably the most difficult to attain. Sonny had been difficult, but then he had enjoyed the ultimate seduction even more. He liked James but he despised softness, and in Sonny's hands James was weak and of little value to himself or to anyone else. Gavin saw it as a small, weak link in Carregan Shipping. Gavin still found Sonny amusing, but his physical urge for her had waned, as it did for all the other women that had come into his life. There was something to be taken from each of them and whatever this was he sucked it down to its depths. He never fell out with his women because he had never fooled them in the beginning. They knew what they were getting and wanted just what they got. Only a few had he been unable to satisfy, but even they were drawn along the path of satisfaction further than they had ever been drawn before. The very young ones thought of him as a potential husband, but then they were very young.

The three ships came into line ahead as they sailed for the quay. They were moving very slowly and James judged that he had sufficient time for a bottle of Piper-Heidsieck. He had never drunk deeply before but there were going to be many first times for him in the future. He had tried what he thought was the correct way and failed, and he would now see whether the wrong way would do him any better. He strode across to the awning which shaded four members of the hotel staff and a substantial supply of champagne. The bill would be quite exciting.

"Fill it up," he said, offering his glass.

"Certainly, Mr Carregan. This must be a big day for your shipping line. I can never before remember three maiden voyages terminating in one day."

"You will see more," said James, smiling at him as he took the full glass, "and each of the ships will have a green funnel embossed with a dolphin. Mr Morgan and I have only just started competing with each other."

"Excuse the impertinence, sir," the waiter said politely – it was part of his trade to talk. "But I thought you were partners?"

"Yes. The best type of competitive partners. The type that makes money. Or so it has done up till now, hey Willie?" Von Brand had his glass out for a refill. "I'll bet you never imagined this eight years ago when we were seen off at the station, brass band blaring and newspapers hoping for blood."

"Thank you," said von Brand to the waiter. "No, and I feel damn stupid in these clothes."

"You look it, Willie, but Morgan's orders are Morgan's orders."

"It's some distance still, but isn't that your grandfather on the bridge of the *Ester Carregan*?"

"Must be. They don't have Commodores that old normally."

"What age is he now?"

"Eighty next month."

"Maybe as well that he's retiring."

"He doesn't think so. Says Gavin has given him a new lease of life. He's right on one point. None of us have been the same since those two boys found us in Bulawayo."

"He did what he said he would do."

"Make us rich?"

"And that we are, Jamie. It's positively disgusting."

"We've all worked our part."

"That was the cunning of him. To see from the start that we would all fit together. He knows how to get what he wants out of people. How big is the party going to be for his twenty-first next week?"

"As big and as ostentatious as I can make it."

"Not like you."

"No, but it soon will be like me."

"What's bitten you?"

"Sonny," said James. "He even made me see Sonny for what she is."

"I didn't want to tell you."

"You should have done."

"No, James. You never tell a friend that he's making a fool of himself. Especially over a woman. By the way, have you noticed how different women look at you when they know that you are rich? I might even try my luck myself whilst in Cape Town. A bit out of touch – thirty years out of touch to be exact."

"You do that, Willie. Now, let's have another drink. Why is it that it takes so long to dock or sail a ship?"

"It's like a woman," said Gavin, having heard the last sentence. "You have to lure them in and then lure them out again. They normally take longer to go out than to come in. By the way, it looks as if we're going to get our war sooner than we thought. Kruger has been given another ultimatum. No doubt he'll clutch his Bible and gun and tell the British to go to damnation. He remembers Majuba. If they can keep their tempers from boiling over for another six months, I'll have the twelve ships I promised myself. I think even now we should stockpile in Cape Town. The interior will become difficult."

"Would you be kind enough," said James, "to stockpile some of this champagne? I'm beginning to find a taste for it."

Taking no notice of James's statement, Gavin looked around and said, "Pretty, aren't they?" He was smiling.

"The women or the ships?" answered James.

"Both. Mingle with the guests," went on Gavin more seriously. "This is not just show. We have here every leading merchant in Cape Town. Over there is the one and only competitive shipping line. We must buy him out. That way we only compete with the British lines. How long do you think the war will last, Willie?"

"If it comes? Six months. Don't underestimate the Boers."

"That should be long enough, though I'd prefer it to carry on a little longer. Sonny is looking particularly attractive today, don't you think, James?"

"I thought the one over there quite acceptable."

"A little coarse. There is more bosom out than in. The more obvious they are in public, the more inhibitions they have at home."

"You think so?"

"My statistics have proved it to me."

"You run statistics on women?"

"Of course. It saves a lot of time. You have a greater chance when you are pursuing the type that would like to be pursued by you. There is no one man that all women like. Now, you see the one over there? Small girl, very neatly built. She is a nurse. Good family, but they're six thousand miles away. Now, I would say that you were for each other. She prefers the older types. She says I am a little too obvious, a comment for which I was grateful, as every man can learn from his mistakes. Come let me introduce you to her. Her name is Virginia. Virginia Webb. A nice girl. Twenty-one. Will you excuse us, Willie?"

"You don't think Sonny will object?" asked von Brand.

"They are not engaged to each other, is that not so, James?"

"That is so, Gavin." Gavin and James looked straight at each other. James smiled first and easily. Gavin forced a smile onto his face but his eyes, dark brown, showed clearly for once that he was slightly off balance. Then he understood, and the expression in his eyes changed to the one of understanding followed surprisingly by one of relief. Gavin hoped that James had at last seen the way to avoid the pains and problems of letting the woman have control of the relationship. Maybe, having been shown Sonny as just a woman, James would treat them with less reverence and realise that if one created problems there would always be another.

This philosophy, as Gavin put it to himself, was one of always remaining in control of any female situation and being prepared, at any time, to move on to another woman. To need women was an integral part of his driving force, but never to need just one, always two. The understanding of this differential in the relationship to women he counted as the first rung on the ladder to power and the first step in preventing the inside of your life being shattered by a cause that had grown beyond your control. For this, with relief, he smiled at James. A cornerstone of Carregan Shipping had become, he hoped, that bit less vulnerable.

They walked among the guests and the waiters that were

topping up glasses. Gavin checked one of the bottles to make certain that it was properly cold, and, satisfied, nodded to the waiter.

"You amaze me for a man of your age," said James.

"You amaze me for one of yours."

They both knew what the other meant and chose to ignore any continuation of the subject. James looked up at the awning. Without the cool breeze coming in off the sea, and the shade, the heat would have been unbearable. James smiled at the chairman of the opposition line as they passed.

"Not often I welcome other people's ships," he joked. He was a little drunk and not holding his drink very well.

They walked on.

"You've got to be able to hold your drink in business," said Gavin as a quiet aside to James.

"Essential," said James, "with luck, that one will make a fool of himself. With all the right people watching it will be good for business. Our business."

"I'll tell one of the waiters to keep his glass topped up."

"Should help."

"Hello, Virginia. Are you enjoying yourself?"

"A little lonely, but otherwise, yes."

"This is my partner. I wanted you to meet him. James, this is Virginia. James Carregan. Virginia Webb."

James took a white gloved hand in his own. Gavin was right. There was something different about this one, in the eyes. They looked straight at you and did not try to look away.

"You are both very young to have such a shipping line."

"Gavin is young. I make up for his age."

"But you cannot be too much older than Gavin."

"Ten years, madam."

They smiled at each other. Gavin excused himself.

"Do you know Gavin well?" asked James.

"Yes."

She continued smiling. He found it easy to smile back.

"Maybe we should have another drink," she said. "You do not seem to have a glass."

"All right. And then, a little way away from the crowd, we can have a better view of the ships and my grandfather. He will have a thirst when he docks, as will the captain of the *Annabel*, Hal Fincham. He and my grandfather have been at sea together for sixty years. They're both old but don't underestimate them, especially when it comes to the drinking."

"What is the third boat called? I can't quite read its name."

"That one is the *Mary Carregan*. She's named after my mother, who died when I was young. The *Ester Carregan* is named after my sister. She became Lady Grantham a few months ago when her father-in-law died. Charming man, but I cannot see his son doing much as the seventh viscount. Her husband lives off my father's money."

"Your father has money as well?"

"Much more than me."

"You are becoming more interesting."

"Up till now I have never had very much interest in money. But something happened today which has changed my mind. Here, have a glass of Piper-Heidsieck."

"Thank you. And what happened today?"

"Do you really wish to know?"

"Not if you don't want to tell me."

"Enough to say that I am free of an image that has stayed with me for several years." He was trying hard to convince himself and not to think how he really felt.

"A long time."

"A long time

"Cheers."

"Cheers."

"Now tell me," she asked. "After whom is the second ship called? Gavin says you insisted on the name because you liked the sound of it. Does *Annabel* have a meaning?"

"Yes."

"But you won't tell anyone what it is."

He shook his head gently and sipped at his champagne.

"I like secrets."

"So do I," he said. "And I like to keep them."

"Do you have a home in Cape Town?"

"Not until now, but I have in mind building myself a house."

"Gavin has the same idea."

"You know a lot about him."

"I told you I knew him well. For so young a man he is surprisingly mature."

"You prefer older men yourself?"

"They know how to treat a woman. Properly."

"And how is a woman treated 'properly'?"

"Unless you know, it cannot be explained. It is like saying that a man is attractive. You can say that he is well-mannered, slim, with a strong bone structure, but it will still not necessarily describe him. There are many men of that description who are positively unattractive. When I say to another woman that a man is attractive she will understand me if she has the same taste in men as myself. So that when I say that I like to be treated properly and you understand what that means and your knowledge of 'properly' is the same as mine then we have an understanding."

"It depends on how you interpret the word 'properly'. In that context it can have the opposite of meanings. To be looked after properly or well or to be looked after in a proper fashion."

"There. You see. It is a matter of individual interpretation."

"I think I know what you mean."

"I hope so," she said.

They looked at each other in silence for a moment. She made her eyes grow larger under the scrutiny.

"The *Ester Carregan* is about to dock," he said, looking away. "Will you excuse me, I have certain duties to perform despite the party atmosphere. Will you be at Gavin's twenty-first next Friday?"

"I've already received my invitation. In person."

"Yes, well, I look forward to seeing you there. In person."

Even as he walked away towards the large brightly painted ship that was edging its way towards the wharf, she watched him carefully, with the tremor of a smile playing around her mouth. Sonny Fentan watched as well, and though she shrugged her shoulders she felt dissatisfied, as though she had had something that belonged to her taken away. She continued with her conversation and then glanced across at James. He somehow looked different even with his back to her.

James watched the gangplank being moved into place. When it was secured, he was the first to take a grip on the two railings and move up quickly to the side of the ship. His grandfather was waiting for him as he stepped onto the deck.

"A slight different thing, lad, since ye first stepped onto one of me ships," said the captain. "That first time yer were more frightened than the ship's cat."

"How are you, Grandfather," said James, shaking the old man's hand with affection. Then they hugged each other and stood back to have another look.

"I'm well, lad. So's Hal. Or he was when we left the Clyde. What's all this shindig on the wharf?"

"Welcoming reception. Publicity. It will all be in the papers tomorrow. The big merchants are here as well."

"Good for business?"

"Yes."

"Gavin's idea?"

"Yes."

"Bright lad. Eye for the opportunity. Needs keeping in hand, mind you. Same as Hal. Always have to keep a strong hand on his shoulder. He was bad with the girls when he was young too. Yer father sends his regards. Not well these days. It's living by himself in the west wing of that ruddy mausoleum that he built for 'imself. Yer sister's 'ad another baby. Son this time. Makes ye laugh, heh. Me, the great-grandfather of the eighth Viscount Grantham. No mind. It was what yer father wanted. Whether it's all what Ester wanted is another story."

"She wanted it to begin with."

"That's how most of the worst things in life begin. Come on. Let's get down and try some of that champagne. I can sense it's cool from here. Don't introduce me to too many people. How's Sonny?"

"All right."

Captain Carregan looked at him and shook his head.

"Oh well. It had to go one way or the other. Nice girl; liked her. Missed her chance. Probably won't get another as good. Now, give me yer arm. Not as steady as I used to be. Make it look as dignified as possible. That's it, me lad."

They reached the ground without difficulty and, once on a level where his knees were more certain of holding him upright, Captain Carregan took brisk steps towards the nearest waiter with a tray. Gavin and Lagrange moved to greet him but he had drunk the first glass of cold champagne before they could shake his hand.

"Nice party," said Captain Carregan. "Hal will like it. There he is. Beautiful. One year off eighty, brought up on sail, and he brings in one of those steam ships with hardly a bump. Well, almost," he finished as the stern of the *Annabel* smacked the wharf head and sent a tremor along the wooden planks and among the guests.

"That's my Hal," shouted the captain. "Knocking the ruddy wharf down in his hurry to reach the champagne."

Everyone laughed and the Captain winked at Gavin.

"Must think quick," he said, and as if in answer a voice came across from the ship: "Ruddy steam engines." The guests laughed again. By the time Hal Fincham had found his land legs, the party was well into its second stage.

"JUST KEEP THEM DRINKING," said Gavin to Lagrange. "Tell the women to circulate. The ten of them are adroit at keeping out of trouble. We want our friends to ogle and imagine they were near to success. Afterwards, they will associate us with something that they want."

"You've thought of everything," said James.

"It is all the small touches put together that make an important whole. They would prefer to talk nonsense with one of those girls for half an hour than to talk business with you or me to make them a thousand pounds."

"Who are these girls?"

"Friends of mine like Virginia Webb. Nice, well-spoken girls who are poor but would prefer to be rich. In this society they have a chance of meeting wealth, so they come along for their sakes as well as for mine. Not all the rich men are that old. Take you for an example. But it's mainly the good time they enjoy. Better being one of that crowd seeing in the new ships and being envied by friends who never met that grain merchant over there, for instance, than sitting at home and feeding a good-looking clerk on your own or your mother's coffee. Then there are my own parties. The smaller ones that I throw for my own enjoyment. You must come to one."

"I might even start throwing them myself. I understand from Virginia Webb that we are building our own houses. Where is yours?"

"Ten miles down the coast road. Just below the last of the Twelve Apostles. I bought the cove and the surrounding hills from the local farmer. The land was no good for sheep. He thought I was particularly stupid building a house so far from Cape Town but the scenery is breath-taking. I'll create a home that everyone will wish to travel ten miles to see. During weekends I'll have it full of house guests. When the war begins we'll be able to entertain the more important military. What we are doing today, James, is a mere nothing to what we must do in the future. It is one thing to have the transport available and another to use it to the maximum profit. And it is profit we want, not just turnover. We need an administrator, by the way. A good accountant. The detail side of the company is becoming too much for three people. Even with Phil working to capacity we are still not watching every detail. We must work on a plan for separating the work. Someone just to check Willie's arithmetic would help, hey Willie? Hell, but you could not have added up figures since you left Germany."

"I haven't."

"Every man to his own job. The trading network you have set up is nothing short of brilliant and the feeder wagon services from the rail heads are the best in Africa. With the new ships, we'll be able to go into Lourenco Marques to trade with the Boers. A pity we'll not be able to do this once the war starts, but we still have time to make something out of them. They're bringing in as much along that railway as possible before the gate is closed. With the new rail open to Beira we'll be able to trade with Rhodesia around the back despite whatever happens in the war."

"Unless the Boers raid Rhodesia," said von Brand.

"Too far from home. The Boers won't go far from their farms according to my information."

"Probably not," agreed von Brand and took a sip of his drink.

"Your champagne has turned to a dark brown," said Gavin in mock amazement as he looked at von Brand's drink.

"You mean my champagne has turned to brandy," answered von Brand. "Champagne gives me indigestion."

"Me too," said Captain Carregan and winked. His champagne was the same colour, as was that in Hal Fincham's glass.

Behind them, the *Mary Carregan* docked and was tied up to the wharf.

The two old men began walking towards her. The voyage was over. James made to follow them.

"No. Let them say goodbye alone," said von Brand as he caught James's arm. "They've come a long way together and I think I know how they feel."

They watched them walk away from the guests, up along the wharf, until they reached the bows of the *Mary Carregan*. They held up their glasses, first to themselves, then to the ship, drained them and threw them hard at the steel plates of the hull. Some of the guests were watching and heard the faint tinkling of breaking glass above the conversation. The two seamen put an arm around each other and came back down the wharf. Captain Carregan stopped just short of the first guests and held up his hands for silence. The noise subsided and everyone turned in his direction.

"That, ladies and gentlemen, was me last voyage," he said in a strong voice despite his age. "After sixty-seven years at sea, sixty of 'em with me good friend Hal Fincham here, I've come to land. If any of ye can look back when yer my age and see the years behind as good as the ones I've 'ad, then they'll be lucky. At seventy-seven I came into this venture. At eighty I deliver them my twelfth ship. It's what I promised. When we know who the new commodore is going to be, we'll have another party to celebrate 'im coming in instead of me and Hal going out. Meantime, drink with me. We're going out the two of us like all good seamen on shore leave. And that's drunk. Two drinks, waiter, and make them brandy. I'm not too good on champagne."

The glasses were filled and carried to the captain and Fincham. The captain raised his glass.

"To the *Ester Carregan*, the *Annabel* and the *Mary Carregan*, God bless 'em and Lord help the crews from those confounded steam engines. To Carregan Shipping."

They all drank and a good many spilt wine down their fronts in their drunkenness, their mouths not being quite where they had thought them to be.

"I've got it," said Gavin in a soft voice that could only be heard by James. "Annabel was the name of my mother."

"You're really quite quick today," said James and raised his glass to Annabel Crichton's eldest son.

4

1899

"I think," said James, "that it is quite beautiful." He sat his horse and looked around him. Below was the cave, the sand, white and gently lapped by a blue sea, patterned by the currents and pushed shoreward by the tide. Rocks, great giants of rocks had been tumbled from the hills and mountains that towered above the sea in their massive show of force and protection. The sea went out forever and sparkled with a metallic sheen from the sun, hot but not unbearable. A miniature of the great Lion's Head that watched the main harbour ten miles behind them watched the cove and the workmen scurrying over the almost completed building. Gavin and James were high up the protecting hill and heard only the echoes of the drifting voices through the heat.

"It is necessary to have more than wealth, James," said Gavin. "It is necessary to have a quality of life, and such quality can only be made by yourself."

"Where did you learn such sentiments? They seem to be contrary to everything else by which you live."

"I had a tutor who made me read philosophy. I only understood some of it. I try to use the philosopher's teachings in whatever I do. A man must have contrast in his life. If business and wealth is a strong power then it must be balanced by scenery such as this. On this hill there is peace in everything, including me. Do I make sense?"

"Yes. You just surprise me. If I had not known your father I would not have believed there was such feeling inside of you. Rhys was the perfect romantic. Some of it must have gone down into you. Can you afford a place like this?"

"Not at the moment but it will ensure that I strive still harder to pay for it. The bank gave me a large loan. They are impressed by the balance sheets and the growth of Carregan Shipping. Oh, and they agreed to lend you the same amount. Build yourself a mansion, James. It will be good for your soul."

"I thought I'd build my last house on Morgandale after the fire. Maybe I should. I have better energy for the shipping line than I do for building things for myself. It was the same on the farm."

"How did you find Virginia Webb?"

"Why do you ask?"

"Lack of good women has something to do with the state of mind of which you complain."

"I found her well. She enjoyed your twenty-first. I took her home and wished her good night. Yes, she was well."

"You must build your own house and then they will not have to go home after the parties."

"People will talk."

"To hell with people. They're jealous. Bring in an old housekeeper to chaperone. Make it look decent from the outside. What you do inside is your business. This Victorian trappery is nothing more than a façade. Take any person and tell them not to do something and they'll want to do it even more. I've seen things you wouldn't believe, James. Right here in Cape Town. And they're nice girls. It's just that we all have imaginations and sometimes we have the chance of putting our thoughts into practice. Do you like the sweep of the hill down to that rock strewn island? The cormorants breed on the island. You must begin to live, James. We're young and rich and obliged by the nature of this to do something about it, to do everything about it, in fact. Soon after the house is completed I shall buy myself a schooner. It will look well in that bay."

"And how do you intend to pay for the boat?"

"By then, war will have broken out and three more ships will have joined Carregan Shipping. We're rich now, but when war chases up the freight rates and inflates the price of everything we have in our warehouses there'll be no comparison."

"If there is a war I shall return to Rhodesia."

"Why?"

"To rejoin the Mashonaland Horse. At home, we are civilians first but soldiers second. They may not have Willie in the army anymore because of his age so you'll have him to maintain the trading posts. Phil, I don't know. That will be up to you. Running a shipping line would be considered an integral part of the war effort. I would suggest you design yourselves a uniform. You may feel uncomfortable in civilian clothes."

"I shall be captain of my schooner."

"Make sure you have a qualified sailor as well."

"It will not take me long to learn."

"No, I doubt if it will."

"You are right about the uniforms. The right image in everything is important. They must be worn a few times at sea."

"That bay down there will be rough in winter."

"Powerful, too. Why haven't you seen Sonny recently?"

"Has that anything to do with you?"

"Only that she asked me to intercede for her."

"I was naïve, Gavin. This shipping venture of yours showed me just how much I had imagined my life related to one woman, a perfect woman, and one to whom I would be the only one in her life. Look around you here. There is a tangible perfection in beauty such as this bay with its crowding mountains. It is there, out there, and its total beauty is shown to us on the surface and we know there is nothing else and that it will not change like a chameleon before our eyes. We can fasten ourselves to this bay and be certain of its constancy. There will be wind and sun, rough and smooth seas, but when the tempers have fallen, and the day is like this again, the bay will be exactly as before. Even if there is a little storm damage it can be exactly repaired.

"I hoped to find such tranquillity with a family on Morgandale. I'd hoped that Sonny Fentan would form the other part of that life, but then I came here and became aware of the reality. People are not honest with each other. They're not satisfied with normality. The utopia that I envisaged would have been boredom to Sonny. She enjoys the game of making men's blood boil and I have every reason to believe that she has made some of it boil properly. With me, she would have been safe, as I would not have known the difference between a virgin and a whore. She did not want me then but she felt that when she grew older I might be necessary; in her own society she would be too notorious, but poor old Jamie wouldn't know what they were talking about. Security would have been bought for the price of a little boredom and I might just have lived in my fool's paradise forever.

"But life is not like that, and I thank you, Gavin, for ensuring that I did not find out the facts of life too late. I was a farmer, and before that I was at Oxford. Of women I have only known Sonny. Now, yes, she would like to come running back as she will always want what she cannot have – so do we all. She will find a husband. She is rich enough with her fifth share in Morgandale. I hope that when this change in our relationship has been established that we can retain a strong friendship. No, I want someone a little more constant for a wife."

"If you can find one like that, she'll have as much emotion as that piece of granite over there," said Gavin sourly.

"True, but that granite does not do me any harm."

"Hell, James, life must have fire. It must have its heights and its depths. There can be no constant flow of mediocrity. Anyway, that is how it is for me. In your frame of mind you must see more of other women. When this house is finished next month we'll have a small and intimate party. If I may, I'll invite the guests. With luck we'll see the reality of people. Ideals are all very well to look up to but you can't go on looking upwards in life. You have begun to go round the one side of a circle, James and when you have travelled the distance you will be back right here, mark my words. Now, do you think I should plant the Cypress trees to the left of the house or to the right?"

"I don't think you should plant them at all. I prefer blue gums."

They both laughed.

"You're right, James. You can't tell anyone how to run their lives."

"I would like to have met that tutor of yours."

"He was a great man."

"I can believe you."

"How is your grandfather enjoying retirement?"

"He has become his age. No, they enjoy themselves, the two of them. They drink each night in the Harbour Tavern and many of the sailors have known them for years. Maybe I should get on with my house so that they have somewhere permanent to live. If I am forced to return to Rhodesia for a long time they can look after the house. There will always be that housekeeper you recommended to cook for them. The new commodore is good. Wilkins will be able to handle the fleet in an emergency, and it will never come to a naval war as the Boers don't have any ships. The line is in good shape thanks to everyone's energies. Phil surprises me with how much work he can get through. I think he is better at the paperwork than he is in the field."

"We shall see."

"Don't expect too much from him, Gavin. He may just be your one blind spot. I hear his eldest sister is coming out for a visit."

"Yes. I hope the house will be finished for her. She may even arrive in time for our party."

"I thought this one was prim."

"Oh, I wouldn't say that."

"You know her that well?"

"It depends how well you mean by that."

"And where will she stay?"

"Down there."

"I see."

"I very much doubt if you do. We'll invite Sonny that night as well, and Virginia Webb. Don't expect too much. Good parties must be spontaneous. You'll be quite surprised at Louise Lagrange at a party. So would her brother be if he were invited, which he certainly is not."

"You have whet my curiosity."

"So did you with the *Annabel*. Unfortunately, there are a lot of people who carry the Christian name of Annabel. No matter. One day I'll find out."

"You will be pleasantly surprised."

5

"War is glamorous until the fighting begins," said Lieutenant Colonel the Honourable John Gilham to Oswald Grantham as their ship sailed purposely towards the entrance of Cape Town harbour. The officers, men and horses of the Sixth and Ninth Queen Charlotte's regiment were aboard HMS *Caithness*. They passed a heavily laden freighter going out in the opposite direction and Oswald Grantham squinted against the bright sunlight to read the name *Mary Carregan*.

"Must be an omen," he said, "but that boat over there is named after my wife's mother. Belongs to Carregan Shipping. I hear they're doing damn well out of the war. No one else has got enough ships and the yards can't build 'em quick enough. The chairman's my brother-in-law. Only met him once but wasn't much taken. Doesn't believe in family."

"Useful to know if we're to be in this damn country for long. Can't stand the heat. Does he live in Cape Town?"

"He has a big house, so I'm told, but he's not here now. Went to join his regiment at the outbreak of war."

"Patriotic for a civilian. Which regiment?"

"Mashonaland Horse."

"What the hell regiment is that? Never heard of it."

"Rhodesian auxiliary force."

"Oh. One of those colonial regiments. They'll be no damn good in this. This is a proper war. White fighting white. Not one of those native skirmishes. Had those m'self in m' younger days in India. Nothing to 'em."

"Do you think Roberts will be able to finish off the war quickly?"

"Everyone else thinks so and they pulled him out of retirement in Ireland to do just that. He and Kitchener. They'll finish it, of course, but don't know how long it'll take 'em. If the Boers would stand and fight we'd have 'em, but they fight and run. Don't have the same logistics problem. We can only fight near the railways. Is it always as hot as this in South Africa?"

"No idea, sir. Never been here before."

"Thought you might have been with all these relations you talk about."

"Not my relations, sir. My wife's."

"Yes, of course. Pretty woman. How's that son of yours?"

"Fine. Very strong lungs."

"Pity yer father didn't live long enough to know the title was secure. With my four sons it doesn't matter what happens to me. What made you join the regiment?"

"For the hunting, mainly. Wife and I enjoy following the hounds. Her father's still alive. When we have the whole of Halmeston to ourselves it will be better. Wife likes to see me doing something. Gives her a chance to have me out of the way, heh. Not that I have any worries of that sort. Too conscious of the name she now carries."

"I say, that's quite something. There's another ship, in fact two, with that same green funnel and the red dolphin. Must be the same line."

"There are said to be twenty ships in the line."

"Many shareholders?"

"Ester's grandfather has two-fifths, which interests me. My brother-in-law one fifth, a bastard who calls himself Morgan the same and a German by the name of von Brand. They have trading posts from here to Rhodesia plus farmland of one hundred thousand acres in the north. My sister is full of the story as her brother left England ten years ago with nothing. Man must have been damn lucky."

"Must be, to accumulate twenty thousand acres and four ships that size that he could call his own. His father gave him nothing?"

"Ran away on his grandfather's ship. He'd finished Oxford, of course. I think my wife must have helped him by the way she tells the story."

"Probably over-extended himself financially."

"They say just that. Morgan owns the biggest schooner in the Cape. Ester says that people are more concerned about being asked to Morgan's or Carregan's house than they are to Government House. They say Morgan is very well in with the army. Doesn't sound right for a man who doesn't even know his own mother."

"You sure of your facts?"

"My wife told me. She's proud of him for telling everyone. Facts well known. All the boats' names are coupled with the name Carregan except for one, the *Annabel*. Story is that that's his mother's name, but to save his mother's reputation Carregan won't tell him her surname. Probably just one of their business angles to have people talking about them."

"They seem to have succeeded. Ask Lieutenant Crichton to have the regiment on alert for landing. We are coming alongside. Smooth journey, really. Not a seaman m'self. Don't like ships. Too damn stuffy."

"I'll have him get them ready, sir."

"Good of you, Oswald. And good luck to you in South Africa."

"And to you, sir."

GAVIN MORGAN WATCHED HMS *Caithness* dock with renewed interest. After six months of sailing the schooner *Cape of Good Hope* he understood some of the intricacies of seamanship. He had taken her deep into the Indian Ocean and once up the coast past Cape Agulhas. He was nearly ready to use the boat for its real purpose but his price for Mauser ammunition had not yet been reached. He had been holding this stock marked 'engine parts' in Oudekraal for three years. No one would remember their purchase and if they did he would say that they had been delivered to the Boers as part of a barter some considerable time before hostilities commenced. He even had the invoices of sale.

Indeed, the Boers had tried to purchase them at the time, as they too had been certain that war was close. Gavin had held out for his price and each time a new offer was made by the Boers his price had gone up. He was now asking for gold, but the Boers had gold enough from the Johannesburg mines. The first consignment would pay for the *Cape of Good Hope* and the purchase price plus three years' interest on the cargo. He would channel the money back into the company, as the profit belonged to the four of them. Von Brand knew his plans and was part of them. James, Gavin thought, would prefer not to know that he was being shot at by ammunition supplied by Carregan Shipping. But the war had been started with a profit motive to get control of the gold mines, and if the whole thing was started for money then he would keep it going just those few days longer and make them all rich in the process.

Anyway, he was helping the British with cargo. The Boers had helped him set up his trading network. They deserved a little help as well. There was great danger in what he did and it was this that gave him the most amount of satisfaction. He liked his successes to come to him with difficulty. On this venture he had trusted no one except von Brand. He needed von Brand to make contact with the Boers and to be the exchanger of goods. A friend of von Brand's from the pioneer march into Rhodesia was the intermediary. Koos van der Walt had also been a close friend of James Carregan's and a member of the Mashonaland Horse during the Matabele wars. Now they fought each other because the British Government and, to an even greater extent, certain of her subjects, required control of the gold on the Witwatersrand.

Gavin watched the gangplank being lowered, checked the piece of paper in his hand and waited for the regiment's colonel to disembark. This meeting of each regiment had been tedious, as had been the entertaining, but the best of the government contracts were his.

Two men stepped off the ship and Gavin checked their rank carefully before stepping forward. He was dressed as commodore of the Carregan shipping line. The uniform looked slightly shabby, which had been his intention.

"Colonel Gilham, I presume. My name is Morgan. The port captain asked me to welcome you on his behalf. What with this build up of shipping he doesn't have much time of his own these days."

"Are you Morgan of Carregan Shipping?"

"The same."

"Your ships appear wherever one looks, young man. May I introduce Major Viscount Grantham. There is a business connection, I believe?"

"James hoped to welcome you himself but he is at present somewhere in the Northern Transvaal. No one has heard of him or his party for three months. He is trying to fight like the Boers and live off the land."

"Sounds a difficult way of winning the war," said Grantham.

"They say he has been very successful."

"We shall see."

"My other purpose is to invite you both, together with two other officers, to my house next Friday. Cape Town is dull without entertainment. It is a ride of ten miles but pleasant enough at this time of year. If you feel inclined to stay the night, you are welcome. There is more than enough room. Shall we say seven thirty for eight? I understand that it will be a week before your regiment goes north. The horses, you know. The house is easy to find, though the road is rough. The estate has no name but people are calling the area Morgan's Bay. Ask them for Morgan's Bay and they will show you to my house."

"We shall look forward to the evening," said Gilham. They shook hands and Gavin took his leave.

"Anything is better than this confounded ship after three weeks," said the colonel.

"Nerve of the man," said Grantham. "Young enough to be your grandson."

"And rich enough to pay your debts," replied the colonel.

6

1900

*J*ames Carregan stroked Garret's ear and the horse responded in the way that it had once responded to Gavin Morgan.

"You're about the nearest Gavin will get to this war," he said to himself.

"Did you say something, major?" asked Lieutenant Roger Quinn, who rode beside him.

"Not to you, laddie."

Quinn looked at him closely. In the last few weeks the man had grown away from them. He talked to himself and ate by himself. This was in complete contrast to the first months after the Mashonaland Horse had ridden into the Transvaal. They had all looked different then. The major's beard was scraggy now, like Roger's dogs on the farm, and the thought of his dogs set him off again worrying. He would not produce a crop this year, of that he was certain. His only consolation was that the Boers had the same problem. To begin with, until they had tried to kill each other, Quinn had had no real quarrel with the Transvaalers. The major had given them reason by explaining the importance of empire and the benefits that everyone derived from its strength. With the charter company taxing him at the present level, Quinn was not sure about the benefits. But like the others, he followed James Carregan and did exactly what he asked despite how unorthodox his methods appeared to everyone.

They did not fight a particular way on a particular front. Their only concern was the finding and destruction of Boer stocks, whether food or armaments. It was a tedious operation and one that they did in complete secrecy. They roamed the Boer countryside, living off the land, shooting food where necessary and avoiding any concentrations of Boer commandos. They were one hundred horsemen and no baggage, all Rhodesians who knew the bush as well as the Boers. The Boers hated this British commando using their own tactics against them. As the discipline in the Mashonaland Horse was equal to that in any regular British regiment, something the Boers had never been able to maintain, the results had been devastating. The Boers had attacked them twice in strength and found themselves thrashing around having lost all trace of the Rhodesians. And when they had been forced to defend themselves or their depots, they had been severely mauled. At given intervals and precise locations, the cavalry unit picked up stores of ammunition and medical supplies together with the forage for the horses. Carregan Shipping knew every route across the highveld and had stores. Koos van der Walt had heard of his friend's methods and had been seen to smile when he was told that James was in command.

"You watch them, *kerels*. They were well trained by us. I showed him myself how to scan the bush and in those days he was looking for Matabele and not for Boers. They will come here and give us trouble. Better the English on their feet than Carregan's Horse. If he was not a friend of mine, I'd go out and get him myself. If I could, that is."

The Boers called them Carregan's Horse and within a short time they were called this by everyone.

JAMES TURNED in his saddle and looked back at his troop. He

appraised them carefully but could find no fault. They looked dirty and unwashed but then they were, and hungry as well. They moved smoothly as one body, each horseman moving easily in his saddle. The horses were well groomed and fed. Apart from the horses there were only the pack donkeys carrying fodder and water. The men carried their food, blankets, rifles and long cavalry swords, the latter carried at James's insistence. They had proved their worth on many occasions. To be attacked by a troop of tramps wielding steel and moving fast on heavy horses had put more fear into the Boers than accurate shooting. The swords achieved little except the one thing that James required. He wanted a reputation among the enemy. He wanted his Horse to be feared. That way he was always in command at the beginning of a fight; the edge of confidence was always his.

James slowed Garret and Captain Hall rode up beside him.

"Not a bloody sign of that depot," said James.

"Country's too flat," said Hall. "He must have been given wrong information."

"Don't think so. The Boers are more careful. Having lost Pretoria and Bloemfontein they're conserving their resources and certainly can't afford to let us find out where they keep the stuff. Our own pick-up point is scheduled for tomorrow."

"The men are hungry."

"So am I."

James smiled at the man and waited until he smiled in return.

"We'll hunt," said James, "when we've found their depot. There may even be food among the armament. It's our way of fighting, Jack. There's never an easy path in anything. Oh, and pass the word that I'll find a way of replacing your crops even if I pay for them myself. We're all farmers, so we have the same problems. This is no worse, in fact a lot better, than '96, when we had the Rinderpest as well as the rebellions. At least all is quiet at home."

Behind them rose a trail of dust that could be seen for a mile. James had been waiting for an ambush for two days. He had known the information concerning the Boer depot was false when he had accepted it three weeks before. He also knew Viljoen was in the area and if he could capture him the war would be shortened by months.

Carel Viljoen was one of the best of their guerrilla commanders and vociferous in his argument that the war must go on. James's plan was simple. Being aware that his informer had sent them into a trap, and knowing the area in detail, he was waiting to find them. He had trained along the Macloutsi River and ranged down into the Transvaal with Rhys Morgan and Willie von Brand before they had joined the column and defied Lobengula in their march to Fort Salisbury. He would turn the trap and attack first. The horses were strong and would last longer than the smaller Boer ponies when he broke off the engagement. He knew the odds would be in favour of the Boers but then they did not know how to attack as a cavalry unit. He was tense and had no wish to communicate this to anyone. He wished that von Brand had been allowed to join the unit. It was lonely campaigning alone.

"We're being watched," said Captain Hall.

James saw that he was worried and this meant that by this time most of the men sensed that they were being hunted.

"We have been for two days," he said, "but I've been unable to detect any large concentrations. At all cost we must appear unaware. I knew it was a trap, Jack, before I came out into it, but if I reverse the trap we have a chance of getting Viljoen. We must find out where they're camping tonight. I know they're close. It's the same feeling I have when I'm close to buffalo."

"They'll roll us up if they know we're here."

"No. Not if I see it my way, Jack. My way, they'll wonder what the hell hit them."

"I hope you're right."

"Yeh. Well, I will be."

They rode on and James made no more display than usual scanning the countryside. Darkness fell but they did not make camp. Instructions were given to muffle the horses. They moved on into the moonless night in silence. James had known there would be little or no moon when they reached the danger area. He had planned for it accordingly.

Two hours after the last vestige of daylight had left the night sky, James called his seven officers aside from the men. No fires had been lit and no noise was to be made. Those that wished could lie down and sleep. Some had taken the opportunity and were spread out on the coarse grass. They were camped in a fold in the ground surrounded by scrub. Even a Boer scout would be unable to differentiate between the scrub and the horses from a vantage point on any of the distant hills that were able to look down into the camp.

"We are close to a strong Boer commando," said James. "They're within ten miles of this camp. They must be located in the dark and attacked in the first light of morning. The object is to capture Carel Viljoen. I've met him twice and we've all seen his posters. Jack, will you split the command into as many units as we have expert trackers? Having located Viljoen's commando, they must be able to return to this camp and lead us back again by daybreak. Everyone is to assemble back here two hours before dawn irrespective. If we can't find them tonight then we'll break out. Each scout to report to me the points of the compass he'll search. To find them and be caught would be fatal to everyone. The sooner we're under way the better."

Within twenty minutes the parties had gone out in all directions. James knew that in the dark it would be impossible to cover every piece of ground. He relied upon the scouts having lived in the bush for most of their lives. They should be able to sense people as much as hear or see them. Frustrated by inactivity, he settled down to wait for their return. As Commanding Officer he had to remain at the point of control. Roger Quinn had remained as well; the remainder had left.

Roger Quinn was twenty-six and had been chosen especially by James for having spent three years as an officer in the Sixth Queen Charlottes. He had disgraced himself by hitting a senior officer and been cashiered following his court martial. Soon after, he had found his way out to Rhodesia and bought himself a farm. He had arrived eight months before Gavin and Phillip Lagrange and since then had taught himself to farm with the help of his neighbours. He never intended to return to England and he certainly never intended rejoining the army. James had helped him with his farming; he owed him not only the debt of knowledge but that of friendship. Rhodesia could have been a lonely place, so when James had asked him to assist in making the Mashonaland Horse into a long range scout unit that was capable of cavalry efficiency, he could only answer yes. James had commissioned him in the field to overcome his previous problem. Even Jack Hall, two ranks his senior, knew that Roger Quinn was second in command of the unit. James hoped to bring him into Carregan Shipping when the war was over. He knew the octopus that was Morgandale and Carregan Shipping required executive staff if it was not to outgrow its strength. They sat and listened to the night and heard nothing. Total stillness. Winter on the highveld. The cold began to settle into their bones.

"One of us should sleep at a time, Roger. I'll keep first watch."

They had trained themselves to sleep when the opportunity arose. Within minutes James was the only one awake in the camp. When his turn came to sleep he rested completely. When he awoke the first of the patrols had come back. They had found a strong Boer commando, had hobbled their horses and moved in on their stomachs as close as possible. They estimated a thousand men with baggage wagons. There were women and children in the camp, as it was the Boer custom for the senior men to travel with their families.

"There is no commando of that size in the area other than that of Carel Viljoen," said James to Quinn. "Surprise, I hope, is now on our side. Tell the others as they come in to sleep. We'll keep watch from either side of that camp."

Well before the sky began to pale, Carregan's Horse were saddled and ready to move forward. James gave the command with his hand and they moved out with the metal pieces of the horses' equipment muffled against noise. They moved across the flat, open ground in perfect formation with the sergeant who had found the Boer commando directing James. They would attack into the light. Within half an hour they were in position. James waited until he could recognise the sergeant's features and then gave a hand command for them to form into their box formation. James rode at the front with Quinn in the middle to control the charge. They moved up slowly and were then given the signal to canter. Shortly after came the order from James to gallop. The ground vibrated but there was no other sound than the hooves of the horses. The box formation loosened to give them room to manoeuvre but the positioning remained exact. James drew his sabre and held it at the ready. The type of fear he had felt on the Shangani Patrol was gone. If someone was going to shoot him they would do so but until then he would maintain the same precision that he required from the others. His mind was free from anything except the task in hand. It would not be easy to detect Viljoen and having done so to capture him alive. He had no wish to kill more of them than was necessary. He fought because it was his job, in the same way that he had fought against Lobengula in '93 and the rebels in '96. He was at war and this was the consequence of war. He heard a shout from the Boer camp and smiled to himself. They were too late. They had thought they were hunting. Maybe Carel Viljoen was not such a good commander after all. As the first shots crashed at them, the formation hit the camp. James still held his sabre at the ready and looked for Viljoen.

"Where are you, Carel," he shouted in the *Taal*.

"It's Carregan's Horse," shouted a Boer in return in the same language.

"Where are you, Carel, you Boer who looks like a baboon."

"No man calls me a baboon," shouted Viljoen as he came out of his tent and sighted his rifle.

James saw him and smiled. An old trick, but it had worked. Garret answered immediately and swung towards the crouching Boer, at the same time increasing his speed. James steadied himself along Garret's neck and switched the sabre into his left hand. He loosened his feet from the stirrups as Viljoen tried to aim again. As he came up he whistled softly in Garret's ear and dropped away from the horse, hitting Viljoen across the shoulder. James's knee hit his face and the Boer lost consciousness.

The camp was in uproar but the swift movement of the horses at close quarters made it difficult for the Boers to shoot straight. Quinn and three troopers moved correctly into position and began circling James and Viljoen. No one attacked them. Garret had brought himself round and James whistled again. When the horse came up, James threw Viljoen over the horse's rump and roped him to the side of the saddle. He picked up his sabre and remounted. James signalled to Quinn, who drew a small bugle and sounded the withdrawal. They spurred their horses. The unit was charging the camp for the third time and the charge carried them out and onto the veld.

The sun had still not risen. James looked behind and could see no one following. Accurate rifle fire hit them until they were out of range. James signalled the canter and when the camp was lost to sight behind them he changed their direction. Over ten miles he changed their direction three times. By noon he had led them to the pick-up point where he found the stores that would take them back into friendly territory. The horsemen ate hungrily while some looked to their wounds. One officer and four men had failed to keep up with the main troop.

"We'll move out again," said James. "We must keep ahead of the word that will have gone out about Viljoen. We'll strike the railway one hundred and seventy miles from here where we'll pick up a British patrol. There will be no sleep until then."

Viljoen, surprisingly for a Boer, was lightly built, which was fortunate for James and Garret. After eating, Viljoen had recovered his senses. His head still ached as did his shoulder. For two hours they rode the same horse in silence.

"When we camp tonight, it is best, man, that you let me escape," said Viljoen to James in the *Taal*.

"Of course," replied James. "At the first opportunity I'll lend you

Garret and forget about five of my friends that have been lost in your capture. Don't be sore, Carel. It is the game of war. You have been caught and you are on your way to Cape Town and from there you will be sent to Ceylon. After the war, you must come and visit me on Morgandale. We'll be able to tell each other good stories and talk about maize and cattle."

"I think you misunderstand me," said Viljoen.

"Maybe, but does it matter?"

"It may matter to your partners. I would have thought you would have known about their negotiations with us Boers."

"No."

"Oh, please, Major Carregan. You, as chairman, I think you call it, of Carregan Shipping, you must know all the significant negotiations of your organisation?"

"Of course I know that we traded with you before the war. It was good business and I have nothing personal against your people. There are many of you in Rhodesia. My good friend Koos van der Walt taught me some of my bush knowledge. Willie von Brand and I have talked at length on the implications of fighting our friends. But it is circumstances. I am still British and for this I must play the part that is required of me by the country of my birth. In the future of my new country we may find it necessary to think only of ourselves. But this is not true now. We are part of an empire. If someone fights one part of that empire they fight all of it. That is how it is. I know nothing that Carregan Shipping has done to breach this principle."

"Maybe you have been away too long."

"Maybe I have. It is over a year now. This war has gone on too long."

"Not for some. We'll go on, if necessary, until the last one of us is dead or until we have no more ammunition."

"Brave sentiment, but no less foolish. If a cause can be seen to have failed then it is only stupidity and arrogance which continues its pursuit. The effort you expend is worthless."

"Not if it inspires our race to remain as one people in the future."

"Again, Carel, that will not be possible. You are too few and the world is forever increasing. There will not be room for small enclaves in the future."

"Leave that as it may. I am more concerned about the present. If you say you do not know then I'll tell you about the first consignment of Mauser ammunition that was delivered by Carregan Shipping last week. Or more correctly by Willie von Brand, I think you call him, who had collected the consignment from a boat called the *Cape of Good Hope* that had pulled into a bay on the Transkei coast. I would imagine the payment gold is being delivered to the boat at this moment. It was a considerable amount. Your Gavin Morgan drives a hard bargain. But then we needed the ammunition."

"That is quite a statement. I presume you intend giving out this information in Cape Town if I ensure that you reach the place."

"Exactly."

"I wish to think. I'll give you my answer when next we stop."

"There can only be one answer for your friends. Treason of that nature in war would bring them in front of a firing squad. It would also be the end of Carregan Shipping. Most probably Carregan Horse as well. I do not see how you yourself cannot be implicated."

"I'll give you my answer when next we stop."

"I'll be waiting."

James knew the statement was correct. It was all too much like Gavin Morgan. Willie? Hell, that didn't sound quite right but then Willie was a German and had no particular alliance to the British crown. It would probably amuse him. Having been left out of the war, he was missing the danger.

Gavin? Oh yes, he would do it for money. Young men in control of large businesses often crash them in the most idiotic of ways. But then if Gavin had sold them ammunition he would have done so properly. He was that kind of man. There would be no trace left behind him of what he had done. Or none that could be proved.

Viljoen? He stood to gain his freedom. If he was lost to the Boers it would be a harsh blow to their morale. But if he uncovered Morgan, what would he have achieved? His people would not receive further ammunition and of this they were desperately short. And he would not have set himself free. To his own people it might appear to have been the action of a frightened man.

And if he was implicated himself? Hell, he wouldn't be the first to be shot for somebody else's actions. And would the British believe Viljoen? His capture would make good news and the name of his capturer would be in every English newspaper. Would the public allow themselves to believe the word of a captured Boer? He didn't think so. If he let him escape? There would be no chance of incrimination. No. He did not like blackmail and five men had died or been captured to put the Boer commander on the saddle in front of him. If he was free, many more people would die. Without people such as Viljoen, they would not use Gavin's ammunition.

They rode on and only stopped to rest at nightfall.

"You are going to Cape Town, Carel, for a number of reasons," said James in the *Taal*. "Firstly, because I don't believe a word of what you say and neither will the British. Even if they do, it will not have set you free. And secondly, it is not in your character to stoop to blackmail. We know all about you. Admire you probably, yes. You are a proud man. You are a Boer. No, you would try to frighten me but you would never tell your story in spite. Anyway, if the story were true, you would not get any more ammunition."

"You are foolish," answered Viljoen. "You do not really know us Boers."

"No, Carel. You are the foolish one. You could have just sentenced yourself to death. Maybe I should let you escape. A little way. And then shoot you in the back. Maybe you should trade your word for your life. A dead Viljoen is just as good to my cause as one who is alive in Cape Town. A pity, because then we would not be able to visit each other's farms after the war."

"You think you are being clever."

"Be careful. I've been fighting the hard way for a year. I've seen some things that I would prefer to forget. I do not hate, but just one word of your invented story may make me do this. Then I would go back and hunt your commando. I would hunt your family. And this time, Carel Viljoen, I would not be taking prisoners. We English are not vicious but if we are made to become that way then we are the very worst of enemies. I wish you a good journey to Cape Town. From now on you will travel in front of one of my troopers. And next time you find plenty of water, wash out your mouth."

7

*G*avin Morgan watched the second consignment of ammunition being loaded into the *Cape of Good Hope*. They were clearly marked as engine parts for a well-known mining company in Natal, whose diamond mine was situated eleven miles inland from Oudekraal, the destination of the schooner. The engine parts had been bought by Carregan Shipping four years earlier and kept in their Oudekraal warehouse. They were difficult to obtain and the Natal company were lucky to have located them. The first consignment of gold had been sent to England on the *Ester Carregan*. It was consigned with the other papers and documents to Carregan Shipping's London office, which was close to the Stock Exchange. The gold would be sold after the war and by then Gavin would have bought an English company that dealt in bullion. At present, they had no need of the money. With the war dragging on to Gavin's satisfaction, the freight rates were climbing higher each month. Carregan Shipping was embarrassingly solvent.

"We'll put in to my bay on the way round the coast," said Gavin to Kevin Grant, the skipper of the *Cape of Good Hope*. "I've not seen Louise for three days and then there'll be the trip up to Natal. We might even catch her up to some mischief."

"The diamond mine is screaming for the parts," replied Grant.

"If they shout a little louder I'll put up the price. This is wartime, Kevin. If you receive anything it's better than nothing and Carregan Shipping always deliver. And on time. It will be up to you to rendezvous in seven days. If you would prefer me to, I'll captain the boat myself. It's just that I have a large amount of paperwork to be done and sailing without the responsibility is my only relaxation. I may be young but I do not enjoy the use of a self-winding motor. Anyway, I thought you wanted one of the larger boats in the line? A few good voyages on the *Cape of Good Hope* must put you ahead of the others."

"We'll be there on time and we'll call at your house."

"Make it just after dark. We'll come in without any lights."

"Sure."

Kevin Grant smiled. He was twenty-seven and ambitious. He thought he understood Morgan and did not know that the reason he was captain of the schooner was because he was one of the most stupid men that Gavin Morgan had ever met.

When the sun was well down in the sea, the three-masted schooner filled her sails and ran before the wind out of Table Bay. Once around Mouille Point the wind changed again and Grant kept her tacking hard against the wind for a long run before bringing her about. He was a natural seaman, one of his very few attributes in life, and he did not spill a drop of the wind, all the time sailing close up against it. He constantly watched the burgee on the tall centre mast for any change in the wind. The wind was fresh and steady and the *Cape of Good Hope* sliced her way through a choppy sea towards Morgan's Bay. The light had gone completely before they were half way, and Grant sailed by keeping the gaunt night shapes of the Twelve Apostles at the same distance from the schooner. At the end of the range of mountains that emerged from the granite mass which began as Table Mountain was Morgan's Bay. Resting at the feet of the last of the Twelve Apostles was the nearest the house would ever come to God.

. . .

GAVIN MORGAN HAD SEDUCED Louise Lagrange when she was fourteen. He was sixteen at the time and she had not been his first woman. She was tight and uncontrollable. She was still uncontrollable at twenty but she was not so tight. Given the opportunity, Gavin believed that she would be able to climax in double figures every day. It was this side of her make-up that he enjoyed the most. He enjoyed women who reacted. When she wished to visit her brother in Africa it was natural that she would stay with him, and as Lagrange was staying with Gavin, it solved everybody's problem. But in the process of satisfying himself with Louise he had made a mistake. He had made an enemy out of Lagrange.

PHILLIP LAGRANGE WAS weak but he was also sensitive. The sister he thought to be like his mother, and secretly despised for it, was a whore, and this had been shown to him by the man he'd thought was his best friend. He'd lost faith in two people at once, but was forced to continue living with them as he did not have the strength of mind to support himself independently. He wished to show the mother whom he loathed that he could do it, and successfully. From the outside looking in it appeared he had done exactly what he had set out to do.

When he was drunk he believed in himself. At twenty-two he had begun the long run down to becoming an alcoholic and the nearer he reached this goal, the more he hated Gavin Morgan. The smallest slights came back to him and grew in his mind's eye. The way he was treated by Gavin after he had run away from the buffalo became a mountain. All these things were never his own fault. They were always Gavin Morgan's. None of this had been missed by Gavin, but despite his ruthlessness he had a great sense of loyalty. He knew that he had made Lagrange what he was because he expected as much from his friend as he did from himself. Gavin had been mindful for some time of James's remark that Phillip could be his one weak link. He kept Lagrange where he was in the company, but made certain that he carried no responsibility. He had him watched. Lagrange slowly realised this and became more frustrated and each night took it out on the bottle.

LAGRANGE SAW the schooner enter the bay with her lights doused. He was seated on the balcony that ran out from his room and overlooked the sea. He was well into the first half of his daily bottle of scotch but he was still sober. He was amused. He had no intention of warning his sister. He would enjoy the spectacle of Gavin being embarrassed in his own house. He watched the schooner from his vantage point high up on the great house and relaxed, something he had not done for many months. He was going to enjoy himself. He watched the dinghy being lowered from the schooner and saw two people climb down into it from the rope ladder. One began to row. The other would be Gavin Morgan. He finished his drink in one swig and poured himself another from the crystal decanter that rested on the marble-topped table and stood at his elbow. He hit back the stopper and returned his thoughtful gaze to the rowing boat that was halfway towards the small jetty some distance away from the house. He was trying to think how he would obtain the most amount of enjoyment out of the moment. He had time to think and savour the situation.

GAVIN MORGAN WATCHED the house carefully. The idea of Louise bedding with someone else increased his own appetite. He just hoped he would be lucky enough to catch them in the act and then realised that at eight thirty at night his luck would not be that good. It was one of his quirks, which he always found at the end of his relationships. Louise was on the wane. She had lasted a long time, which was the strangest thing of all. He normally grew bored with a woman after a month. When the younger sister arrived, he would make a play at that one and see what happened. He had never had two sisters. The complications, he told himself, could be quite exquisite. Poor Phil. He would really hate him after that, but then he would hate him anyway so there was little point in not trying his luck. He sat back in the boat, facing out to sea, and drew in the lines of his schooner silhouetted against the night sky. Perfect beauty. He turned back and looked up at the vastness of the dark mountain which guarded his house. He wanted to stretch out a hand to caress its craggy top. It was good to be alive, he told himself as the boat bumped gently against the wooden jetty. He jumped out onto the strong, wooden planking.

"Come back in an hour," he said softly.

"Aye, aye, sir."

The boat turned on its way back to the schooner while Gavin began the walk up the path towards the mansion that other people called *The House at Morgan's Bay*.

Phillip Lagrange made up his mind again. He walked to the edge of his balcony and looked down at the drop. He felt fear and, if he had not drunk so much whisky, he would have funked the idea. The bedroom next door to that of his sister was unoccupied. The distance between the balconies was the same as the one he now contemplated. The drop down to the rocks below was also the same. The house had been built into a forty-five-degree incline with the edge of the house poised above a vertical cliff. Below were the giant boulders, not even sand or sea. He swigged at his drink and made up his mind for the third time. From the balcony he could hear everything and he had to hear it all to regain some of himself, to see Gavin brought down through jealousy. He might even kill the Englishman, and with Louise not being his wife they'd hang him. He savoured this thought and experienced a deep pleasure in the pit of his stomach. Saliva cloyed the back of his mouth. He got away from the balcony and put down his empty glass. He moved quickly through his bedroom before he could change his mind. It was pitch dark in the corridor.

·　·　·

LOUISE LAGRANGE TURNED towards Oswald Grantham, gently turned his head towards her mouth and bit his ear.

"Do it again, darling," she said.

"I don't think I could just now. Give me a few more minutes and I'll try."

"Let me see how few minutes you really need."

Slowly she ran the tip of her tongue around the edge of his ear and then forced it in hard. She felt him stir under her left hand and lightly flicked her tongue around the strange pattern of his ear for the second time. She was excited.

Louise was a small girl who had been made in a perfect shape. She looked her best when naked and she knew this better than anyone. Her small face shone out of a series of soft, tight curls and her eyes were the same chestnut brown. The nose, above the soft, large mouth, was very small, as were her ears when they were found by men, fondling and pushing back the soft curls of her hair. Her breasts were hard and small like her bottom. Surprisingly, she had a mound of pubic hair which gave away the secret of her passion. She had never been satisfied by any man, though with Gavin she had fallen asleep more than once through sheer exhaustion. She brought Oswald round on top of her and felt him go inside. He was not particularly hard, which was a shame.

GAVIN MORGAN TOOK up the lamp which rested on the hall table, lit a taper from the Tilley lamp above the hat stand, and put it to the lamp. The hall light was the only one burning in the house. He smiled to himself. She had gone to bed if nothing else. With an easy step he walked to the spiral staircase and began the climb up to the bedrooms.

PHILLIP LAGRANGE TRIED NOT to look at his sister lying underneath Oswald Grantham. But at the same time he was fascinated. They had not drawn the curtains and the little light that came in from the moon showed them to him entwined on the bed. Their noises made his imagination leap and showed him the gaps his eyes were unable to see. He was still frightened following his lunge from the adjacent balcony and the effect of the Scotch had worn off immediately. He would never be able to go back the way he came. The French window into his sister's bedroom was half open but the sea had drowned any sound that he might have made if either of them had been in a position to listen. He heard the door click and the light swing into the room some moments before the couple on the bed apparently did.

"I wonder who it is?" said Gavin Morgan, holding the light above his head to enable him to have a better look. "Must be English, the bottom's too white. Louise," he said loudly, and Lagrange moved back from the French window, "won't you introduce me to your friend?"

From the point of sensual exclusion, Louise brought herself back to reality and looked straight at Gavin over the shoulder of Oswald Grantham.

"Who is it?" said Grantham through clenched teeth. He felt ridiculous.

"Gavin," she whispered, then, louder, "You've no right to barge into my room."

"Come, come, Louise. Since when has that been the case?"

Grantham had shrivelled and he pulled himself away from the gap between the wide open legs. He rolled over onto his back and tried to bring the sheets up over both of them. Gavin began to laugh and the lamp shook in his hand. Lagrange came closer to have a better look and was thoroughly disappointed. Gavin was enjoying himself but he was the only one in the room in that frame of mind. Lagrange went white with fury. Gavin had cheated him out of what he was sure would be his revenge.

"Fancied a touch of the old nobility did you, my love?"

"You have no right to talk like that," snapped Grantham as he forced himself back into type. "You are not her husband."

"Neither are you, my lord, neither are you."

"I have a good mind to challenge you to a duel."

"The cause would not sound right. Especially when the Carregans own everything you spend. Get dressed. It's a long way to Cape Town but I am sure the ride will improve your spirits. Oh, and Phillip, come in off the balcony. You don't know me well enough even now to realise what I really think of your sister. Run around to your bedroom and have another whisky."

"What are you doing there?" said Louise, sitting up in alarm as her brother ran past them for the door, unable to say a word.

"He came to watch my fit of jealousy. He must have seen the *Good Hope* come into the bay. We're on our way to Natal."

"And what made you call in here?" said Louise. She was beginning to enjoy the sensation of conflicting feelings. She was the cause of everything.

"To see you."

"Are you satisfied?"

"Not yet. Come along, Oswald. If you don't dress quicker than that I'll mention this evening to James. And then again your colonel would not find the ethics particularly amusing."

Gavin put the lamp down by the side of the bed and walked out onto the balcony. Sails furled, the schooner rode gently in the bay. A good moon showed him the clarity of her lines. He heard the door slam shut and he turned back to the French windows.

"What are you going to do?" said Louise.

"Make love to you."

"Good." She pulled back the sheet and squirmed her shoulders into the pillows.

"Have a bath, first. I have no wish to contaminate myself with Oswald Grantham."

She got up and moved to the bathroom. She had never felt more excited in her life.

AN HOUR LATER, Kevin Grant ordered the anchor to be weighed. The sails were pulled up to their mast heads and the schooner got under way. Gavin Morgan relaxed in his luxury cabin and felt the breeze come up through the portholes as the *Cape of Good Hope* sailed out of the protection of the bay. The wind caught in the full set of sails and the schooner came over at an angle to the sea. The smack, smack of the waves on the timber hull became rhythmic and strong. Fully at peace with himself and the world, Gavin got up out of his sea chair, opened the cabinet where the bottles were held in wooden rings, took down the bottle of old Cape brandy and poured a liberal amount of the golden liquid into a crystal tumbler. Having exactly caught the angle of the deck, he stood looking through the porthole to where he watched the moon playing on the surface of a black sea.

SIX DAYS LATER, the schooner dropped anchor off Oudekraal. The weather was fine without the trace of a cloud in the sky. Inland, a dust cloud hung above the dry veld. Gavin was met off the schooner by the mine captain, who was a little disappointed to find that there were no women on board.

"We'll bring some up next time, Chris," said Gavin. Chris O'Connor had last seen a white woman when he had met the schooner after its first voyage to Oudekraal. "The parts are coming off in a few moments. How are you getting on with putting that mine back into operation?"

"It's a long job. The whole sifting and sorting plant was rusted together. If we could have got them, it would have been cheaper to install a new plant."

"Wartime, Chris. You were lucky to find the parts."

"How many more consignments complete the order?"

"Three. But you may need more spares after that."

"You've got them?"

"Sure."

"How did you know we'd need them? And at these prices?"

"I didn't. It was the luck of trading. I have stacks of other equipment that may never be used. Before war broke out I bought up anything I could buy cheap."

"Do you enjoy these trips?" asked O'Connor, looking at the *Cape of Good Hope.*

"Only relaxation I get. Last trip, though. Kevin will see you next time. We'll put the cases in our warehouse. Willie will bring them out to you tomorrow. Come up to the office and we'll sign the papers."

The paperwork was correct. Gavin, von Brand and a few Boers were the only ones who knew the reality of the consignments. Satisfied, and after making his farewells, Gavin went back to the schooner. The return cruise the following morning would be a pleasure, as would be his meeting the following week with Sarah Lagrange.

AT TEN O'CLOCK THAT NIGHT, Willie von Brand was rowed out to the *Cape of Good Hope.* The two partners greeted each other with warmth. Von Brand's negotiating had brought them a high price for the bullets and the danger had always been his.

"Any problems?" asked Gavin.

"Only one."

"What's that?"

"James has captured Viljoen."

"What extraordinary luck. I hope he doesn't talk."

"So do I, my God, so do I. Is our cover good enough?"

"I think so, Willie. If it isn't, it wouldn't have been for lack of planning. Just don't get caught on your way to delivering this consignment to Koos van der Walt."

"The ammunition cases will be marked as engine parts to a mine much further inland. Further than my meeting place with Koos. There's no reason why anyone would open the cases."

"What extraordinary luck that James should catch him."

8

*B*y the time James Carregan reached Cape Town with Carel Viljoen, the word had reached all corners of the British Empire. He had been asked to escort the prisoner to army headquarters in Cape Town while the rest of the officers and men of the Mashonaland Horse had been given leave. Roger Quinn had accompanied him on the train, on which a British armed guard had taken charge of the prisoner. James had not spoken to Viljoen on their long journey through Boer country, nor on the train. He'd told no one about Viljoen's threat either, even Quinn. It was a family affair and, as yet, Quinn was not part of the family. James had invited him to spend his leave at Ship Corner, the house he had built for himself overlooking Table Bay. His grandfather and Hal Fincham found it satisfying to watch the ships come into the harbour and spent many hours of contentment on the large veranda, looking way down into the bay, discussing the ships as they came and went, especially the ones with the green funnel and the red dolphin.

There was a reception of press photographers waiting for them at Cape Town, but as none of the press knew the looks of James it was not difficult for James and Quinn to stand back while the prisoner was escorted down the platform. By the time the photographers had taken their fill of Carel Viljoen, James and Quinn were in a hired cab on their way to Ship Corner. They were in uniform but so were a large number of other men.

The cab took them up the long driveway to the large house. In building a large house, James had listened to Gavin as much for the sake of his grandfather as for the image of Carregan Shipping. It was a good house and he liked it, but nothing compared to the house he had built with his own hands on Morgandale.

As the cab came to a halt outside the house, he wondered whether Viljoen had taken his advice. There was nothing more he could do except visit Gavin as quickly as possible. He presumed that von Brand was still supervising the trading posts and ensuring that the managers were producing a crop on Morgandale. He would not be in Cape Town. A year of fighting had been a long time. The thing he wished for most, as he stepped out onto the gravel driveway, was to go home to Morgandale. Maybe after a rest he would not think that way. There was his Cape Town social life to distract him for a while, and Carregan Shipping, maybe Sonny, certainly Virginia Webb, and then the war to get back to. It would be some time before he found his way to the farm.

Two strangers he had seen when Ship Corner first came into view now walked towards them from the far side of the house. They both carried cameras.

"Quite a house," said Quinn. "And this looks like the reception. Maybe we were not so clever at the station."

"You must be Major Carregan," said the reporter.

"Yes."

"Congratulations."

"Thank you."

"By your expression, you're not familiar with the news to which I'm referring."

"Viljoen, I suppose."

"Not only. They've put you up for a Victoria Cross."

"Have they now?"

"May we take your photograph?"

"If you wish. But if you'll excuse me after that, I have a lot to do."

"Of course. Now if you would stand over there like that. Turn your face away a little. Now, if you could hold it just like that."

"Never thought ye'd come to posing," said Captain Carregan from the balcony above. James looked up and saw his grandfather and Hal Fincham smiling down at him.

"Don't move your head."

"Sorry."

"Hold it... that's fine. Many thanks, Major Carregan."

"My pleasure. Come on, Roger. We both need a long drink after that damn train."

"A VC is quite something."

"Yes. I suppose it is. Unfortunately I have bigger problems on my mind at the moment."

James noticed that his grandfather did not come down the steps to meet them. When he reached the veranda he saw the reason why. In a year, his grandfather had become a very old man. The sparkle was still in his eyes but the rest was bent and old and the movements were slow and troubled. It must have shown in his face.

"Do I look that old, James?"

"Not at all. You look well. No different from when I last saw you."

"Not possible, laddie. But nice of ye to say so. Come on in. The housekeeper will get ye a drink organised if she can keep from biting me head off for a minute. Women. Marriage to yer grandmother was never as bad as this."

"Can I introduce Roger Quinn. My grandfather, and Hal Fincham. Hello, Hal, you look well."

They all shook hands and a servant was asked to fetch the drinks.

"When ye've done something about yer thirsts I'll tell ye the family news. A lot has happened, lad, while ye've been up north. You from the north, too, Mr Quinn?"

"I farm near Morgandale. James coerced me into Carregan's Horse."

"He's my number two," said James. "In reality but not in rank. Had a bit of trouble with his regiment in England."

"What did you do, lad?"

"Socked the CO."

"Not the best way to promotion."

"It got me out of the army."

"Pretty fast I would say?"

"Yes. It was pretty fast."

"Here are the drinks," said Captain Carregan. "I hope ye like 'em. Orange and lemon juice plus rum. A sailor's drink I learnt in Jamaica when Hal and I were sailing the old *Dolphin*. Good days, they were. Well. Cheers. Glad to see ye back. Bit of a hero, now. Not that it'll turn ye head... right. First things first. Yer father's ill. Last message from Ester was that there was no point in ye going home. She thought he'd be dead before ye reached England. He's my son as well as yer father so we don't have to talk on that one. Funny, I never thought I'd live longer than Ernest. He seemed indestructible. He'll be glad to have heard about you in the papers before he died. Oswald's out here with his regiment. Ester will follow if yer father dies. Gavin's living a life of debauchery, so I hear."

"Is he?" replied James. "Is he in Cape Town?"

"He returned last week from Natal. He's out at his house. Phillip's younger sister has arrived on a visit. Phil's drinking too much. He'll have to talk to him. I don't get to the office much now. Me bones all seem to have locked together. No matter. They did me well. Willie's still up in Rhodesia."

"Carregan Shipping?"

"Doing well. But it would be difficult not to in present circumstances. Gavin runs a good business. Even in times like these he expects and gets his top efficiency. We have a lot of money in the bank and more to come."

"The man must be crazy."

"Why should Gavin be crazy?"

"Oh. Just something rather stupid that he's done. Nothing

important. Or, rather, nothing that I can't sort out in my own quiet way. Any news of Morgandale?"

"A good crop. The cattle ranch outside Bulawayo is doing well. They are selling sooner than they intended but with meat prices at such a premium, Willie is right to sell. The maize is fetching a good price."

"Everything seems to be rosy."

"Everything is rosy."

"I hope so."

"Ye've been fighting for too long."

"Yes. Maybe I have. This drink is good. What do you think, Roger?"

"No complaints."

"Which regiment is Oswald?"

"Sixth, Ninth Queen Charlottes."

"Another coincidence. That was Roger's regiment. Do you know my brother-in-law, Viscount Grantham?"

"He was not in the regiment during my time."

"Do you feel like a drive, Roger? I wish to see Gavin. Talk a little business. As chairman, I think I should be brought up to date. Will you excuse us so quickly?" he said to his grandfather. "We'll change into civvies first. Where did that cab driver put our trunks?"

"In the hall."

"Good. Nice seeing you both again. We'll all have dinner together tomorrow night. I'll spend tonight at Morgan's Bay."

"Sonny's there."

"Interesting. Are there any women in Cape Town who are not at Morgan's Bay?"

"Ye'll have to see for yerself, lad. A year's a long time. In wartime people don't behave as they should and Gavin was always a good one for taking an opportunity."

"Yes. He is. Very good, in fact. Cheers, again. The second half of a good drink always tastes better than the first. Or so Willie says, and he's a connoisseur. Or at least he used to be one."

.   .   .

AN HOUR LATER, they were seated in a trap on their way down the coast. The weather was clear but cold and James pulled his fur-lined coat close around him and moved his toes around inside his boots. Normally he would have taken pleasure in the scenery around him but instead he sat silently and let the horse take its own pace. If Viljoen had talked, they were all finished. He should have been a coward and shot the man on the highveld. He told himself that he didn't give a damn about Gavin. He knew the consequences. It was Willie who concerned him, and his grandfather and everyone else who earned a good living from Carregan Shipping. The man was too young to have got where he had. Youth has energy and ideas but age is the only way to wisdom. That had always been. Maybe it was his fault not to have seen it. But then, without Gavin they would not have had a shipping line.

"You're quiet, James," said Quinn next to him. "Is something worrying you?"

"A family affair. You'll be able to see Morgan's Bay around the next corner. This road is pretty bad but it serves the purpose."

"If you need any help, then let me know."

"Thanks, Roger. I hope it won't be necessary."

They reached the stables, which were situated some distance behind the main house. James gave the horse and trap over to a groom.

"Bring our cases up to the house," said James to the groom. "We'll both be staying the night."

"Hope there is room, baas. The house is very full, just now. Army, you know. And then there's Miss Louise's sister from England and Miss Sonny and another young girl whose name I don't know but as I see it she's pretty all right. Two other girls but I've never seen them before."

"You seem to know the family business."

"Well, you know how it is, baas."

"Yes. All too well. Just leave the word that I've arrived with yourself for half an hour. I wish to be a surprise."

"I think you will be, baas."

"Yes. Well. It has been a year."

"Baas Gavin knows how to entertain. Never been like this in the Cape before."

"Thank you. I am sure that will be enough." He turned to Quinn. "Come and meet my partner, Roger. He's quite something. Oh, and bring the cases up in half an hour on second thoughts," he said over his shoulder to the groom. "Good people," he said to Roger, "but forever inquisitive. Sounds like quite a house party."

"Sounds too good to be true."

"That's what I am afraid of."

A maid opened the front door and let them into the hall. They could hear that the drawing-room was full of people having drinks. The maid thought they were invited guests and took no further notice of them. She shrugged and went back to the servants' quarters. The noise was high spirited and it was obvious, even from the hall and with the door to the drawing-room closed, that people were enjoying themselves.

"Only one answer," said James. "Take off our coats and join them. There will be two good fires burning in there. Do you like Gavin's taste in architecture?"

"Yes. I do. Rather grand, but he's done it well. Must be quite something in the summer."

They opened the door but nobody turned and noticed them. They were too engrossed with each other. All the men except Gavin were in uniform. Roger looked at the women and saw a series of hard, pushed-up bosoms. He swallowed gently and then looked straight into the eyes, which were incredulous, of Lieutenant Colonel the Honourable John Gilham. Roger looked away quickly into a steady, frontal gaze from Louise Lagrange. Beside her was a young man who was obviously drunk but nobody seemed to take any notice. Quinn was unable for a moment to look away from the soft, brown eyes.

"We expected you, but not quite so soon," said Gavin, coming across to James. "Welcome to the party."

"Thank you for the invitation," said James. "This is Roger Quinn, Lieutenant, Mashonaland Horse."

"Carregan's Horse, don't you mean," answered Gavin.

"That's the press. The army still prefer Mashonaland."

"Ah, Colonel Gilham," began Gavin, but he was cut short by the colonel.

"That young man should not be allowed into a military gathering."

"Oh. Really," said Gavin. "Well, may I first introduce my partner, Major Carregan. This is Colonel Gilham, the Commanding Officer of the Sixth, Ninth Queen Charlottes."

"How do you do," said the colonel as shortly as manners permitted.

"Nice to meet you, sir. This is my second-in-command, Lieutenant Roger Quinn, though I seem to imagine you have met before. But, just in case of misunderstanding, I commissioned him myself in the field and it was ratified later in England. If I may say so, sir, you trained an excellent cavalry officer. Without him, the Mashonaland Horse would not have reached its small successes. I hope you will permit your previous grievances to be forgotten."

"Never seen anything like this before, meself," answered the colonel.

"Yes. Well, there is always a first time," said Gavin. "Wartime, you know." He even took on a little of their accent.

"Hello, James," said Sonny.

"Hello, Sonny."

"You made good headlines."

"Did I?"

"I hope they give you the Victoria Cross."

"Yes, jolly good show," said Gilham. "Must have been quite tricky capturing Viljoen. Come and meet some of my other officers." He was recovering himself. "I've always said what a help the colonial regiments would prove in time of war."

"Let me introduce you to the women," said Gavin to Quinn. "Have you set your eye on any one in particular?"

"The one in the white dress."

"You must mean Louise. This is Sonny Fentan, by the way. Such on old member of the family that we are sometimes inclined to take her for granted. This is Roger Quinn, I think it was. Sonny Fentan. I'm sure we'll be seeing more of you, Mr Quinn."

"Roger."

"Gavin. Never know with these army types. What did you do to the colonel?"

"Hit him in the face."

"Good for you. Any reason?"

"Not really. We were drunk. Unfortunately we were also in uniform."

"Nasty."

"Yes, it was."

"Go and save James, Sonny. Those army types will eat him, VC and all. Come, Roger, and meet my friend, Louise Lagrange. The unsteady gentleman next to her is her brother. Also a very good friend of mine. The very best when he's sober." They moved across the room.

"Darling, this is Roger Quinn. He's just arrived with James. Straight from the Transvaal and capturing the notorious Carel Viljoen."

"How exciting," said Louise.

"This is Louise Lagrange."

"Charmed to meet you, madam."

"This is her brother, Phillip."

"A pleasure," slurred Lagrange.

"Look who's here," said the Colonel as he guided James into the middle of a group of officers. "Oswald. Did you not see your brother-in-law arrive?"

"Hello, James."

"Hello, Oswald."

"Sorry about your father."

"Doesn't sound good. Ester well?"

"Was last time I heard. She's coming out."

"So I heard."

"This is Captain Firth, Captain Gore-Rupert, Lieutenant Berkeley and Lieutenant Crichton. Lieutenant Crichton's grandfather was Lord Levenhurst. This is Major Carregan of whom we have all heard so much."

"Nice to meet you all," said James and shook their hands.

"Have you been here before?" James asked Crichton.

"Many times. Gavin and I have become good friends. There is less than two years between us."

"How did you meet?"

"Through Colonel Gilham and Major Grantham. He thought the regiment would be posted up country again. He had six months up there and now we've been back again for three. Without Gavin's hospitality we'd all be bored stiff. Not a place, South Africa, really, if you like the English way of life."

"There are a lot of compensations," said James with a smile. "Will you excuse me for a moment. I must talk to my partner in private. A year away has kept me out of touch with my business and I am impatient to learn the news. I'll be back within half an hour."

"Have a drink first."

"Thank you. Thank you, waiter. That Scotch with a little water will see me fine. Cheers, everyone. A fine night for a party. Cold outside and the wind's coming up but warm enough in here with the fires."

"Hello, James. It's been a long time."

"Virginia! How nice to see you. Do you know everyone? Good. Yes. A long time. The farewell party to my grandfather seems a whole lifetime ago."

"I'm so glad about the decoration."

"I think it's only because they want to make this damn war look glamorous. It turned out to be one of the easiest operations we had undertaken. Viljoen was caught unawares. In fact, he thought he was hunting me."

"Nonetheless, it makes good reading."

"That's my point."

"Will you be here for the weekend?"

"Until tomorrow. This was a business trip. I'll be back later. Look after... no, don't bother. Louise has found him already. By the way, who is that girl over there?"

"Nice, isn't she?"

"Yes. You could certainly call her that."

"Phillip's other sister, Sarah."

"Not very like Louise."

"Not at all. Not in any way."

"You mean there was one sensible one in the family who didn't fall into the shadow of Gavin Morgan?"

"Give me time," said Gavin softly, having come up behind the group as was his habit. "She's not even been here a week. I imagine you want to talk business, James?"

"It was my reason for being here."

"I thought so. After a year, you must be anxious to hear the state of the company."

"I hope it's good," said James, smiling for the sake of the company.

"Yes. Will you excuse us? We can use my study on the top floor. The view, at night and in winter, is magnificent."

They went out of the room together and up the spiral staircase.

"Is what Viljoen told me true?" asked James after Gavin had firmly shut the door.

"Yes."

"What the hell made you two get up to a stupid thing like that? Wasn't Carregan Shipping and the damn farm making you enough money? Are you that greedy?"

"The deal had certain attractions. The excitement probably most of all. The rewards were high."

"So are the penalties. And not only for you, damn your eyes. Willie? How did you get him into this?"

"He was left out of the war."

"And wanted a little of the fun."

"Something like that."

"What I don't understand is your conscience. There's me and a good number of your friends being shot at and what does Morgan do? Supplies them with the bloody ammunition with which to kill us. And what for? Profit? Bloody money?"

"I think, James, that if you wish to look at that aspect of the problem we must go back a little in history. Take you and my father. Willie too. In '89. Had Rhodes any incentive other than profit to occupy the country that you now call Rhodesia? He thought there was gold, King Solomon's mines, in fact, and he spent years tricking an old savage like Lobengula into selling him his birth right. Then Rhodes gave Lobengula arms as part of the Rudd concession and what did the old savage do with them? He used them against you, and don't tell me that Rhodes did not envisage that when he delivered the rifles. My father was almost certainly killed by one of those guns. And who sent everyone running off to steal old Kruger's land? Rhodes again. For what? Profit. I've had this ammunition for four years. You knew about it, you just thought it had been sold to the Boers before the war began. And what difference would that have made? They would still have killed Englishmen, only this way they'll kill a few Boers as well, since the ammunition's old and may not go off as they expect it to. The real difference is the price Carregan Shipping has been paid, and in gold. We're merchants, James. Buying and selling at the right time and delivering it where it wants to be sent. And if we don't deliver it, they'll soon find someone who will."

"And what about Viljoen?"

"In all my calculations I must confess I didn't expect you, of all people, to bring him back in a British train. He tried to bribe you?"

"Yes."

"And you told him to go to hell."

"Yes."

"Would have done the same myself. Don't like blackmailers. He wanted what he was getting."

"You amaze me!"

"Why?"

"Your principles. Blackmail, no, but treason, that's different."

"Well, it is, and I explained it to you. Have I stated anything untrue?"

"No. But your argument still doesn't stand true."

"Because one man cannot make profit from another man's death? It's been done, year in and year out, since the world began. And just maybe I agree with the Boer cause. Am I not allowed my own freedom of mind? What have they ever done to you, for instance? What has Koos van der Walt ever done to James Carregan?"

"Nothing. He is a friend of mine."

"And yet if you caught him in a Boer commando you'd have shot him just the same."

There was silence.

"You met Koos?"

"Yes. Willie and I negotiated with him in the beginning. Willie talked to Viljoen after that."

"You used the *Good Hope*?"

"That's what I bought it for. It was not bought to titillate the women. Most of them are titillated enough."

"We seem to have a situation," said James after a while.

"Do you think he will talk?"

"I don't know. Apart from spite, he stands to gain nothing. However, we did not become friends."

"Do you want a drink? I keep some up here."

"Thanks. A whisky. If you had a sense of humour, you'd call this damn funny."

"It will be funny. Here, take this," he said, handing James the drink. "If we get away with it."

"If he talks, can they prove anything?"

"I planned the sale with someone talking in mind. The two shipments were documented correctly. Unless Koos stands in a court with Viljoen I can't see how they can prove anything."

"You still have Mauser ammunition? I gathered that from Viljoen."

"Good stocks, in fact."

"Send it to them little by little," said James. "That way they won't wish to blow you up. You'll be worth more to them than my scalp. And, anyway, would a jury believe the word of an enemy?"

"The Boers could only find out if Viljoen opens his mouth. They may have to back him to save their face. I'll show you every detail of the operation in the office on Monday. There are manifests, bills of lading, invoices, to show quite clearly what we have been delivering to Oudekraal. Carregan Shipping is a big operation. There are thousands of other transactions which appear to be exactly the same."

"When is the next consignment?"

"Tuesday."

"Are you going?"

"No. Kevin Grant. Two trips in one month by me would look unnatural."

"Can you rely on him?"

"He knows nothing. He's a good sailor but stupid. All he has to do is meet Willie at Oudekraal, land the so-called engine parts, and come back again. The real consignment was put into our Oudekraal warehouse three years ago."

"How did you manage the documents?"

"Simple. The *Cape of Good Hope* shows clearly on her manifest that she has shipped ten cases of engine parts. These are landed at Oudekraal under the nose of the buyer's mine captain. He receives a copy of all documents, including the invoice, which is specific in detailing the contents of the cases. He signs for them and signs a further, separate order for Carregan Shipping to move the cases inland to the mine. We sell the parts CIF to the mine. This way, they don't ever become his property until they reach the mine. We ask for him or a mine employee to watch the unloading from the schooner. Willie then explains he'll take them the following day as only then will it fit his schedule. The cases go into our warehouse.

The next day Willie loads ten cases of engine parts onto the wagon, having taken a normal consignment of assorted goods for the interior. You see, Willie completes all orders at Oudekraal at once. In fact, the *Good Hope* landed ammunition, the engine parts were already at Oudekraal and the normal consignment is bullets for the Boers."

"What happens if the British stop Willie on his way to Koos?"

"That is where I hope the name of Carregan will stop them looking. This VC of yours may be just what we need to counter Viljoen."

"He may remain quiet. I made some threats of my own."

"Good. Cheers. And sorry, James, I really did mean to keep you out of this one."

"How much will the total consignment be worth?"

"Half a million."

"Christ!"

"The gold goes to London. We won't sell it for years. The sale of Boer gold, or gold of any kind, would be the only way to trip us up."

"You've thought about this carefully."

"I hope so. Dinner will be served in half an hour. I'll put you between Sarah and Sonny. Should be fun. I'll ask Jasper Crichton to move out of your room. He'll have to go in with one of the others. Good sort. Never minds that kind of thing. I like Roger Quinn. Do you want to bring him into the business?"

"Yes."

"He's our type. I'll get to know him better. There's one small room left for him. After a year in the bush I expect you'd both enjoy some privacy."

"Thanks. See you at dinner. Send Roger up to change. It'll have to be in uniform. My old evening clothes no longer fit me. I seem to have lost all my fat, which, by the way, is more than can be said for you."

"Too much good living."

"An understatement. What are you going to do with Phil?"

"Draft him in the army."

"I'll give you some help. He'll die in a bottle if we leave him as he is."

"He's half dead already."

"You caused him to be what he is."

"Yes. I know. You can't make a silk purse out of a sow's ear. I thought you could. Or I thought that I was so bloody clever that I could make anything work. I'm learning a little, James. I'll be twenty-four next month."

"Jasper Crichton. What do you know about him?"

"Not much."

"I met an Edgar Crichton when I was last in England. Think I met him through Oswald. Could be the father."

"Must be. By all accounts Jasper is rather different to his father and they all know Oswald. Good connection, that one."

"You're not serious?"

"As a person he is a trifle pathetic, no offence meant to your sister, but as a name he is useful. People like their titles."

"Yes, I suppose they do."

"Dinner's at nine. Come down when you're ready. Your suitcase will come up to you. You know the room?"

"Yes. I know the room."

"Bottoms up."

"Nasty expression."

"Current military. How's Garret?"

"That horse can do anything but talk. Not a scratch. Can I buy him from you?"

"You've got him as a present. He was the only horse I loved."

"Sentimental Morgan. This is a new side."

"I think I liked that horse better than any woman I've met."

"Yes. I think I prefer horses as well. They don't change and they can't be influenced."

They laughed but without any great hilarity.

They finished their drinks and James found his way to the room he had always occupied when he stayed at Morgan's Bay. It was the same room that Lagrange had used to gain entry to his sister's veranda. James found the cupboard full of Annabel's second son's clothing. Strange world, he mused to himself as he ran a bath. A knock on the door brought a servant and his clothes came in and Jasper Crichton's went off somewhere else. The whole thing was not so surprising really. The connection was Oswald, himself and Rhys.

He let the bath run and opened the French windows. The gas lamps threw a good light around the room. He stepped out onto the veranda and held his face to a strong wind. The smell of seaweed was heavy. He stood there for some minutes, enjoying the cold and the smell of the sea. It would be a pity to lose all this, he told himself. He went inside to find his bath almost overflowing. It was too hot, and he let out the plug and gushed in some cold water. The plumbing was good; the tanks were some way up the hill at the back of the house. Good planning, he thought. A strong head of water.

"THIS IS QUITE LIKE OLD TIMES," said Sonny Fentan as James took his place beside her at dinner. "You look quite different in uniform. Have you met Sarah Lagrange? This is James Carregan, my dear. He is not as bad as the Boers and the British make him out to be. Sarah has just arrived."

"Hello," said James.

"Hello."

"Are you enjoying your stay?"

"I find some of the company a little unusual. My sister, for instance."

"She enjoys herself, yes, but is that wrong?"

"It depends, Mr Carregan, in which ways one enjoys oneself. I have asked my mother to come out immediately. My sister, being over twenty-one, and a woman of means, prevents the normal parental action. Phillip, too, is a disgrace. The man positively lives in a bottle."

"They say he's going into the army."

"Who are they? Mr Gavin Morgan or whatever his surname should be."

"Morgan," said James softly. "His father was my greatest friend."

"That may be so, but his son has turned out no friend of my brother or my sister. Look at them sir, and this is only what you see at the dinner table."

"I think this subject better left to a private occasion, Miss Lagrange. Then, and at your convenience, I'll be happy to discuss your brother. He's an employee of mine. Your sister, unfortunately, can be no concern of mine. No doubt your mother will deal with the situation adequately. I've heard she is a very capable woman."

"Of that, I can assure you." She looked up as a bottle of sherry appeared over her right shoulder. "No wine for me, thank you waiter. I was taught not to drink."

"Thank you," said James to the waiter and saw his glass filled to the top with an excellent dry, Cape sherry. Sonny giggled and James nudged her knee under the table.

"Did you have a good voyage out from England, Miss Lagrange?"

"Yes, thank you, Mr Carregan. It was very pleasant."

"The soup is pleasant also."

"I am finding it so."

James turned to Sonny and let Jasper Crichton take up the difficult dialogue with Sarah Lagrange. People like Jasper Crichton, he hoped, were more used to conversation for conversation's sake.

"Do you know, Jamie, you've become quite famous," said Sonny. "They say you're one of the first self-made millionaires to have been put up for a Victoria Cross, or anything like it for that matter."

"I do not consider myself a millionaire, my dear. A reasonably rich man seems to be the case, but let us not exaggerate."

"You must look at the books."

"Has business improved that much in a year?"

"Yes. With purchases of two shipping companies in America, your only opposition company here, you now control a fleet of fifty ships and they're not only trading in South African waters. Gavin is using some of his war profit to cut up competitors on other routes. He wants a prosperous shipping line when the war is finished."

"Sounds good business."

"He has the Midas touch, that boy," said Sonny.

"That, certainly, is an understatement."

"Gavin has finished with Louise."

"He really does go through them at an alarming rate. Nonetheless, that one lasted the longest of any. The only one. What other scandal can you tell me?"

"Virginia Webb has been pining for you. You must talk to her after dinner. I mean, she is quite a nice girl."

"After all these years, are you jealous, Sonny? This is not like you."

"I was young and didn't know what I wanted."

"But now you think you do?"

"Yes."

"Let's talk about it tomorrow. In the cold light of a cold day. Dinner parties and wine are not conducive to clear thought on such subjects."

"I won't sleep."

"I would, if I were you." There was silence for a moment.

"When will you know if they've awarded you the medal?" asked Sonny.

"I have no idea. I've only heard from other people that the matter is under consideration. I can see no reason why there is all this fuss."

"Where are you going to live when the war is over?"

"On Morgandale."

"Not Ship Corner?"

"I'll come down once a year when the crops have been reaped."

"What about Carregan Shipping?"

"That's for Gavin to attend to. I prefer farming. There are fewer complications. When Gavin first brought up the subject, he explained that Morgandale was too small for us both. So is

Carregan Shipping. Whatever its size. There can only be one man in successful control of one enterprise."

"Don't you prefer the way of life in Cape Town?"

"No."

"I am sure you will change your mind once this war is over. You have been through a hard year. It has changed you, as did Cape Town, but you'll change back again."

"I'm grateful for your confidence."

"If I did not know you so well, James, I would say you were being sarcastic."

"How well do you know me, Sonny?"

"After eight years? Better than you know yourself."

"Would you like to try the Riesling with the fish?" he said, changing the subject.

"Why not. Everyone drinks around here."

"Not everyone," said James, and turned to smile at Sarah Lagrange. She was deep in conversation with Jasper Crichton.

James looked across at Quinn, who was not listening to the subaltern on his right but watching Louise instead. Phillip, on Quinn's left, was having difficulty in locating the fish on his plate. When he drank, the liquid slopped dangerously in his glass. Colonel Gilham had recovered his good humour after being faced with Roger Quinn and was talking at great length to the girl on his right, who was trying not to be bored. James winked at her and, understanding him, she winked back. Gavin was trying to seem interested in the girl on his right, but his mind seemed to be far away from the dinner. James thought to tell Gavin to send the schooner in next time with real engine parts and drop a case while unloading in front of the mine captain to spill the proof of its contents at his feet. They would have to think of everything. He wondered if Viljoen had already told his interrogators about the ammunition. Meanwhile, Sonny was still talking to him. He answered her when it seemed necessary but heard nothing of what she said.

· · ·

James excused himself as soon as the party left the dinner table. He had slept little on the train from Bloemfontein. The worries, if there were to be any, would start later, but for the moment he had learnt all that he wanted to know.

In his room upstairs he opened the French windows, latched them firmly to the wall and tied the curtains against the wind. The sound of the heavy rollers on the shore below thundered into the room and within a short time of getting into bed they had lulled him to sleep. Surprisingly, he slept through the night and remembered none of his dreams when he woke to a grey morning.

James found Sonny at breakfast. The others had kept to their bedrooms. He looked under the large silver tureens and helped them both to what they wanted. His large breakfast cup was filled to the brim with black coffee. Neither of them talked. He hated conversation at breakfast. Half way through, Gavin joined them at the table. They greeted each other and then went on with their meals.

"Why don't you go for a walk," said Gavin when he saw that they had finished. "The Cape in winter has as much for me as it has in summer."

"Suits me," said James.

"Me too," said Sonny.

"Well, you might sound a little more enthusiastic."

"Early morning, Gavin," said James. "Come on, Sonny, it's walking time. You'll need a coat, but after last night's rain it's not that cold."

"Morning everyone," said Gilham as he briskly came into the breakfast room. "Damn good party. Enjoyed the port. You two going out?"

"For a walk."

"Humph. Bit damp. Enjoy yourselves."

. . .

"You didn't have to come for a walk," said Sonny when they were outside the house. "Gavin seemed to be pushing us."

"Probably was. The walk will do us good and I haven't seen the sea for a year. We can talk if you want to, but let's wait until we're down on the beach. The path isn't too steep but just look where you're putting your feet."

"It's a grey morning," she said.

"El Greco would have painted it well."

They descended the winding paths to the rocks below and then walked in and around them to the beach and its soft, white sand that had been dulled by the heavy rain overnight. She took his hand and felt how hard it had grown. He saw no reason to take it away. Great, green waves rushed in at the beach and as they crested, the wind spumed a white sheet of water back at the running sea. Then the wave crashed and gouged up the sand and ran in towards the two small figures, hand in hand, dwarfed by the massive mountains that grew out of the green slopes that ran and then dropped to the sea.

The sea reminded James of his voyage out to Africa on the *Dolphin* more than ten years earlier. He had hardly known his grandfather then, never met Willie or Rhys, never heard of farming, Sonny or Carregan Shipping. The winter sea was what he'd wanted at that moment. It toned in with his aches for the future.

"When do you think the war will be over?" asked Sonny.

"They should have given in months ago, after Bloemfontein and Pretoria fell. They're stubborn. They fight for survival like the tribes of Israel."

"I hope you come back alive."

"Does it really matter to you, Sonny? It never seemed to before."

"As I said at dinner, I was young. Now, I want what you want."

"Do you really? Or do you want what I have apparently become? Apparently, because I've not changed in eight years. Grown a little older but nothing else. Would you be content with Morgandale?"

"Yes."

"You say so now because you think you would be able to

persuade me to live in Cape Town. Once, you could have persuaded me to do anything. Not now. That affair you had with Gavin; oh yes, and don't emphasise what you thought was my naivety by protesting. You did what you wanted at the time and that was your business, not mine. But with that I saw your reality, and subsequently the reality of all human relationships. Like all else, it is a barter. You want me now because what I can now barter is wealth and, so you say, fame. This balances your book. I am now sufficiently attractive. I don't say you have come to this conclusion in a deliberate fashion, though at twenty-six you may have decided upon a marriage and looked at each man to find most of what you wanted in one of them. I wanted something spontaneous. Something that happens in the way that I first felt for you. When I met you, you became something so positively special.

"I do not want a bargain, a deal, I've had enough of those in recent years. When I marry, and of late I am qualifying this by saying that if I marry, then it will be to someone of feeling and not some picture that fits with my social life who will do sufficiently well to be taken. To compromise, yes, that is important, but I do not wish to negotiate the mother of my children."

"What will you do with what you have built up if you do not have any children?"

"There you are again. It's what I have that concerns you, not me."

"No, not only. I did not want to marry young. I thought it necessary to know other men so that I would not look back on my life without any comparison and think that it had been wasted, or think that I could have had something better. Was it wrong to want to do a little living? After mother died there was only me. Maybe I lost more than I thought I had gained."

"Did you gain anything?"

"Yes, James, I did. I regret nothing. Knowing what I know now, I would still go back and do the same things. Too many good things in life pass too many people by because they are always counting the costs in terms of the future. They're also too frightened to do what they want to do. Conformity can be very dull. I thought, looking at you, that you were enjoying a good bit of this way of life before you went off to the war. Maybe you didn't have enough. Give it another go. You'll be old, James, before you know it, and then you'll be finished."

They thought about this for some time.

"Funny how the image of women appears so much better at a distance," said James. His mind had rambled on from the thought of becoming old.

"How do you mean?"

"Well, take this Sarah. When I first took a look I said to myself that she was something unusual. Then she started to talk. Unusual, yes, to quote her own words, but not the type of unusualness that I had hoped to find."

"You look too hard. Expect too much. Too intense, Jamie. Relax a little. You may even have to compromise, as you say. Now. Come on. Let's race to the end of the bench. They'll all be still in bed with big fat heads, or each other, so no one will be watching."

They ran. He let her get a little way ahead and then stopped to watch. She flew with the wind and her long hair ran out in the same direction as the spume from the crests of the waves. After a moment, he began to amble after her.

9

*T*hree weeks later, they gazetted James's Victoria Cross followed by his promotion to Lieutenant-Colonel. Viljoen had sailed for Ceylon without incident. The *Cape of Good Hope* had dropped a crate of engine parts at the feet of Chris O'Connor, who'd seen exactly what he was getting. There might have been some bad language except that Virginia Webb and her best friend, Emily Hargreaves, were watching. Gavin had taken the boat himself and had also been able to bring Willie up to date. After Cape Agulhas, the weather had been good. The girls Gavin had picked were good sailors. They all spent a night on the mine and the next morning Willie brought in the engine parts. The dropped case had been repacked. There was no damage, and the schooner departed Oudekraal that afternoon leaving everyone happy. Willie left on the boat. The three of them were to confer in Cape Town.

COLONEL GILHAM SENT his respects to Colonel Carregan and asked for his company at the regiment's dining-in night the following Monday. The senior officers were housed at the newly opened Mount Nelson Hotel, which had been appropriated for use as British Headquarters. Lieutenant General Sir Richard Thackeray, the senior British officer in Cape Town, was also invited. The invitation stated seven thirty for eight o'clock. Number one dress. The Colonel secretly hoped that James would not know the protocol, but his hopes were in vain. "May I introduce Colonel Carregan to you, Sir Richard. This is General Sir Richard Thackeray, James. Colonel Carregan recently won the Victoria Cross."

"Damn fine show, Carregan. Must have shortened the war. Plucked him out of his own wife's arms, as I understand. Damn fine show, Anyone given you a glass of sherry? Don't mind this South African stuff but still prefer the Spanish. Price of war, you know."

"I always said the Colonials would be worth a lot to us in this conflict," said Gilham.

"Did you. Distinctly heard you say the opposite, John."

"Well. Hmph."

"Don't make noises. What did you say?"

"I wasn't sure of their worth. Then, that is."

"Wasn't sure. Sounded like you were damned adamant to me. Hell, just to prove your point I've seconded Carregan and that man Quinn to your regiment to show you how to fight the Rhodesian way."

"But, sir. Quinn was cashiered from the regiment."

"Don't tell me what I'm doing, Colonel. Believe he hit you at a mess function. Says he was drunk. Wants to apologise. This is war and unless we finish it soon my head will roll. And I don't like rolling heads when one of them is mine."

"Yes, sir."

"Good. Then I'll have another glass of sherry."

"Steward," said Gilham, sounding relieved. "Another sherry for the General. And put this one on my card."

"Good of you, John. Glad you can still afford to stand me a sherry. Poor show, what, if you couldn't?"

"A very poor show, sir."

"Now tell me, Carregan. Where did you go to school?"

"Wellington."

"Place is not up to Marlborough. Never mind. After that?"

"Oxford."

"Reading?"

"History."

"Bit strange for a historian to win a Victoria Cross. Ah, well, Wellington makes the difference. Now, where did this partner of yours come from? Heard some rumours. Not sure of his mother, or something. Heard it the other way round about other people. There are some in the cabinet who make you think. They even say you know his mother. Morgan? Must be Welsh. Never come across many of them meself. This sherry's not bad, John. If your card can take it, I'll have another. You have one, Carregan. I always say the first part of these dinners are so damn tedious that the only thing to do is drink. Can't even smoke. Not that sherry can do much harm. Carregan Shipping? That's you, so they say. Also hear your father left you a million. My condolence on his death. Lot of money, a million pounds."

"They say it may be more," said James with a smile.

"What the devil are you going to do with it all?"

"Quite frankly, sir, I haven't the first idea."

"How many ships have you got?"

"Sixty-one at the last count."

"Big ones?"

"Big ones."

"You must have had a million before your father left you another one?"

"Some people say so."

"And your pater left you the lot?"

"All of it. I am to look after my sister."

"Sorry for being personal, but it's a damnable lot of money for one man."

"Then there's the farm."

"What farm?"

"My farm."

"How big is that?"

"One hundred thousand acres. It may be more. Difficult to measure."

"This is in Rhodesia?"

"Yes."

"Give him that other sherry, John. He can afford to drink it. Your brother-in-law can't be too happy about that will, eh, Lord Grantham," said the General, finishing his glass. He looked at Grantham, who was trying not to be noticed.

"Not unhappy," said James. "We understand each other, which is more than can be said for my father. To begin with they were all right. At the end, not so good. Pity, Oswald, you should have persevered a little more."

"Poor old Oswald," said the General. "Well, never mind. You've always got your career in the army. The war's not over yet. Still have time to cover yourself in glory. Now, where's that confounded sherry of mine?"

"Steward," said Gilham sharply, and the offending drink was found immediately.

"Cheers, Carregan. Damn good show. You should go into politics."

"Cheers, sir. I prefer farming."

"Hope to retire to the family estates, meself."

"It's a good way of life."

"Will be when we finish this war. I want this regiment to fight the way you fought. You can't fight a few horsemen with a major offensive. They've gone when you get there. Find the leaders. Put them away and the rest will go back to their farms. Kruger's in Europe, Viljoen in Ceylon, a few more of them out of the country and the war will be over. Do you agree with me?"

"A war of attrition will only cause bitterness," said James. "It was why I went for Viljoen. They know they can't win and it's only leaders like Viljoen who are holding the commandos together."

"They say van der Walt has taken over Viljoen's commando. Friend of yours?"

"Yes. We went into Rhodesia together. He helped me set up my farm. I knew nothing about farming in those early days."

"What do you do if you come up against him?"

"I doubt whether he knows what to do either. It is a situation that I hope will not arise. We are both what we now call Rhodesians."

"But you are English."

"Yes, that as well. In the end it will become a new country. A mixture of Morgans, Carregans and van der Walts."

"You don't really hate the Boers?"

"No, sir. I know too many of them. It was why I captured Viljoen and did not kill him. We hope to visit each other's farms when the war is over."

"Not quite my sentiment, but then I'm a professional soldier. You think you can convert this regiment to your tactics?"

"Yes. But I'll need all my men to help. In the field, I would like one of my men to act as scout to each of the units that I shall create from the regiment. That way, everyone will have the immediate benefit of our years of experience in this type of warfare. And my people have all lived in the bush. Our method is hunting, General. To hunt well, you need skill and experience. The fighting comes right at the end of the trail and is often the easiest part."

"I wish you luck. Now, John, don't you think it's near enough to eight o'clock to take us in to dine? Don't mind drinking on an empty stomach, but I prefer doing it on a full one. I'd like Carregan on my left and you on my right. We'll have none of the imperial forces taking preference over the colonials. We should have listened to them a damn sight earlier than we did. Don't you agree, John?"

"That's what I always said, sir."

"No you damn well didn't. You must point out which one is Levenhurst's grandson. The man was a friend of my father's, fine man. Left a lot of money. Pity he didn't have any sons."

.   .   .

WILLIE VON BRAND adjusted his cravat in the mirror and smiled at himself.

"Not a day over fifty."

"What did you say?" said Gavin, who was already changed. He was still worried and had wished to talk over every detail with von Brand.

"Not a day over fifty."

"Who isn't?"

"Me. Who else?"

"Oh, yes. Not a day over fifty."

"Stop thinking about it, Gavin. The man's been gone to Ceylon for weeks."

"Maybe he told them. Maybe the British are waiting to find some proof."

"Maybe. Where are they going to find some proof?"

"That's what I'm trying to outthink them on."

"Forget it. It was a scare. As James pointed out to him, he had nothing to gain and something to lose."

"People are not always logical."

"Where's James now?"

"Some military function."

"Popular lad these days."

"Yes."

"Is he coming out afterwards?"

"Yes."

"Pour yourself one of your own drinks. You'll feel better. I like that Mrs Dalton. She may be forty-five but she doesn't look a day older than thirty. Pity about her husband. She told me last week that she likes farm life. Good start, don't you think? Bought the evening dress clothes to celebrate. Like it?"

"Sure."

"How are you getting on with Sarah?"

"Terrible."

"As a host, you're going to be a flop tonight."

"Let's hope it's only as a host."

"Look, Gavin, don't start losing your confidence at this stage. You're not the only one who is likely to be shot."

"You're right. We'll fight it, at the worst."

"That's better. Now, come on and let's go down and start the drinking. We have a reputation for debauched parties to maintain. The ladies will be joining us shortly. I always said that I didn't want to live out my old age alone."

MRS BETHANY DALTON WAS, in fact, forty-nine years of age. She had aged well, but then she had looked after herself. She had come to South Africa to see the burial place of her dear husband; or, more exactly, to make certain that he was really dead and had not used the war as an excuse to avoid his creditors. He had, she discovered with relief, died accidentally. It had never been his intention to expose himself to danger. Captain Hugo Dalton had been involved in one of the first motor car accidents in Cape Town, run over and killed by a motorised car in Adderley Street. Since at the time of the accident he had been on Her Majesty's Service, they had given him a military funeral. Mrs Dalton was perfectly happy with his death, but he had left her one problem. Money. What did a lady of leisure do, at the age of forty-nine, to earn sufficient income to live in the way that her husband had been able to by borrowing? Some of his creditors, and they were the larger ones, had even insisted that as his widow she had inherited his liabilities as well as his assets. If Hugo had only died in action, she would have been able to reproof them with his sacrifice for the nation. Adderley Street motorised cars did not seem to have the same power.

She had decided, therefore, to remain in South Africa. She would find a rich old man to charm and of this she had plenty. Her success had been minimal until she'd met Willie von Brand. He was rough, too large and German. But he had his compensation. He was rich. They even said that he was worth a million, though for the life of her she couldn't see how. To have money, one either inherited, the best and surest way, or one had a great skill, such as a surgeon did, and one turned it to profit. Nonetheless, she would change him. She had discreetly checked up on his wealth. He would become putty in her hands. With all that money she could pay off Hugo's debts and go back to England. She could even drop a few of her lower class friends, the ones who had been the most tedious about money. First, she would curtail Mr von Brand's drinking habits, but only after she had become Mrs von Brand would she explain to him the changes that were necessary in his character.

She spread just the right amount of rouge on her face and put a good layer of red lipstick on her mouth. Satisfied, she dabbed at her hairdo and looked at it carefully in the mirror from all directions. She stood up. Her corset made her feel faint. The price of success, she told herself, and patted the whalebone flatness of her stomach with satisfaction. They made them so well if you found the right shop.

It was time for her entrance. With so many young and attractive women in the house, it was necessary to play every move carefully. Mrs Dalton was not a woman to underestimate her opposition. She would make them look too young and too frivolous. A mature man needed a mature woman.

She sailed down the corridor and staircase at a steady speed and checked to compose herself as the servant bent to open the door to the drawing room. She allowed the door to remain open for a moment, then swept over the threshold. She nodded at those she knew slightly, smiled sweetly but with a hint of superiority at Virginia Webb, caught the eye of von Brand and sparkled him a smile before getting under way in his direction.

"My dear Mr von Brand," she said, putting her gloved hands into his. "How nice to see you. I had no idea you would be here. These house parties are such fun if one finds the right company."

"The pleasure, Mrs Dalton, is, I am told, mine," said von Brand and immediately he had the feeling that he had somehow put it a little wrong. The charming woman only smiled; for her, his ignorance of etiquette was not important.

· · ·

'MUST TELL HIM ABOUT THAT WOMAN,' said Gavin to himself as he watched Sarah Lagrange come into the room. If the damn woman despised his way of life and what he had done to Phil and Louise, then why did she accept his invitations? At least the threatened mother had not arrived, which was something. He would make a play tonight despite the frigid way in which she talked to him. With a body and a face like that, she must be a woman underneath. And being far away from home she would want to do something about her curiosity. This time he would ignore her for the evening and see how she got on with that. He always became irritated with women who did not respond to his advances within a reasonable amount of time.

Gavin had another drink and felt better. Even if they came after him now it had been a good run. Not many people his age made sufficient money to entertain in the way he was doing. Everything, he told himself, had been a risk, and everything would be. He had almost panicked and that must never happen again. Panic made wrong decisions. If it came, if they were faced with their problems, their success would lie in their ability to bluff. This the three of them had agreed. They would use their money if it became necessary. All they had done was trade. They had sold no secrets and, as yet, told no lies. An opportunity had shown itself to make a large amount of money. The only thing he had forgotten was the final penalty and for that he had no wish to be shot.

"IS IT TRUE," said Louise to Roger Quinn, "that you are taking my brother into your regiment?"

"Not exactly. We have bought him a commission in the Queen Charlottes who are to be trained in guerrilla warfare by the Mashonaland Horse. I believe your sister had words with James. Phillip will come directly under me."

"Do you think he will be all right?"

"Away from Gavin, yes. To begin with he tried to keep up with Gavin and found it impossible. From this he decided he was no good for anything. To compare oneself to Gavin is not a fair judgement for anyone."

"I have merely been lucky," said Gavin, who was listening to the conversation. "If it was possible to buy a commission for Phillip, would it not be possible to buy one for me?"

"You in the army?" answered Quinn.

"I can ride a horse. Garret was mine before James. I have taken a lot from this war. Maybe I should put some of it back. Being a soldier in Africa seems to be a prerequisite of life. It will be good experience. Also, I am getting fat, which is disgusting at twenty-four."

"Your birth may give us difficulties."

"Well, find a regiment that is not averse to the odd bastard. If viscounts can do what they do, then bastards should be able to do a little of their own."

"I'm sure you can get into the army," said Louise quickly.

"It could be fun. Yes. Find me another regiment. Better not tread on poor Phillip's toes any longer. There must be a Rhodesian force that would welcome the son of one of their first heroes. Failing that, I'll put together a troop of my own."

"That might work the best. Offer to form and finance a new Rhodesian regiment. Governments are always short of cash. With your reputation, you shouldn't have any difficulties with volunteers."

"What will the women do in Cape Town?" said Louise in mock despair.

"Out of sight is out of mind," said Gavin. "This new idea might amuse von Brand."

"But not Mrs Dalton," said Louise.

"Yes, the more I think of it, the more I find it a good one. It will solve so many problems at once. The crew of the *Cape of Good Hope* can join up to start with. The jobs undertaken by the schooner can be done by another member of the line. As a cargo boat, she was a failure. It merely gave me an excuse to go for a cruise. I'll go and tell Willie."

"He makes his mind up fast," said Louise as she watched Gavin walk across to von Brand.

"It's the way to do business."

GAVIN PUT his left hand on von Brand's shoulder and smiled at Mrs Dalton.

"We're joining the Army, Willie."

"Good idea. What did you say?"

"I'm forming my own regiment, attached to the Rhodesians. We've been out of the fighting for long enough and I'm bored."

"They won't let me in at my age."

"Of course they won't," said Mrs Dalton.

"We'll tell them you're under fifty. I'll sign the papers."

"But that is perpetuating a lie," said Mrs Dalton.

"Don't we all, Mrs Dalton?" asked Gavin.

"But Willie is over sixty."

"And he's fitter than half the regular officers. Experience? They could never know as much as Willie von Brand, and if you can find ten officers in the British Army who can shoot straighter I'll give you fifty pounds."

"What about the business?" said von Brand.

"Yes. What about the business?" agreed Mrs Dalton.

"It will run on its own. It may not grow. It may go a little backwards, even, but it will run. The war cannot last for that long."

"I'll come," said von Brand, warming to the idea. Suddenly he felt uncomfortable in his new evening clothes. Maybe it would even stop him feeling old. "We'd better make this a damn good party. I hope James doesn't arrive before I get drunk."

"Do you always get drunk at parties, Mr von Brand?"

"It would not be a party otherwise, Mrs Dalton. Can I fetch you another drink?"

"Well, under the circumstances, I think you'd better."

Von Brand winked and brought a twinkle to her eye.

"A large one?"

"Why not."

"That's better, Mrs Dalton. I think we are getting to know each other." And, as he went by, he gently tapped the hard corsetry of her otherwise fleshy behind.

"DID YOU SEE THAT LOT?" said Louise.

"I think it's earmarked for Mrs Dalton."

"I hope she has a head for drink."

"She'd be the last to admit it and the last to say that she enjoyed the stuff but I'll bet she enjoys her drink and her food. She'll get on better with Willie like that. She would not have been able to fool him for long."

"You can't fool anyone for long."

"No, Louise, you can't."

"Not even you, Roger?"

"Least of all me, Louise."

"I see."

BY TEN-THIRTY VON Brand was at his correct level of alcoholic intake and Mrs Dalton was a little drunk. They had enormously enjoyed themselves and Mrs Dalton had decided to change her tactic. Anyway, if it succeeded, it was a far more pleasant way of achieving what she wanted. The door opened and for a moment the noise subsided. It was the first time they had seen James in ceremonial uniform and the first time that any of them had seen a Victoria Cross. He waved and walked across to the bar. For once he was less than sober despite the hour and a half drive he had undertaken to Morgan's Bay. Forcibly, General Thackeray had kept him drinking drink for drink and James had never liked port.

He reached the bar and poured himself a small Scotch and soda. He turned, leaning a little backwards, and looked at the crowd. He felt like having a woman, but in the age in which he lived, this was not always possible. On the surface, that is, he told himself. Maybe it was the port or just the time of the month. He took sight of a new, rather tall girl and decided to try his luck. Gavin came across to him as he was making up his mind.

"Glad you came. I'm joining the army."

"Good."

"So's Willie."

"Good. Who's that tall girl over there?"

"That's Lillian Dalton. Mrs Dalton's daughter."

"That would be fun. Becoming Willie's stepson."

"Are you thinking of marrying her?"

"Not before we've got to know each other properly."

"They're not all like that."

"Just my luck."

"You did hear I was joining the army."

"Yes. A good cover."

"Attack them before they attack us. I'll have to try and do something spectacular."

"These things are pretty easy," said James, tapping his medal.

"Not everyone has your luck."

"True."

"Something, anyway."

"If our problem is uncovered, it'll help. Now introduce me to that girl."

They walked across. Gavin was a fraction less sober than James.

"Miss Dalton, I'd like you to meet a friend of mine. Colonel Carregan, Miss Lillian Dalton."

"Not so formal, Gavin, I'm not that old."

"Sorry. Lil Dalton. Jamie Carregan."

"How did you know my nickname, Gavin?"

"Quick brain. Can't do a thing without it."

"Hello, Miss Dalton," said James. "Excuse all this stuff, but I've just come away from the army."

"I've heard a lot about you."

"Was it good or bad?"

"A little of both."

"I hope you didn't believe a word of any of it. Never believe anyone these days."

"Oh, but I don't. I believe in finding out for myself. Are you staying the night?"

"It's too far to go home. They've given me a job at last but it won't begin till next week. Then I go up north again. I may stay for a few days if Gavin will put up with me. He's joining up as well. So is Willie. That puts us all in the army. If I were the Boers, I'd surrender immediately. Too much competition, especially with Willie coming into the war on our side. He could always fire three shots to one of mine from under a wagon. He frightened Lobengula into giving us Rhodesia."

"You've known him for long?"

"We share the same farm, the same wars and the same bottle of brandy."

"Where did you meet him?"

"In a tavern."

"Seriously?"

"Seriously."

"Which one?"

"The Harbour Tavern."

"Here in Cape Town?"

"Here in Cape Town."

"Cheers, Colonel."

"Cheers, Miss Dalton. What do you do for a living?"

"Nothing. I follow my mother."

"A good occupation."

"Sometimes."

"Do you know," said Roger Quinn to Louise, "you haven't looked at another man tonight."

"I must be getting old or something."

"Just maybe you've had enough of the way of life you've been leading."

"Is it possible to change? I think I'd grow bored. The same face, the same habits, the same old routine. Take my mother. She's followed an identical pattern for years. I couldn't lead a life like that. This way I may end up with a reputation but Cape Town is a long way from home. Virginia says the same. If we have to go back to the accepted society in England, no one will know us for what we may have done. Such habits do not even form part of their imaginations. No. We'll be just like all the other girls, except that we'll have travelled. This in itself is a status in that society. They'll imagine that we've seen all the old masters in Italy or something equally idiotic. And when they think of this war they'll think of a Florence Nightingale. Very patriotic. No. I'll go back when I have to, but not before. Who as a girl in England could imagine a way of life like this? The company is young, the money unlimited and the setting delicious."

"You've not been north, have you?" asked Roger.

"Not out of Cape Town, in fact."

"When this war is over, I'd like to show you Rhodesia. It's wild and not always friendly, but it has a great power. There's no chance of boredom in such an atmosphere."

"Rather uncivilised, though?"

"Come and see for yourself."

"First you have to finish this war."

"Something that becomes more difficult every time we think we have the situation in hand. The Boers are tenacious. I can't say I like the idea of putting the women and children into camps and neither do the Boers. Makes them fight. It may have stopped their provisions coming from home but it has given them something else. They can live on the smell of an oil rag. Provided they have a horse, a rifle and ammunition, they go on fighting. Guerrilla warfare is difficult to bring to a conclusion from either side. It's something that can just go on until one side grows bored and disappears. At the moment that's just what the Boer does, and regularly. The poor British soldier trudges along behind. They never find the phantom. It's like trying to swat a fly with a pick-axe. The one is too fast and the other too heavy. Stupid war, this one. The British government thought it would be over in a few weeks. How could they believe that unshaven farmers could defy the British Empire? They probably wonder why they started it all now. But they'll finish it; the British always do. So, that is war. Did you enjoy the crayfish tonight? They were taken from the bay. Gavin says there are enough to feed an army."

GAVIN MORGAN TOOK a drunken look at the gap between the balconies. He knew what was down below so he did not have to look. He had seen it done before, and by Phillip, so the jump was certainly possible. If he fell, he told himself in a sozzled mixture of thoughts that floated through the fumes of his mind, then he would have fallen in the pursuit of his favourite cause. Women. He imagined that he steadied himself and then launched. In fact he swayed, lurched and ended up all of a mess on the floor of Sarah Lagrange's balcony.

'That's my boy', he giggled to himself, and tried to rise to his feet. His bottom came up but his head stayed down. He pulled up his head and looked at the doors. He leered in self-congratulation and managed to get to his feet. One of the French windows was open. It was the British way of life above a certain social level; they always slept with their windows open.

He moved to the seaward side of the balcony and forced himself to draw in and down quantities of cold sea air into his smoke-encrusted lungs. He had no intention of spoiling his final and perilous effort by being drunk. He waited and slowly his brain began to clear. It began to rain and he could hear thunder a long way across the water. He went on waiting, as he wished to be in full control of himself. Vicious lightning bit into the horizon. He watched each flash and waited for the thunder. He was looking forward to going to war. It had been his best idea for a year. It would be cold, bitterly cold on the highveld at night. The fires, when they could have them, would be big and warm. A hard life, sleeping on hard ground, but he'd grown sick for the moment of what he'd been doing. He wondered how well he would do in a real fight. The storm was coming closer. The rain, forced in under the awning which protected the balcony, slashed at his face. He ran the back of his hand across his wet mouth and turned to the open French windows.

It was a new approach even if it was a little direct. It took a moment to let his eyes grow accustomed to the darkness. Lightning flashed and showed him her face asleep. Her expression was calm and soft. He sat down on the edge of the four-poster bed and rainwater ran off his face onto the bedclothes. She was sound asleep. Strands of brown hair had strayed over her face. He waited for the lightning and pushed the hair gently away from her face. Her mouth was slightly open but she made not a sound in her breathing. He waited for some time as the storm come closer. He was sober and enjoying himself. She was even more desirable where she lay and slept. The thunder built up and she woke with a start.

"It's all right. It's only thunder. The Boers have not reached Cape Town."

"Who's that?" Her voice was small and pinched. Very frightened.

"Gavin. I came to see if you were frightened of the storm. My room is next door."

"Get out."

"That is no way to treat a man who has come to comfort you."

"I'll scream."

"You'll need good lungs to compete with this storm."

"You've no right to come into my bedroom."

"On that you are right."

"How did you get in?"

"Over the balcony. Your door was locked."

"I don't trust anyone in this house," she said in disgust.

"Don't you trust me?"

"You, least of all."

He bent across swiftly and touched her lips with his own before she could move her head away. He looked down at her from a few inches above. She saw the amusement in his eyes when the lightning flashed.

"Thank you for the compliment," he said.

"You frighten me. There is nothing you won't do to get what you want."

"Nothing."

"The only way I could give to any man what you want is when he has married me first," she said.

"Are you proposing to me?"

"I wouldn't marry you if you were studded with diamonds."

"Do you want a bet?" He bent and kissed her hard. Before she could recover herself, he'd unlocked the door and let himself out into the corridor. Amidst the storm she could hear him laughing, as though he was thoroughly enjoying a joke with himself. Then he shut the door gently behind him. Thunder crashed just above the house. She hid under the bedclothes and tried to pretend she was back in England.

PART II

1

*G*avin Morgan worked his way out of his sleeping bag and cursed the bitter coldness of the Transvaal night. The air was sufficiently cold and clear to cut with a sabre. There were no fires burning and most of the camp was asleep from sheer exhaustion. Gavin picked up his rifle and walked to the perimeter of the camp. There were sixty men. Rhodesian auxiliaries. In exchange for his private army, they had made him an acting captain. The rank made no difference, as the men belonged to him and von Brand in other ways. They were mercenaries and the best paid troops in the allied army. They all knew the bush except for the crew from the *Cape of Good Hope*, Kevin Grant having been made captain of a small coaster that ran up to Durban.

From these trips, Koos van der Walt found he was not short of ammunition. He was sending more than half of the new consignments through to the other commandos. Three weeks earlier, he had heard that Gavin Morgan had crossed the Limpopo into the Transvaal. The situation had provided him with his first amusement for months.

Gavin moved further into the bush. Having gone a hundred yards, he whistled softly. The answer came back and he moved in the direction of the noise.

"Morgan," he said softly when he estimated he was close enough.

"Over here, Gavin," said von Brand.

"You shouldn't be standing sentry," said Gavin when he joined him. "You must be the only captain on sentry duty in the whole damned army."

"This is our first night within contact of the Boers. I want to smell them first. Maybe the others do not have the experience. If I had your father posted on the other side of the camp I would feel even happier. We used to hunt like that together in the old days. We had our fights but never surprises. Your father was a great hunter."

"Did you two hunt in these parts?"

"Many times. It was outside the control of the Boers or Lobengula. Karma lay claim to the land, but we hunted it just as we wanted."

"It's been a long ride."

"Good training. But we're still raw at this type of fighting. Before, I've only shot natives when they had it in mind to shoot me. On our way to Bulawayo in '93, they attacked the wagons seven times. It was slaughter. You cannot successfully attack a well-armed laager. Even the king's regiment found that to their cost."

"Willie, it's important we make a success of this venture. Hatred breeds well in captivity. Viljoen has had six months to think and fester."

"If he hasn't talked now, then he won't. But we'll do what we can. It's cost us enough money. I now know why Rhodes sent in such a small army to Rhodesia."

"We must get into the press so that we have the public behind us."

"You have a fixation, Gavin."

"Maybe."

"Check the sentries and go back to sleep."

"When are you going to sleep?"

"I don't do it as well as I used to. One of the problems of getting old. Five hours is enough for me and I'm usually lucky to have that amount before I wake up."

"Do we move out at first light?"

"Yes. I want to move up into the hills. We'll wait up there until we see their dust trail. They say De Jong is hard pushed. This time he'll be caught."

"I hope so. Just make sure that our name is mentioned in the report."

"It will be, Gavin. He'll have guided the British into closing the trap. Go on. Get some sleep. I'll tell you what to do when anything happens."

"Thanks, Willie. We've done all right in the army together so far."

"We haven't started yet. We only will when we see that dust from De Jong's wagons."

"We'll find him."

"Let's just hope that he doesn't find us."

"We travel light. Horses, pack mules. Exactly as James directed. How can they find us in this expanse of veld?"

"I'll take a bet that they knew the day we crossed the border. It's how they've stayed alive and in the war for so long. They know this country. We're the foreigners, despite how many elephants I've shot in the area."

"I'll sleep well for the thought."

"Just don't forget, Gavin, that we're new in this game. They've been at it for two years." Gavin went back to his sleeping bag and tried to sleep. It was his first experience of war and the glamour was beginning to wear thin. They were ill trained and, Willie aside, badly led. But like so many of his gambles in life, he felt it had been a necessary one. He believed implicitly in looking at any problem from every angle and as far as each could be taken. He analysed the consequences of every one of his actions and took evasive or precautionary measures if he could see that it was possible for something to develop to his disadvantage. He was building up a dossier in his defence and he believed in public opinion.

The army in Cape Town envied his way of life, despised him and would do anything to squash him if the opportunity arose. He had been too successful. He did not have a family. They did not like an exception to their rules. They thanked him for his entertainment and laughed behind his back. It gave him no worries, as he had expected nothing better. He despised a lack of ability in a man as much as they despised a lack of breeding. They lived for each other. He only lived for himself and only did for his friends. But they ran with the herd. Their opinion was always that of the majority. They liked to be popular and they liked to be saying and doing the right things at the right times. If luck was with them here in the bush, Gavin told himself, they would gain their own experience without all being killed. The man next to him was snoring but, despite him, Gavin went back to sleep.

WILLIE VON BRAND walked through the camp and no one stirred. Some of them may know the bush, he told himself, but when it comes to war they know nothing. As he looked over the camp, he was puzzled as to how at the age of sixty-one he had come to have as his defence sixty of the least experienced troops in the area with the veteran of Boer veterans not further than fifty miles from where they slept so soundly. Despite Gavin's intentions, he would have to keep them out of trouble, and to do that he must keep them well out of De Jong's way. He sighed to himself and went back into the bush to watch and to listen.

THE DRAKENSBERG MOUNTAINS stretch for a long distance and then well on into Natal. De Jong had entered this range to find himself a valley that he could easily defend and easily escape from. The war of attrition had been hard-going for the Boers and De Jong wanted time to recuperate. He was weighed down by many of the burghers' families travelling with the commando to prevent them being forced into a concentration camp. They needed rest and there were parts of the Drakensberg where he knew the British would never find him.

It had been difficult to make the older burghers do what he wanted. They knew better. They always knew better. The great *berg* was too far. The wagons would not climb up into the mountains. And if the British found them and attacked them in force, they were finished. He argued they were finished if they remained in the open veld where their dust trail could be seen for five miles. Eventually, he'd won his argument. He wished many times that he was a dictator, but that was not the Boer way. They elected their commanders. They were free men. They followed who they wished and they listened to old men. That was good in times of peace. But not now when half a day's trek meant freedom and the chance to come out again and smash the British supply system. He'd done a lot of damage and would do a lot more. He knew these passes like nobody else. His patrols scouted around the trek for miles. They would know if they were being watched and would have time to move out of the way of a superior British force. They were three thousand strong, not to mention the women and children, wagons, cattle, goats and all the other impediments of a small army on the move. They had two big guns they prized above all their possessions. The war would go on, and every week was costing the British millions.

WILLIE VON BRAND watched the vast snake of the Boer commando as it made its way up into the mountains. They had found it completely by mistake.

"Don't use your glasses," he told Gavin. "They'll see the reflection from the sun. Send Porter back to warn the main troop. The Boers will have scouts out all around that column. We did the same when we went into Rhodesia. They'll have men ranging out for twenty miles in all directions."

"We must send a report back to the forts," said Gavin. He was openly excited. "From now on we must never let them out of our sight."

"I hope we know what we're doing."

"Of course. This is exactly what I wanted. If we can guide the British to De Jong we'll be in every newspaper in the British Empire."

"Provided a few of your well-supplied Mauser bullets do not end it here. If they start hunting us we'll never get out. They could not afford to let any of us leave the mountains. They're looking for somewhere to rest. The war has been bad for them recently. They're angry men down there."

PORTER LEFT them and skilfully guided his horse down the mountain path away from the crest where they'd been able to look down on the Boers. The Rhodesians were to keep out of sight, show no fire and make no noise. He was scared. The whole valley was full of Boers. He had kept out of the war on purpose and had only been brought into it by Morgan's money. The crops had been bad and it had seemed the war was nearly over. He had certainly thought the danger was over. He looked around the surrounding hills and was certain he was being watched. He wished he and his horse could disappear right out of the Drakensberg Mountains. He waited for the first bullets to hit his back, but nothing happened.

He reached the troop hidden among the trees and passed on the instruction to acting Lieutenant Tenant. The news spread quickly and the swashbuckling confidence disappeared from the troop. Their bluff had been called. They might have to fight. Their confidence ebbed as low as their feelings. More than anything else they needed a leader in whom they had confidence. They would have to rely upon the German and hope that Morgan took his advice.

Two of the troop left on their way back to make contact with the British troops. Tenant wondered if they would be believed. People had been looking for De Jong for months and now here was

Morgan with his luck – good or bad they would have to wait and see – finding the Boers on his first patrol.

TEN MINUTES LATER, von Brand and Morgan joined them among the trees. Von Brand called them together. He was big enough to stand above any of them.

"De Jong, as you know, is on the other side of that mountain. Most of you thought this war was over. Few of you thought you would have to fight. Hell, right now, you may have to for no other reason than to save your own lives. Now, I'll tell you something about us. We may be green in this type of warfare but every one of us knows Africa, which is more than a lot of the British can say for themselves. And in country like this it will be men behind rocks and the ones who shoot straight will be the ones who come out alive. Every one of us is a marksman. We'd have been dead in the new country from starvation if we weren't, as Rhodes helps those who help themselves." There was a small snigger and he let it run.

"I am the only one here who went into the new country with the Pioneer Column," he continued. "Many of them were green then, much greener than you; and none more green than Colonel Carregan. He had never even fired a rifle before he came to Africa and that was just weeks before he went up to help defy Lobengula. You say I'm old and Morgan's young but I know these hills and I know how to hunt like the Boers and Captain Morgan never does a damn thing without asking me. And then we use our brains together. And if any of you have enough brains to do what Morgan's done in five years then I'd like to see you repent his performance. We are untested, but so was everyone before the first shot was fired.

"All we have to do is keep out of De Jong's way until the imperial forces make contact with us in strength. Right now, there are Boer patrols all round us, guarding their column. They range for long distances. Our advantage is that we know they are there but they know nothing about us. There is no reason why we should not succeed and have this war brought to an end. Apart from De Jong, there are only seven major commandos still in existence. You can say that the valley is ten per cent of the Boer war effort. Just imagine there's a wounded buffalo around every tree and the Boers will never surprise you. We stay here till nightfall. Then we follow that column. Every day, two men will go back to the imperial forces to report their new position."

"How near are the British?" someone asked.

"I have no idea," said Morgan. "But one or more of the patrols will either find a fort or the railway line."

"At best, how long will it take to bring up a British force?" asked another.

"A week," said von Brand.

"How many men has De Jong?"

"They say three thousand, but a lot have been deserting and going back to their farms."

"We'd better keep out of his way."

A few of them tried to laugh, but without any conviction.

SECOND LIEUTENANT GORDON HARRIS of the Twelfth Kings Own Rifles was bored in the way that he had been for seven weeks, ever since he'd taken command of the small, concrete line of pillboxes and forts that ran out straight across the veld with a heavy fencing of wire in between. The Transvaal was being cut up into segments and each area then cleansed of Boers. The war of attrition was reaching its final stage. Harris was twenty and had been in South Africa six months. He preferred the army in peacetime, the social life, the element of glamour in uniform, the people you met. He was of good Irish stock but had been unable to buy himself a commission in an Irish regiment. The Twelfth Kings Own Rifles was not quite up to his mark, but there would always be time to change afterwards. To reach his goal he required action, but couldn't afford to make a mistake.

When the first patrol sent out by von Brand reached the wire two days after leaving the mountains, they were immediately escorted to Lieutenant Harris.

"We've found De Jong," said the trooper, who had forgotten to salute. He was tired, thirsty, hungry and out of temper after three days of travelling.

"Don't you salute an officer, young man?" said Harris.

"We're not regulars," explained the trooper. "They didn't teach us anything like that."

"The first thing a soldier learns is to salute an officer."

"We're Rhodesian auxiliaries."

"Which regiment?"

"We're attached to the Mashonaland Horse."

"Impossible, young man. Colonel Carregan and his men have joined with the Queen Charlottes. They are some seventy miles behind us, not in front of us."

"Nonetheless, we have found De Jong."

"Am I to believe you and make a fool of myself?"

"Use the telegraph. Tell Colonel Carregan it's Morgan and von Brand. De Jong's in the Drakensberg. We're hiding during the day and following at night but it's dangerous. If they come to us we are only sixty men."

"I'll relay your message but I'm bound to give them my reservations. How large is the commando?"

"An estimated three thousand men."

"And I presume you require ten thousand imperial troops to run off to the Drakensberg."

"Exactly."

"It's ridiculous. Positively ridiculous."

"No. Not if you arrive in time. They've been chasing De Jong for months. Could we have some food?"

"First you give me these extraordinary stories, and then you want food."

"We left our troop three days ago."

"Sergeant! Give them food and attend to their horses. Send for the telegraph orderly. You say your officers' names are Morgan and von Brand?"

"Yes. They are Carregan's partners in Carregan Shipping."

"You'd better be on call if they wish to ask any questions. Sounds very odd to me. And anyway, what is a shipping line doing in the Drakensberg mountains?"

"COMPLIMENTS OF LIEUTENANT CRICHTON, sir, but a message from the wire. Two auxiliaries say they've found De Jong. Used your name. Say their officers are von Brand and Morgan."

"Tell them to keep the line open," said James.

"They're holding on for instructions."

"I'll be right across."

He put on his hat, moved out of his tent briskly and walked to the command telegraph office. Crichton was waiting for him.

"Must be Morgan's Mercenaries," said James to Crichton. "But I want to make sure. They're all Rhodesians or should be. Ask them with whom Morgan's father was killed. If it isn't Morgan then it's a good way of the Boers taking off the heat. Where are they meant to have found De Jong?"

"In the Drakensberg," said Crichton as the telegraph chattered. "Makes sense. He must by now need time to regroup and rest. Does Willie know the mountains?"

"I think he hunted there with Gavin's father but I'm not sure. It would have been well before my time."

"Compliments, sir, but man named Thorpe of Inyanga sends his compliments to you of farm Morgandale and says that Rhys Morgan died with Allan Wilson on the Shangani River in '93 and he also asks how the skins look in your new house."

"Compliments to Jimmy Thorpe as follows. 'Thanks. Give last position. Will move immediately. State De Jong's strength. Tell line to expect further patrols from Morgan.' Looks like we've got him," said James to Crichton.

"Unless he gets Morgan first."

"No. Willie's too clever and Gavin is too lucky. But we must move fast, however. Give my compliments to Colonel Gilham. Ask him to inform the commanding officer. I think De Jong has three thousand burghers. If he has, we'll need ten thousand troops and they'll take some moving from here to the Drakensberg."

Koos van der Walt was more tired than he could remember ever having been in his life. For nine months he had been hunted, had fought, retreated and been hunted again. It was all over, he knew that, but it had become a habit not to give in. He looked around at his fellow burghers and saw what he must look like himself. Dirty civilian clothes, half-fed pony, ammunition belt slung over his shoulder, Mauser rifle, kit for sleeping, eating and everything else just above the horse's rump, unwashed beard and tired, sunken, old eyes.

He still had a thousand men but unless he could give them rest they would go, just begin to disappear during the night. They only fought when they wanted to. They had no big guns left, just a few wagons and the families that had come along with them because there was nowhere else for them to go. They were what was left of the Boer people, together with a few other similar commandoes scattered through the remoter parts of what was once the Transvaal Republic. They had all done their best, but what could twenty thousand do against five hundred thousand? They would just go on until they were dead or caught.

Carel Viljoen was lucky. The hills of Ceylon had a good climate and food and sleep. Once you were caught, you did not have to force yourself to go on. Honour and pride were satisfied. He wondered if he would ever be able to join up with De Jong; then they would rest and come out again as new men. The Germans would come into the war on their side. The British public would throw out their government and, out of shame for what they had done, they would give them back their republics. They would yet ride back to Pretoria in triumph. But for all this to happen they must hold out and he must find De Jong and rest.

His commando moved up slowly into the Drakensberg. So far they had missed three rendezvous because they were too slow. But he could not hurry them up any more. He tried hard to keep his head up straight and succeeded. He had seen this before in his men and then seen them fight for hours and win. The wagons slowed their pace as the incline up into the mountains increased. Scouts ranged out on all sides of the column but there was nothing to report. If luck was with them they would join up with De Jong the next day. Koos van der Walt believed that he still had some luck left to him. He had already gone through the pioneer march, a war and a rebellion. He no longer found it strange that in those days, which were so far back over the horizon that he sometimes had difficulty remembering them, he had worn a British uniform. He probably would again one day if someone saw fit to attack Rhodesia. Nothing made sense except reaching De Jong and putting their forces together and resting and then coming out again.

They trudged on, pulling themselves up the pass. The scouts guarded them but no one in the column bothered to watch the surrounding hills. Their thoughts went as far as their feet going forward and the slack reins to the pony that followed beside. There were no fat men or fat horses in the column. Children walked beside the big, jolting wagons and they were barefoot like their mothers. Lean dogs and cattle, goats whose rump bones stuck out of their mangy fur, followed at the same pace. Chickens in wicker baskets, hung from the tail boards of the wagons, had an easy, swaying journey up into the mountains as they watched the harsh, rock-strewn track go by beneath them a foot below; they had stopped laying eggs some months before.

Koos tried to remember the good times when they had been winning. The great fight in the Tugela Basin, Spion Kop, the siege of Ladysmith. This normally produced in him a little strength but this time there was nothing left for him to draw upon. He looked across at his wife, who walked over on his right, next to their wagon. They had met in Pretoria soon after he had come down from Rhodesia to join his commando, Viljoen's commando. She was Carel Viljoen's daughter. When they had met she had been young and plump and, when her father allowed her to, which was only during times of festivity, she had worn coloured ribbons in her long, black hair.

Hanneli was the third daughter of seven. Her elder brothers had fought alongside Koos. Johan had taken a bullet in his mouth, Christo had been lying on his belly when the lyddite exploded a few feet above him, and Piet was still with the column. Hanneli looked too old now to bear children, and yet she was only nineteen. When the war was over, and he could take her back to his farm in Rhodesia, then she would grow back to being what she was. They would have a large family like all good Boers and there would be many sons to help him farm his land. He looked at her carefully now. Hanneli would look better when they reached De Jong and could rest. He caught her looking round at him and gave her what best he could make of a smile. She came across to him.

"It is better than a concentration camp," she said in the *Taal*. "There is no disease here. We do have some chance of being alive. So don't look at me like that. All this is not of your making."

"We'll be all right when we reach De Jong," he said. "The British will never find us. None of them know where to find the tracks through the passes that will take us up into the heart of the mountains, where the valleys are rich and cool and a man and his wife can rest and watch the stars above them in peace."

"How long will we stay?"

"Until we are strong again. There is still game to be hunted, so food will be plentiful. A small haven it will be in a dangerous world. But it has always been like this for us Boers. For a short while we find rest and the reality of all our hopes and we make our families and farms until it is time to fight again. It makes no difference whether it is natives or British. The one want our land and our cattle and the other want our freedom. Maybe it will always be like this, but then why should it change after two hundred years?"

"How far are we from De Jong?"

"Five miles. Maybe ten. We shall only know when we find them. But we will find them, my little love. My luck has not all gone out of me."

"I wish this war were over," she said with bitterness.

"Now. You know we can't talk like that. The war will be over in God's good time and He will deliver whichever of us He thinks worthy. We are only the instruments of His will. But God has always been with us. In all our times of wandering in the wilderness of Africa, away from the British, has not God always been by our side?"

"He was not beside Johan or Christo."

"But that was His will."

"Sometimes I do not like His will."

"That is blasphemy."

"I am too tired to know what it is, my husband."

"Maybe, because of that, He will forgive you for your words. Tonight, when we stop, I shall pray that He will."

"You pray, my husband. It is good for you to pray. It takes away some of the age from your eyes."

Her long skirt, right down to the ground, was dirty, the ends frayed from tearing at the rocks. Her long, black hair was tangled and matted, as dirty as the skirt that had not been washed for weeks. She did not want to think of these things, as there was nothing she could change. There was no end in what she saw. Nothing that was good. Only the road, the dirt, pain, hunger and the wagon wheels going round ever slower. Maybe the whole thing would stop and they would all go to sleep for ever.

"THOSE ARE SCOUTING PARTIES," said von Brand. "The last two we sent back must have been caught. Our luck has held for five days, Gavin, five days longer than I expected, so for this we must be thankful. From now on we are being hunted. My plan is simple. We are outnumbered. We cannot stand and fight, so we must fight like the Boers themselves. If we are engaged by a smaller force then we fight hard and quickly to show them that we can kill. We then disengage and move away fast. By the look of their horses from here, they are far weaker than ours. Ours will be able to go further and much faster.

"The advantage of the guerrilla is still ours for the moment. If we are attacked by a superior force, we'll disengage immediately and use our speed to get out of the way. But we need discipline. This was where James always succeeded. Carregan Horse moves as one man. You must explain to them that anyone not keeping up with the troop will be lost in the mountains and if they are not found by the Boers, they will not find their way back to civilisation. This is bad country if you don't know where you are going. The sun is coming up now and we must keep in among the thickest trees, but by nightfall I know where they will be; there is only one pass they can take and it is not the one there," he said, pointing. "That one seems to give an easy passage between those hills but further on a ravine cuts across the pass. The ravine is fifty feet wide. No one can cross. They must take the one over there. We'll catch up with them easily tonight."

"How will the British find their way?"

"When the Boers stop to rest, I'll go back and guide them. I think I know the valley that De Jong is looking for. It has five exits. We'll have to stop up each one before we attack. When that is done De Jong will be forced to surrender. We can surround him with big guns and fire down into him in the valley. With extreme luck there will not be any bloodshed. The British will have to move fast. If our first pair have made contact I would expect word by the day after tomorrow."

"Their scouts will pick up a large British Column. There will be no time to block the exits and a British force of size will be moving as slow as the Boers."

"I've thought of that. All the exits except one will bring the commando back in this direction. I can have British forces waiting for them in ambush. The one exit that goes the other way we'll block ourselves."

"With forty men! By then, nearly half will have gone back to give the directions."

"It is a very narrow passage. For a good while, and until they outflank us, we can dominate the heights. They will have no protection. With plenty of ammunition, which we have, we can hold them up for hours. They will have to scale the cliff to come after us and if we fire fast and accurately they will think we are many more than we are and will try to withdraw in the other direction. We'll have forced them back onto the British."

"There will be problems," said Gavin as he put his logical mind to work on the proposed situation. "The Boers will be aware of the British Column when it is twenty miles from their valley. They will therefore not retreat into a larger force. At that point they will try and get out through the pass that is furthest away from the British, through us. They will have to force us. It will take the British at least ten hours to get into position and longer to bring up the big guns. By that time we'll be dead and the Boers will go out like water through a burst dam. They have two guns themselves. We've seen them. They'll blast us out of our highland fortress."

"The cavalry will be able to get into the valley within three hours. They'll be outnumbered at first but will have to fight for time. This will take some of the fighting from us. But in all this you suppose the Boers will have good warning. James will have to hunt their scouts."

"They'll hear the shots."

"If James is quick there'll be few enough for the main force to think it a hunting party. When the scouts fail to return they'll think again, but by then the troops will be coming up into position. Yes. I agree. The guns will have to come after to stop the slaughter."

"The worst job seems to be ours."

"It is. But the thing we have in this mercenary force of yours is some of the best shots in Africa. You'll notice how all the seamen have gone and they were the worst shots. With luck we can make our forty sound and feel like two hundred, and the Boers will know that we can hold that pass forever with two hundred men.

You'll receive your publicity, Gavin, have no fear. I'm glad we taught you and Phil to shoot on our way back from Bulawayo in '96."

"So am I," said Gavin, and he managed to force a smile.

"Look down there. They're sending a small force this way. We'll not engage intentionally. We'll withdraw ten miles and then lay up for the day."

"Do you think they've seen us?"

"No. I've watched buffalo many times before like this and they have even better eyes than the Boers. The buffalo did not see me."

"I HOPE your interpretation of the situation is correct, Colonel Carregan," said General Farrow. "I never like leaving behind the guns."

"We have four thousand mounted troops including a machine gun unit. Speed is more important than fire power. Even with that number we'll have them outnumbered. They are tired, General, their horses are tired and we'll be firing from the heights. We must catch De Jong. With his commando smashed we'll be able to count towards the last days of this war."

"And if he manages to smash us, the war will go on for another six months."

"There is always a chance in everything," said James with an easy smile.

"I hope it is not your reputation that is influencing me, Colonel."

"There are only two decisions. To do this or to let him go. With your permission, sir?"

"Yes. You may go."

"We require speed. By pushing them along I can make the column move that much faster."

James saluted and moved back down the column. It had taken him a long day to persuade the General and his staff to move out with a flying column and let the guns come up behind as best they could with the infantry. Even with only a slight superiority he was confident that they could force De Jong to surrender.

GILHAM, Grantham and Crichton were riding together. They all rode a good horse and looked exactly what they were. British cavalry officers. Some fifty yards behind them and again on the wing of the advancing column were Quinn and Lagrange. Jack Hall rode behind them alone. He was searching the surrounding bush and moved easily in his saddle as he turned. At the first sight of an enemy scout party he was to lead out his troop and stop the scouts reporting back to De Jong. They were a day away from the mountains and did not expect anything, but James took every precaution. Von Brand had sent word back that he would join them that evening and lead them up into the mountains. Morgan had remained with his mercenary force to keep watch on De Jong in case he moved further than the valley in which he was expected by von Brand to make camp. The trap, as well as it could be, was set. James expected to engage the enemy in two days' time. He had drawn off his own force as the action they would take would be a classic military engagement, similar to many that Gilham had commanded on the north-west frontier of India.

It took him half an hour to circle the column, at the end at which Garret was snorting down his nostrils.

"This could be another excellent chapter in the history of the Charlottes," said Gilham as he surveyed his regiment. The men were in exact formation, with their officers jogging along at a steady pace in front of each squadron.

"Shows what years of discipline can do when the time's required."

Neither Grantham nor Crichton were certain which of them he was speaking to, so neither replied.

"The regiment hasn't seen a full-scale engagement since Omdurman, and those dervishes didn't have much of an answer. Fine looking regiment, Grantham."

"Yes, sir."

"Let's hope they look fine when the bullets start to fly," said Quinn to Lagrange. He was now twenty yards behind the Colonel and had heard his last remark. "The Mashonaland Horse may look a trifle sloppy in comparison at the moment but they change into rigid formation when they come under attack. But a straight engagement will be new to us too. You not feeling too good, Phil?"

"I still have an imagination."

"Think all the time. Look where you're going and watch the enemy. Luck, when it comes to a fight, is something that can often be created." He looked around them again. "If they've sent scouts down to the foothills, they'll see our dust trail for miles. We'll have to scout carefully ourselves to avoid an ambush."

"That's our job," said James as he brought Garret's pace in line with that of Quinn's horse. "This is exactly how it was when we entered Providential Pass on our way up from the lowveld in '89. Only then, we had the Matabele to worry about. Let's hope history repeats itself and we get up there without being molested. We start scouting in the morning, by which time we'll be up into the foothills and I'll have had a talk with Willie."

"CHRIST," said acting Lieutenant Tenant, "that's another bloody column of Boers and by my sense of direction I'd say they're going to intercept De Jong. This must change some of von Brand's thinking, but by now he'll have joined up with the British. Come on, Frank. We're going back to Morgan. This is where he has to make some decisions for himself."

"WELL, we can't stop them joining up together," said Gavin when Tenant had given him the news of the second commando. "You say it looked a quarter of De Jong's size? We can't do anything about a commando that big except watch them and report the information back to the British. You'll have to send out two more men."

"That brings us down to thirty-eight."

"Yes. That brings us down to thirty-eight. We'll know by tomorrow morning whether De Jong has stopped in the valley. He still doesn't know how long ago he was spotted. He may yet try for a few days' rest."

"He may come out after us."

"He would if he knew where to find us. Even his scouting parties have failed to make contact. When the two men have gone, we'll move onto his other flank. We'll be in a better position to plug the other end of the valley."

"I wish I'd stayed on my farm," said Tenant half under his breath.

"I expect you do. Maybe we all do. But for the moment we have a problem on our hands and until it is successfully finished we'll be unable, any of us, to return to our farms. But return we will. I'm far too young to end up as a corpse in these bloody mountains. So we'll think and go on thinking carefully until the whole engagement is over. If you feel like funking at any stage, then just hold my hand."

"You sure you don't want a hand to hold yourself?"

"That, I assume, is meant to be rude? No, I've never held anyone's hand in my life and I see less need for it now, or in the immediate future, than many other times in my life. If you see me behaving in the way you expect, Lieutenant Tenant, the way of the rich when the situation is not to their liking, then you have my permission to shoot me in the back. Likewise for you all. You might get that message across to the others for me. This is not a well-paid buffalo shoot. This is war."

"WE HAVE MADE CONTACT," said Wilhelm Cronje to Koos van der Walt in the *Taal*.

"Thank God for that."

"They have sent us a warning. A small mounted force is said to be in the area. De Jong does not think they are British, as they cover their tracks and behave like hunters. Scouting parties have been trying to make contact with them for two days but without success."

"It can't be," said Koos almost to himself.

"No. It's not Carregan. He and his whole unit were reported, a week ago, to be with Farrow."

"Show me where to find De Jong. We must talk. The commando will come on afterwards."

"THERE IS ONLY one man who could be up in those hills without you being able to find him," said Koos to De Jong in the *Taal*. "Willie von Brand. They say at one stage he hunted these valleys with Selous. I wonder how long he was watching before you noticed he was there. They came across from Rhodesia a month ago according to my reports. Sixty of them. And most of them know the bush as well as you and I. Maybe von Brand knows it better."

"And what difference is it if they saw us some time ago?"

"You are tired. If they saw us some time ago they would have sent back word and a British force under Farrow will be well on its way by now."

"They'll never find us in these mountains."

"With von Brand leading them?"

"Not with anyone. If he goes back, he loses contact with his own unit. He then has to find them again."

"He could do that with his eyes shut. He's a hunter, kerel. Thirty years he hunted. I came up with him in '89. He, Selous and Rhys Morgan guided the column. Us Boers, and there were many of us, followed. They knew their business better than us. In '93, three hundred of us chased Lobengula out of Bulawayo. They were caught once. On the banks of the Shangani River. Once in twelve years is a good record. We must go on, kerel, we cannot stop here."

"We must stop in the valley," said De Jong. "For a day, two days, maybe more. My people cannot go on without a rest."

"Neither can mine, but they must."

"Even if word was sent back a week ago, it will still be another week before they can come up on us. We will rest for three days. Eat some fresh meat. Graze the cattle and goats. See to our horses and our families. Then we'll go on, Koos van der Walt. If you wish to go on now by yourself you are welcome. But when we are rested, us two together can have fun with a large cumbersome British column in these mountains. We can ambush them in every suitable valley. It will be them who won't come out of the Drakensberg. But first we must have our rest."

"Two horsemen," said von Brand to James. "They must be from Gavin."

They were ahead of the column, scouting together, while von Brand showed him the gaps and explained the patterns of the distant hills. They rode out across the veld to meet the horsemen.

"Yes," said von Brand. "Two of ours. That means Gavin has only thirty-eight men to plug that damn valley."

The men tried to salute but von Brand nodded his head towards James.

"Colonel Carregan," he said. "Another damn Rhodesian."

"We've located a second Boer commando that was about to join up with De Jong," said the trooper. "By now they should both be in the valley. Our estimate of strength is now three thousand, five hundred fighting men."

"Damn," said James.

"Makes the numbers even, anyway," said von Brand.

"No. It's not only that. The other commando must be Koos."

"Let's hope they don't want to fight."

"Yes. Yes, that would be a better way, but life is never like that. We had better tell Farrow, Willie. He is not going to like me for this."

"Under these new circumstances, Colonel Carregan," said Farrow, "we will have to bring up reinforcements."

They continued to ride forward at exactly the same pace with four of the general's staff in line abreast ten yards behind them.

"We still have a slight superiority in numbers," said James. "We'll have the height and the cover."

"I cannot afford to lose."

"Can we afford not to go on? With respect, sir, if it becomes known that we have found De Jong and van der Walt, and then retreated despite them being numerically inferior, the situation at present may not in retrospect appear so dangerous."

"He may have guns."

"To fire up into mountains is not so easy as firing down or using them on the open veld. There will be no concentrations of men."

"What sort of surprise are you going to bring me next?"

DE JONG WATCHED them making camp in his valley. It was very beautiful. Tall mountains that sheltered the lush greenness of the valley with its river that ran clear and fast along its course. As they had entered the valley, a small herd of impala had made room for them, slowly and without fright. The buck were still grazing on the far side of the valley. He would have preferred to leave them there, but they needed the meat. A hunting party had been despatched to come around them from behind. Their instructions were to slaughter the whole herd. The meat alone would improve their spirits.

The thin, lame cattle had moved away from the wagons and were now tearing at the new, sweet grass. The chickens had been let out of their coops and were furiously disturbing the ground with their three-pronged feet in their search for grubs. Some of the men were sitting and staring, as though they had no idea where they were. The women were making the camp, slowly, tediously, out of habit. A good meal of venison and a sleep, that would take them right through the night, De Jong told himself, would see them recovering the following day.

If the British were following them, the commando would not

have been able to outdistance them in their present condition. They had run before the British many times and got away, but they had always had a little strength left in them back then, strength enough to come around the back of the British and attack their supply columns, taking the food and the fodder for themselves.

If they were attacked in the valley now, De Jong would hold back the British at the passes while the wagons got away at the end of the valley. He knew the place well. But he did not expect the British in these parts for another six days and by then they would be rested and well out on their way. He would then circle the British and attack them from their rear. He put down his rifle on the grass and lay down beside it; the peace and gentleness around him was almost painful. An eagle swooped down from the mountain, circled the camp and flew off again. He could hear the water moving swiftly in the river and for a moment it lulled him to sleep. He woke to the noise of the last wagon being outspanned.

Christiaan De Jong was only forty-five, though his heavy black beard was flecked with white. Before the war had brought him out with his gun and his pony he had farmed in the Orange Free State, the older of the two Boer republics. The British argument had been with the Transvaal, but it had brought in the Free State once words had fallen to war. Back then, he had been a man of peace who only wished for his farm to use as he wanted. Now, his family was scattered, his wife and younger children he hoped were still alive in a concentration camp somewhere, his eldest daughter and her children in another. Two of the boys were dead, the eldest with them.

The price of war, he had said at the time, but the price kept rising higher and there was more to pay. Johanna would not be able to have any more children, so he prayed every night, and often during the day, that one of his sons would survive the concentration camps and the war. When the older boys had died fighting with him he had been thankful that the other two were too young to fight. But then had come the camps and their disease.

Well, he had almost come to his own end. There was not much

fight left in any of them, but with his country finished, and with it everything in his life that was of value, he could see nothing else but to go on with what he was doing. If he gave himself up, there would be nothing to live for. And there had been miracles before.

He heard the shots from across the valley and hoped they'd killed each animal with one shot. They were short of ammunition despite what van der Walt had brought them. Ah, yes, he would soon be smelling the flavour of roasting venison. Saliva came up under his tongue at the thought. Venison and cold, clean water from a mountain stream. Maybe this was his miracle.

The winter sun was warm on his tattered clothes. There was not a breath of wind in the valley and only the echoes of gentle sounds as the women made their camp. De Jong sat up slowly, leant on his elbow, and pulled a blade of the long grass and chewed at its succulent end. He saw van der Walt walking towards him and was relieved to see there was no urgency in the man's leisurely pace. Van der Walt sat down next to him and together they watched the dead impala, twenty-three of them, he counted, being brought back to the camp.

"There will be enough for everyone," said De Jong in the *Taal*.

"The bones will make soup," said Koos.

"You think we'll have time to cook them?"

"By your estimate, we have plenty of time."

"Maybe the whole of time. This valley is so peaceful."

"It was a good place to come."

"Mountains are always clean, as are their rivers. I would like a farm here. Right here in this valley. I could hold it away from all the world. There would be fat cattle in this valley."

"When the war is over, you can come back and lay your claim."

"Who from? The British? They would give me a small piece of this valley, enough only for me and my bones."

"There are many valleys like this in Rhodesia. Yes, maybe they'll take away my farm for having fought against them. I was still a Transvaal citizen, so they will not shoot me for treason. There will perhaps be another chance for me and Hanneli. We are young."

"More than I can say. Old? Yes. This time I am feeling my age. At your age I might have gone on with the commando. Not stopped. Left this valley behind me. But there are many others of my own age. They will be thinking like me."

"It must have been difficult bringing the big guns up into the mountains."

"It was. But they are part of us. Maybe the last of our republic's possessions."

They lapsed back into silence and watched the new camp take shape. Big fires were being made in pits, and the great spits were standing ready for the carcasses. Each animal was skinned and gutted and while it was still warm from its own blood the steel spit was thrust through its centre and the whole was hoisted up to rest over the fire. The sun would be going down when the meat was ready.

"HOW FAR OUT ARE THE SCOUTS?" asked van der Walt.

"Ten miles. Maybe more. It would take a British column at least six hours to reach the valley. We would have a good enough start."

"A column big enough to want to fight us could only come the one way. Even von Brand could not find them another one."

"That is how I see it."

"Nothing we can do."

"Except eat and sleep."

GAVIN MORGAN SMELT the meat and his mouth watered. He had not eaten a cooked meal for a week. He was half a mile away from the fires but the wind was into his face and had blown straight down the valley. They were in position, thirty-six of them. Two had been sent back with the information that De Jong and van der Walt had made camp in the expected valley. The fight would begin sometime the following day. Gavin had chosen each man's position as von Brand had directed. There was nowhere the Boers could get to fire down upon them. If they scaled up from the valley, Gavin would still be above them when they came within range. His men would be spread around the crest of the mountain that was split by a gap less than a hundred yards wide. He was careful to have no concentration of men that would make a target for the two big guns he could see down in the valley. His hope was that James would complete the last few miles at speed to engage the Boers before they swamped him. The ammunition had been split equally between each member of the troop. Their instructions were to rapid fire with as much accuracy as possible. To Gavin's eye, the whole valley was full of Boers and the sight of them killing all but three of the impala in one volley had not increased his optimism. And then the three that had lived had managed a few paltry yards before they were dead and meat like the others. His men had been equally impressed.

"It would be pleasant," said Tenant next to him, "if we could make a fire for some tea. Once the sun goes down it's going to be cold up here."

"The sleeping bag will keep you warm," said Gavin.

"Don't think so. It's my nerves. They're stone cold."

"Soon warm up when the firing starts." There was little confidence in his voice.

GENERAL FARROW HAD MADE his last inspection and spoken the customary words of encouragement before they went up into the foothills. James and von Brand rode in front. They had been riding for half an hour when the light faded and within a short while it was totally dark in the pass that led them up into the mountains. They had rested during the day and James had finally convinced the general to ride through the night so that they would be able to attack at dawn, with the sun behind Gavin and his thirty-six men and in the faces of the Boers. It would be more difficult for the Boers to shoot up accurately into the sun. It had taken Farrow a short time to decide to go on despite the arrival of van der Walt. He had concluded to himself that his reputation would look worse if he retreated than it would if he went forward and was beaten. The valley sounded to him like a good trap if the few mercenaries could hold the far end as they had been instructed. The thing he liked least was being led by a damn bunch of amateurs. But their true colours would show when it came to a fight, he told himself.

2

*D*awn had not yet broken when De Jong was rudely woken from his long sleep.

"The khakis," said a burgher. "They're within two hours of reaching us. Cavalry only. No guns. They're moving very fast and exactly in this direction."

"Well, then," said De Jong, getting up quickly and looking around the sleeping camp. "If that's the case, we must go. And quickly. When they come here they must find nothing but the ashes of our fire. Send round the word to inspan. I want van der Walt and five hundred of his men and five hundred of mine to cover the entrance to the valley while the wagons are being got away. We do not want any of their flying columns among the wagons. The women have seen enough fighting without that."

Within minutes, the camp was astir. They had completed a similar exercise many times before and there was no time lost in their preparations to depart. The oxen were inspanned to the wagons and within ten minutes the column was under way and van der Walt had left to protect the entrances. The sky was paling into dawn as the Boers moved towards the one exit that would lead them away from the British.

.　.　.

GAVIN MORGAN HEARD the noise of the camp being broken and sent his men off to their positions. He went round and checked each one carefully as he watched the Boers drawing nearer. Dawn had broken and shown him the Boer column split into five commandos. Four were streaming towards the valley's entrances, which clearly told Gavin that the British had been sighted. The main column was coming towards him. He estimated they were outnumbered by a hundred to one and he smiled ruefully at his own stupidity. He would certainly receive his publicity, but whether he would read it himself was another matter.

"Fire when they are in range," he called softly to the man thirty yards away from him who would pass on the word. They were on one side of the ravine and also curved round to face into the valley. Each man had built a wall of stones in front of his position with firing points at intervals. They hoped that they would be showing as little of themselves as possible to the Boer marksmen. They waited on their stomachs and every one of them felt the first cold shuddering of fear as the tension mounted.

KOOS VAN DER Walt rode for the main entrance to the valley and with him went his fears. They were fighting people that understood them. Even by his calculations, it was impossible for a British column to have reached them so quickly, even the advance guard of cavalry. They would have to hold the passes all day and then make their break to re-join the others during the night. He felt refreshed after the food and sleep. Despite their new predicament, De Jong had been right in making them rest. They would be able to fight, which was more than they would have been able to do the previous day.

He sized up the pass in front of him and began to assess the method by which he would make his defence. The sheer drop from the mountains gave way to a slope that ran down to the floor of the valley on both sides of the pass. Small and large boulders had dislodged from the cliffs and scattered themselves at intervals down the slope. He would put his men behind the boulders at the top of the slope. They would have a clear line of fire down into the valley. It would be extremely perilous for anyone to enter the valley in pursuit of the wagons. Each man took with him his ammunition and water bottle. They would be on their stomachs in the same place all day. They took up position and waited.

They had been lying in the gentle warmth of the morning sun when heavy firing broke out from behind them, from the far end of the valley.

"They can't have gone round that far already," he said out loud, with only himself to hear. "It must be Morgan. Runner," he shouted in the *Taal*. A young burgher whose age had been given as seventeen but Koos knew to be fifteen came up to him at a run. The firing from behind was brisk and was now being answered by the Boers. Koos looked back and saw that the wagons had been brought to a halt.

"Go back to De Jong," he said. "Tell him there can't be more than sixty of them blocking that pass. The British could not have outflanked us that quickly. He'll have to storm them. It's only the patrol that found him, and if my thinking is right they'll be commanded by Morgan, who's never fought a battle in his life. Tell him it's my thinking that von Brand will have gone back to the British, especially considering the speed at which they've caught up with us. They must clear those heights within an hour."

"THE FIRING HAS BEGUN, GENTLEMEN," said Colonel Gilham, without flinching or altering the pace of his horse. "Got 'em this time. Must be in the valley. Hope Morgan can hold 'em till we get there. Tricky position that lad's got himself into. Now what's that fellow Carregan up to, Oswald? Trying to win another damn medal, it seems. Go and get the general's permission for us to follow him. Can't have this damn Mashonaland Horse winning all the glory. I mean, they're not even a proper regiment. Be quick about it, they're drawing well ahead of the main column."

"Yes, sir," replied Grantham, and he cantered off down the right flank of the column.

JAMES KEPT Garret going up the slope at a trot. They still had an hour's ride before they'd come upon the Boers. "How long do you think Gavin will be able to hold?" he asked von Brand, who was riding beside him at the head of the Mashonaland Horse.

"Couple of hours. Three, maybe. Depends how quickly the Boers decide to storm the heights. If they think there are two hundred men on the mountain they may hesitate and only go in when we open fire on their rear-guard. Let's hope Gavin can make his guns appear to be as many as possible. By the sound of it, their firing rate is as I hoped. The Mausers don't seem to be answering them much. Ah. There go their big guns. I hoped they'd try that first. It'll damage Gavin, but it won't knock him out. It should give him an extra hour or so."

"I'm glad I'm not on those heights," said James.

"So am I. But it was the only way of bottling up De Jong. And Gavin wanted his name in the papers."

"He'll get it, but most likely in the obituary column by the sound of those big guns."

The Mashonaland Horse moved up the pass at a steady pace. Von Brand turned in his saddle and looked back at them.

"Looks like Gilham following us," he said.

"Good. I didn't have time to argue with Farrow. Surprised he let Gilham follow us. Must have used the ploy of not allowing the colonials to be a jump ahead of the imperials. He's catching up, too. I'm glad we taught them how to shoot straight. We may need their fire power."

"With Gavin holding their only way out," said von Brand, "they must try and stop us reaching the valley before they have sent out the wagons. They must fight a rear-guard. There will be men at all the entrances to the passes. For us, it would be better to scale the heights and fire down on them."

"How long will that take?"

"An hour."

"Maybe too long for Gavin. We want the pass open for the main column by then."

"If we ride straight into the valley, we'll not breach it anyway. And by then Farrow will have lost his numerical advantage."

They rode on in silence while each of them explored the alternatives in their minds. The Charlottes closed the gap and joined up with them.

"Didn't want you to feel on your own," said Gilham as he rode alongside together with Grantham and Crichton. "Five hundred of us might well be enough. By the time Farrow arrives, we'll have their baggage. My men are looking forward to a fight."

"I'm not sure they will be in half an hour," said James. "The passes will be blocked, but unless we unblock them before Farrow arrives, Gavin will have stopped preventing their progress at the other end. And being cavalry, we don't have sufficient provisions to follow them."

"Simple," said Gilham. "Ride straight in. A good cavalry charge will frighten 'em off. That'll make 'em surrender."

DE JONG WATCHED the bombardment for fifteen minutes, then ordered the column to advance. The wagon wheels began to turn. 'If there were only sixty, there can't be many now', he told himself. The few of the Boers who would die would be the price of their escape.

"LET them into the pass before we fire," said Gavin. "No one to fire until I give the order."

'They will think their guns have killed us,' he thought, 'If I can make them turn around inside the pass it will be chaos. It will take them longer to organise a scaling party.'

"Three dead and one wounded," said the man next to him in

reply to the message Gavin had sent down the line ten minutes before. "Gerry says he can still use his gun but not so fast. The ammunition went up with the men. Direct hits from the guns."

He watched the valley and the wagons moving towards them. Some of his fear from the bombardment had subsided; he had been able to see nothing around him except smoke and the flash of new explosions. He had felt that a shell would land next to him but nothing had. He preferred their rifle fire, since he could fire back at whoever was shooting. Anxiously, he looked at the other passes into the valley. He could see the Boers in their positions but still the British had not attacked. Was he wrong in his assumption? Had they merely blocked the passes as a normal precaution? If the British had not attacked before the Boers scaled the heights, he would withdraw his men. There was no point in blocking the valley for nothing. He looked at the other passes again and hoped the cavalry would not ride unknowingly into the traps that had been set for them.

KOOS VAN DER Walt gave out his instructions carefully. The first wave of British were to be allowed into the valley unmolested. Only then would they open fire. He turned and looked back at the moving wagons. The guns had done what was asked of them. The heights were silent. They were either dead or withdrawn. For a moment he felt sorry for Rhys Morgan, whose line was now finished. They had both died violently, father and son.

GAVIN MORGAN WAITED for as long as his nerves permitted.

"Rapid fire," he shouted, and himself began to systematically shoot at the men moving beside their wagons down below.

Their shooting was rapid and accurate, and no less severe than it had been before the bombardment. If anything, it was stronger, he thought. Fear was driving them all in their desperation. At first, the wagons tried to go on and the Boers fired back at them from the flanks, as much, Gavin thought as he went on firing coldly and automatically, to assure their women and themselves that something was being done as it was to have any effect on the heights. Gavin watched the wagons stop and saw the Boers trying to lead the oxen round to go back into the valley. There was little order in the pass, and even with Gavin's limited experience he knew that with another two hundred men he would have been able to defeat the Boers before they were able to extricate themselves from his accurate rifle fire. He saw one of the oxen go down. The effect was to prevent the wagon being turned. Men were trying to unharness the dead animal.

"Fire at the oxen," Gavin shouted, and turned his own fire on the animals.

Within minutes, all the wagons had stopped and the Boers were retreating, leaving the wagons behind. After another two minutes there was nothing left within range to be shot.

Gavin turned his face away from the mess down below and lay on his back. He watched the clouds and tried to bring his mind up towards them. He wanted to be sick, and without realising what he was doing he got up and walked away from the lip of the crest and relieved himself. After a few moments, he was in full control of himself again and began the rounds of his men, standing up as he did so and ignoring the Boers, who he knew were out of range. Next would come the guns or the assault by scaling the mountain, and he wasn't sure which would be worse. He took a long look at the other end of the valley, but there was nothing to be seen. He could not even see the Boers waiting in ambush. He went on, explaining one by one what he wanted of his men, and he made sure that each had his bayonet ready to fix if necessary. Their faces lit up when he told them that they would retreat if the assault began before the British arrived at the other end of the valley.

"We'll scale that mountain," said De Jong to an elderly burgher.

"There will be too many of them. Koos is wrong. Sixty men

cannot kill so many. This is a bad day. If we climb that mountain, they'll catch us coming up wherever it is and they'll wait for us with their bayonets. A man climbing that face will have his Mauser slung on his back. He'll have no way of killing the man with the bayonet."

"There's no other way," said De Jong. "We must win back our wagons. There'll be easier places to make the top. You cannot see them from down here. Once some of us are on the heights they'll be able to shoot anyone who stands up to use his bayonet."

"Today is a bad day."

"There have been many such days before, but we are still fighting."

"*Ja*, man, we must go up."

"There is little time. I'll lead them up myself."

"Then many will follow."

De Jong looked up at the crest and frustration bit hard into the walls of his stomach. Without those men up there they would have been away by now. He would be telling van der Walt to withdraw to the same pass and man the same heights to keep the British back in the valley. It would have been British dead where his wagons lay sprawled. There was still time to storm the heights and take everyone through. He gave the order and led five hundred of his men towards the slopes.

The Boers moved up methodically and with purpose. There was no rush, since they wished to retain their strength for the top. As the mountain came nearer they searched its face for the easiest way up. Cracks appeared in the face that had seemed smooth from the bottom. From the ground, it appeared that they disappeared into the very face of the mountain.

"WHAT I WANT," said Colonel Gilham, standing up in his stirrups, "is a tight square. We'll go into that pass in parade ground order but as close together as it is possible for you to ride at maximum speed. I want the regiment to be in that valley and among their baggage before the rear-guard can have any effect. Keep down over your horse and don't draw your weapons until I give you the order. We'll appraise the situation when we are into the valley. By my reckoning, they're storming the heights, otherwise their big guns would have restarted their bombardment. It is our job to block the other entrance. Thirty-six men – and there will be fewer of them by now – cannot hold back an assault. Messages have gone back to General Farrow to speed his advance. We cannot destroy their rear-guard. He will have to do that himself, but when we've blocked the other end he'll have time to outflank them."

The regiment took up their positions with the Mashonaland Horse holding the rear. James and von Brand took up their positions at the back, centre of the square. Hall commanded the right flank with Quinn on the left. The pass was half a mile ahead of them. Spasmodic firing could be heard from the valley.

"YOU'LL BE ALL RIGHT, PHIL," said Quinn. "The first time is always the worst. This time you're going to win back what you lost when you came to Africa and Gavin will have the best view possible of what you're doing. None of us have any limitations. These are only set for us by ourselves. This could be the last major fight of the war and it's going to be a good one. After this, you'll never have to say that you funked the war or anything else. The numbers are almost even, but we have them in a corner. They'll fight hard to get out."

"You still don't think I can do it?" said Lagrange.

"You've done it. You're here. You can't go back now."

"No, I'll go that way," he said, pointing ahead, "with my ears shut."

"We'll yet grow old together in Carregan Shipping."

"I hope so. And, thanks, Roger."

"NEVER THOUGHT I'd be doing this at my bloody age," said von Brand, his eyes blazing with excitement. He was more impatient than his horse.

"You really do like a fight, don't you Willie?" said James.

"Always have done. Nothing malicious or sadistic. My blood just gets up and it's the only way of cooling it down. You think Gilham knows what he's doing?"

"He's one of their death or glory regulars, the glory not for himself but his regiment."

"That won't help us."

"But it might help Gavin."

"Pity Rhys isn't here."

"Yes."

Garret pricked his ears up und looked round at James.

"What do you want, lad?" He leant forward and patted his neck. "You're just about to meet your lawful master." James looked at von Brand. "You must have sited Gavin well to have him hold them back for this long."

"It's a good position and they can all shoot straight."

"That must be an assault. The firing is too spasmodic. Not many targets."

They sat for a while waiting.

"Bloody stupid us, trying to kill Koos," said von Brand.

"That's how stupid life can be. We don't have much sense, sometimes. I think Gilham is ready to go. Good luck, Willie."

"Good luck, James."

"Everyone in position, major?" said Gilham.

"Yes, sir," said Grantham.

"You ready, Lieutenant?"

"Yes, sir," said Crichton.

"Very well, gentlemen. We'll go. Good luck to you all."

"Good luck, sir," they chorused. Then Gilham raised his hand and let it fall sharply. The Charlottes, followed by the Mashonaland Horse, began to move forward, then broke into a trot. They watched their officers for the order to canter and when it came they increased the speed of their mounts and waited for the order to gallop. The regiment's pennant streamed ahead of them as they used their years of training with an automatic, precise skill.

Koos van der Walt heard the thunder of hooves and realised immediately that his trap was not a surprise. 'Von Brand again,' he said to himself, 'or Carregan. Better to fight with, than against.'

He stood up from behind his rock and filled his lungs to the brim. The thunder of the horses was loud.

"Fire at the horses when they come into sight. Don't wait for them to get into the valley. They know we're here."

He looked behind him to see how far the scaling party had reached up the mountain, but it was too far to gauge whether men were going over the top. He could hear that Gavin was sniping at them, but nothing else. He smiled at the thought of him being shot with his own ammunition, of Willie too, for that matter.

"Stand up and shoot. They're going too fast to fire back."

He watched his men rise, each ready with his rifle. Some had hats against the sun but the glare would be in the eyes of the Englishmen. The leading horse swept into view and he fired.

Gavin watched the Boers get to their feet and saw them take aim at the entrance to the pass. The thunder of the horses' hooves echoed down the valley and bounced off the cliffs around him.

"Do we retreat?" said the man next to him.

"Not anymore."

"The Boers will be on us before that lot can give any help."

"Nonetheless, we hold for as long as we can. Enough people have died. The sooner it's over, the better."

"I'd just like to be around when it happens."

"So would I," said Gavin as he closely watched the progress of De Jong. Then the firing started from the other end of the valley. The Boers who were not scaling the heights down below took up defensive positions behind the limited amount of cover. They brought the two guns round to face the cavalry. Gavin grimaced as horse after horse began to fall in the charging square and the close, protective formation was forced to spread so that it could pass the fallen. The Boers were not given enough time, and within moments the leading horses were out of range. The Boers fired into the box formation until the rear-guard was out of range. The leading horsemen drew their sabres and Gavin could see that they were preparing to charge through the main camp. He didn't envy the Boers who were crouching behind their tufts of grass. The big guns fired but their range was wrong. He watched for De Jong, to see if he would climb back into the valley, but the few Boers he could see, the ones who were out of range, kept coming. He contemplated using his bayonet but none of them had practised properly. Anyway, they were marksmen, not swordsmen. He got up and surveyed the ground to see where best he could put up a shield to protect their flank and still have enough fire power to prevent the Boers from retreating in front of the cavalry.

"RIDE STRAIGHT AT 'EM," shouted Gilham, looking around. "They've not got enough cover."

Out of range, the horses were back to a canter. The horsemen ran in a mass over three hundred yards. A few horses cantered with them, riderless. A shell landed well in front of them. Oswald Grantham found it difficult to believe he was still alive, as all the Boer guns had seemed to be pointing at him. There was a thousand yards to go and then the guns would fire at him again.

"Where's Crichton?" the colonel shouted at him.

He looked around him.

"Don't know, sir."

"Pity. He would have gone a long way."

Grantham shuddered and prepared himself for the next ordeal.

"WASN'T SO BAD, WAS IT?" shouted Quinn, but Lagrange was unable to answer him. A bullet had taken him through the arm and he was having difficulty riding with his sabre held in the same hand as the reins. He had not worked out yet how he was going to use the sword.

"A bit to go yet," he managed as he brought up his knees and continued to ride in the manner of a jockey. 'That's it,' he told himself. He would hold on with his knees.

"WE'VE LOST FEWER than I expected," said James as Garret continued his easy stride.

"About fifty men," answered von Brand, "and we'll lose more if we charge straight at their main force."

"Once we're among them, the horses will trample them to death."

"That's obviously Gilham's idea. This is what he terms a cavalry charge."

"Some of them are moving back into Gavin's pass."

"Gavin's firing again. Let's hope they have enough ammunition."

"Is there a way round the back to the heights?"

"Still a good climb, but the horses will take us up half the way."

"Some of the Boers are going over the top now. We'll flank the main force. Hold this line. I'll talk to Gilham."

James spurred Garret to a full gallop and came up through the middle to behind Gilham. They were five hundred yards from the Boers.

"Permission to flank and climb the heights," he said.

"Good idea. Morgan won't hold them much longer. Permission granted."

James pulled in Garret and soon dropped back to his own troop, where he signalled them to follow his flanking movement. The Mashonaland Horse wheeled and James drew them into a fast gallop as he pulled away with the ninety-three horsemen left to him. He swung them around the Boers, who had begun to fire in two directions. The big guns had the range of the Charlottes. By the time Gilham galloped over the first Boer, James was in front of the main force and galloping past the wagons and away from the Boers who were trying to get out in spite of the gunfire from the heights above. Von Brand, trying to forget his age, kept to the front with James. They looked behind at Gilham as the Charlottes crushed through the Boers, hacking from right to left with their sabres.

"That man Gilham doesn't lack courage," said James to von Brand.

"Neither does Phil. He's been hit, but he's still holding his own on that horse."

"We'll dismount at the last moment. Save our strength for the top."

"Can we hold those heights even if we get there in time?" said von Brand.

"Hope so. We'll find out when we get there. If we can't hold the position, we'll pull back with Gavin. Good, Gilham is being sensible as well as brave. He's going to ride out of the valley and defend our backs. We'll hold those heights. He'll give us reinforcements if needed. No, he's not, the fool. He's bringing them round to charge again."

Koos van der Walt watched the second charge and cursed. He had not been able to move away from the passes for fear of the main British force that he knew must be following up on the flying column. He waited impatiently. They had split their force so well that three hundred cavalry were able to cut their way through the main force. And if the horsemen who had outflanked the main force got on to the heights before De Jong was able to kill Gavin, it would go badly for him as well. And against the main British force there would be little he could do, split as he was over the defence of four passes. He looked back again and made his decision. They would ride back and attack the cavalry. Van der Walt gave the order to mount. He ran back with the others to where they had hobbled their ponies.

. . .

HAVING COME through the second charge, Gilham saw the Boers sweep out towards him from the far end of the valley. He knew his horses were spent and would not stand up to a long ride and then a charge at the advancing Boers. "Better give Carregan help. You all right, Oswald?"

"I think so."

"That's good enough. We'll bring the regiment back into box formation and ride around to follow Carregan. Don't think we'll have much trouble from the lot we just attacked. Never seen anyone like a cavalry charge when they're lying down."

"Their casualties were heavy, but so were ours."

"But not in the same proportion. By the time Farrow gets here, he won't be needed. If he hurries himself up, the Boers will surrender when he comes into the valley. That last lot have had enough already. Afraid the mess is going to be quiet after today. I can only count seven officers left on their horses." Jasper Crichton was among the missing men.

DE JONG LOOKED down into the valley and saw everything that meant something to him being destroyed. Those who had tried again to leave the valley had again retreated away from the wagons, and too many of his men who had faced the horses lay trampled and crushed. He would go on up and take his objective because he had been doing it for two and a half years. He looked back and saw van der Walt trying to come down on the cavalry. Then Gilham withdrew into the pass and De Jong knew that it would be he who would face the cavalry. They were reaching the top and as many as possible would go over at once. He adjusted the Mauser to cross his back more carefully. They were short of time.

"Over," he shouted in the *Taal* and heaved himself up the last six feet of the cliff.

To his surprise, nothing happened. He moved in behind a rock and waited. There was total silence on the heights. He told himself they must have withdrawn, but in this fight he no longer accepted things as they appeared. Van der Walt had been right. From their first encounter with the patrol they had seen their own methods used against them. Except the cavalry charge. The women and children were safe, he had seen that. The British had only trampled his men. He continued to wait, but nothing happened. He stood up and began to move forward. More men had arrived on the crest and they all began to creep from rock to rock. De Jong sensed that the heights were not friendly. He knew, as he sometimes knew when he was hunting, that he was being watched.

VAN DER WALT watched his quarry ride out of the far end of the valley and cursed. He looked behind again and expected to see a great column of the British riding in after him but there was nothing there. His pass was still empty. He could not pursue the cavalry in front of him, as he would be decimated from the heights. The quiet, as De Jong led his burghers over the crest, had not made him any the happier. Van der Walt reached the main force. Two thousand men had been ridden through twice. The sight that met his eyes was carnage. He had seen death but it had always been clean. A bullet or at the worst a bayonet. But these, his friends, had been hacked open or had their bloody entrails kicked out of them by the heavy, flying hooves of the cavalry horses. There was no stomach for fight in any of the survivors he looked at; their eyes showed horror above the dust-caked filth they called their beards; the women and children watched their men with pity and looked to those who were not yet dead.

"I'm sorry, Hanneli," he said to his wife in the *Taal*. "We could not hold them. They knew where we were and came at us too fast. They were well trained and well led."

"We are finished, aren't we?" she asked.

"Not if Christiaan can gain control of the heights and stop the cavalry coming up."

"And if the rest of the British do not come too soon."

"And that," he agreed.

"What are you going to do now?"

"Go home."

"To Rhodesia? Do you think they will let you?"

"Who can know? Maybe my friends will not want us either. It is not a good thing to try and kill someone. Good friends have been known to keep away from each other after a fight."

"Are you sorry you came back to fight?"

"No. Unless each race defends itself, its laws and its beliefs, then it will be destroyed. Each member of that race must play his part. We cannot accept the benefits of protection without paying for its price. To me there is always a just price for everything. Maybe the British will one day pay their price for this war. Maybe one day we will pay the full price for our arrogance and our blind zest for independence."

"I hope they will let us back into Rhodesia."

"Yes. So do I. We'll be luckier than the others, as I may find my house and my barns not burnt to the ground."

Still there was silence from the heights, which made van der Walt begin to puzzle.

"YOU'D BETTER NOT CLIMB with that arm," said Quinn.

"The bleeding has stopped," said Lagrange. "But if I go too slowly, you go on ahead."

"Come on then."

With his rifle slung across his back, Quinn followed James up the cliff. They were two hundred feet from the summit and strung out across five hundred yards of cliff, each man having chosen what he hoped would give him the easiest climb. Von Brand was flagging already and Quinn wondered what a man of over sixty was doing climbing mountains with a rifle on his back. "Take it slowly, Willie," he called. "You're not as young as you were."

"Fine bloody place to remind me of that one. But you're right.

My climbing days are numbered. It's my knees and my weight. The one won't hold up the other."

"You'd better go down, Willie," said James next to him. "This is a vertical climb."

"I'll get there in my own time. There are probably Boers as old as me going up the other face."

"I don't like the silence from the top."

"Maybe Gavin withdrew."

"No. He'd have come down the way we came. I'm going on ahead. I don't want anyone else to reach the top before me."

"Might ruin your reputation?"

"Something like that. Come up as best you can."

"Thanks, and good luck."

'THIS,' thought Gavin as he waited, 'is a long way from Cape Town and the Lagrange sisters. A long way from your comfort and your wealth. Now, lad, you have a gun for your wealth and nothing else. Likely your old wealth would put a bullet in you,' he chuckled. Not out loud but just in his throat. In joining the fight, he'd intended to ease his conscience, not sample his wares. Irony.

Gavin watched the open space in front of him. He had watched the Boers moving towards the semi-circle he had thrown out, with instructions for the fifteen who were watching the pass to move across and cover the exposed flank if he gave the order. That way he intended withdrawing the fifteen that semi-circled back to the crest and the fifteen lined up in the opposite direction facing down at the pass. He wanted as many Boers in the open space in front of him before he opened fire. He had seen James circle the wagons with von Brand and hoped that they would be climbing up the back way right then. The first to come out was an old Boer. He sniffed the air as if he was hunting. Gavin waited until eleven Boers were in the open and coming towards them in crouched positions. He took aim at the one centre of his line of fire.

"Fire," he shouted and shot the man forty yards in front of him through the right eye. All his men had come up from cover and fired at the same time. They waited but nothing happened. Five minutes went by but no one else approached. Gavin called across to Tenant,

"Hold the line. I'm going to see what's happening on the flank. They must be going around us."

THE WORD SPREAD BACK along the heights that De Jong was dead. They had all seen the destruction in the valley, and while they were waiting for Gavin to show himself they had seen the advance guard from Farrow come up on the heights at the other end of the valley and signal back with a heliograph that the pass was clear. The Boers were waiting for a lead which never came, and then word went back among them that the cavalry had arrived on the heights. As Phillip Lagrange pulled himself over the crest, the first of the Mashonaland Horse to do so, he saw the white handkerchief go up. He climbed up and stood in the open.

"Get down, you fool," said James behind him and slid himself over the crest.

"It's all right, James. It's all over up here. Gavin didn't need us after all."

Lagrange began to laugh. He even managed to wave the arm without the gun when Gavin stood up, fifty yards ahead of him, turned round and grinned. The Boers were standing up as well.

"Step out and stack your guns in the open space," said James in the *Taal*. "Is De Jong or van der Walt among you?"

"De Jong is over there. Dead. Van der Walt is in the valley," one of them answered.

"Where's Willie?" asked Gavin. His knees were shaking with delayed fear.

"It takes him longer to climb these days."

"That was a pretty fine charge of Gilham's," said Gavin to James. "Demoralised even this lot. What's the matter, Phil? Can't you shake hands without putting down your gun?"

"No, Gav. Someone tried to shoot me."

"Thank the Lord they didn't. Sarah would never have forgiven me for that."

"No. She probably wouldn't."

"THEY'VE SURRENDERED," said van der Walt in the *Taal*. "And with five hundred men on the heights, De Jong will be able to prevent the cavalry from reaching the top. We still have time, Wilhelm," he said to Wilhelm Cronje.

"Are you sure it was Morgan surrendering and not the other way?"

"Five hundred against less than sixty? No. But we'll find out. It must have been Morgan. De Jong would never surrender. He'll make the break. Get everyone moving. The British have still to enter the pass."

"It's too late, Koos. We could never take the wagons with us and we've too many wounded."

"You think this is the end?"

"Yes."

"Then De Jong must say so. Christiaan," he shouted up at the heights. "Do we move out of the valley?"

"Who is that?" called someone in the *Taal*.

"Van der Walt."

"Not today, Koos. It's all over. De Jong is dead."

The voice floated down to him.

"Who's that?" he shouted back, but not so strongly.

"Me and Willie."

Silence.

"We won't surrender," said van der Walt.

"You must, Koos. This damn war has been stupid enough as it is. You can wait if you want, but don't go through the pass. I've three hundred rifles up here and I've taught most of them how to shoot myself."

"You'd never fire."

"I would."

"On women and children?"

"We would try not to hit the women or the children. But even if you get out, where will you go?"

"We'll go on fighting."

"Then I won't let you out, Koos.."

"Then we'll fight our way out."

"It's me, Koos. James Carregan. Not some British colonel. I don't want to shoot."

"But you will?"

"Yes."

"Then you'd better start shooting, as I'm going out through that pass."

JAMES WATCHED and a sick deadness formed in his stomach as he saw the Boers gather up what was left of themselves and begin to move towards the pass.

'Damn the man. He's going to make me kill him,' said James to himself. "I want every man to rapid fire in the dust around the Boers until they surrender," he shouted.

"Or until you change the order," said Willie, who had come up onto the heights short of breath.

"Or until then."

The Boers came within range at a slow speed. Some of the Charlottes were on the heights and joined in the firing. The Boers went on.

"Damn him," said James. "Damn the man's bloody pride." He looked around him. Some of the men were watching for orders. "Shoot to kill," he ordered and looked away. The dust stopped kicking around the Boers and the screams came up clearly to the heights together with limited rifle fire. James looked back into the valley and saw the column waver and stop. He gave the order to cease fire as Gilham strode across to him, having made the climb from below.

"Told you we wouldn't need that fellow Farrow," he said to Gavin and shook his hand. "Damn fine show, Morgan. Never been in the army before, have you?"

"Never, sir."

"Hell, if you want to join my regiment, I have some vacancies after today."

"Despite my birth?"

"Oh, we'll find some damn way around that."

"The white flag's gone up," said Tenant.

"You the other officer with Morgan?"

"Acting Lieutenant. Yes. Sir. Name's Tenant."

"Consider yourself substantive rank."

"Thank you, sir."

"Ah. Here comes Farrow." They all turned and looked across at the other end of the valley. "Bit late, don't you think?" said Gilham.

3

"I don't suppose this is the correct behaviour, coming to see you of all people," said Annabel Crichton to James in the hall at Ship Corner, "but you were with Jasper when he was killed."

"I was close, but not with him," answered James. "The Mashonaland Horse were behind the Queen Charlottes and Jasper was in front with his colonel. Won't you come in? We can sit on the veranda if you do not think it too hot."

"I'm not intruding?"

"Any friend, of whatever nature, of Rhys Morgan's, is a friend of mine. I explained to you our relationship when I met you in England in '93. It was not necessary for you to insist on waiting in the hall until the servant found me in the garden. From what I remember of you in Cheshire, it seems a little out of character." He smiled to encourage her.

"So many things have changed."

"It could have been any of us in the Drakensberg."

"Yes, I know. But it wasn't. It was Jasper."

"You still have your other son, if my memory serves me right."

"Yes. But Kinsley is not the same. Not the same at all, in fact."

"Let me lead the way. You will be able to sit under an umbrella."

"This is all very kind of you."

"As I said before, you're very welcome."

James led the way through the morning room to the French windows that let out onto a large veranda with a view over the lawns and the fish ponds. The afternoon sun only came onto the back veranda, which unfortunately did not give them a view of the harbour and the ships. It was very peaceful, and since he had returned from the Transvaal he had spent many late afternoons and evenings in the garden. He came home from the office early by other people's standards. He believed in rising at dawn to go down to Carregan Shipping. Early rising with the sun had become a habit of his on Morgandale. He enjoyed the solitude of the early mornings overlooking the harbour as he drank his morning coffee, watching the mist lift off the sea and the distant grey outlines of ships becoming freighters, sometimes his own; these were the ones that stood out in the bay and waited for room to dock at one of the piers. Then the afternoon in the garden.

He had needed his solitude. His hair was very grey and though he disliked it, it made him look distinguished. Sonny Fentan had found it most attractive, though she noticed he took little notice of her personally; seeing her, yes, but keeping everything away from the personal.

James was on his own downstairs, Hal Fincham having died and his grandfather having kept to his bed. He should have found it lonely, but he didn't. Willie had felt the same and gone back to Morgandale after Gavin had disbanded his mercenary force. He had received all the publicity he needed. James had been recalled to Cape Town and would, otherwise, have taken his leave on the farm.

"Would you like a drink?" he asked Annabel. "The sun is near the horizon. We call them sundowners."

"They sound very nice."

As they went through the French windows, he pressed the service button and then made her comfortable in a deck chair. He would never have recognised her, which probably explained her reluctance to appear unannounced in the garden. She looked an old woman but by his reckoning she was only forty-two. Her hair was not grey but completely white and it was very difficult to imagine the attractive woman she had been under her present layer of fat. She had grown to look like what Rhys had most likely wanted her to become and that was a contented farmer's wife. She had the outward appearance of jovial good nature but after a few moments it was clear to James that she was not contented. Anything but.

"I am sorry about your father," she said. She was obviously embarrassed and this had merely been something to say.

"It was some time ago."

"Ester told me."

"She's coming out."

"So I believe."

"Ah. Here comes my friend, Kosa, with the drinks tray. Press the button at this time of day and you get the drinks tray whether you like it or not. Can I suggest something?"

"Please do."

"I always take a long drink in the summer. Gin, sweetened fresh lime juice, a little Angostura bitters and soda water. We keep it in the cellars so it is always cool."

"That will do fine."

"Where are you staying?"

"Quite frankly, I've just come off the boat."

"Then you will stay here with me and my grandfather. He is not very well at the moment. I think he is dying. He didn't retire till after he was eighty and once he stopped working he was never the same. How does that look for a drink?"

"Delicious."

"That sounds more like the person I first met."

"I'm glad all of it hasn't gone. No, don't think you have said something wrong. I can read it very clearly in your eyes."

"Does it show that much?"

"Yes."

"Do you want to tell me what happened? To have spoken to Jasper too much might have led me to say things I had not intended. I know very little about you."

"Jasper never knew about Gavin?"

"Neither did anyone else."

"Thank God."

"Gavin and he became very friendly but they had no idea they were brothers."

"It's really Gavin that has brought me to South Africa. And the pain of losing Jasper. I thought that if I came to the country where he died I would be closer to him."

"Try your drink first."

"We couldn't put in a little more gin?"

"Of course."

"It will help me to tell you my story. Not that it is interesting to you."

"There is no hurry. Do you like my garden? All this has been done in two years. Everything grows so much faster in the Cape than it does in Cheshire."

"What are you going to do with Halmeston now your father is dead?"

"Oswald and Ester can have it. It's no good to me. I never intend living in England."

"Do you think Oswald has changed?"

"Yes. And for the better. An army life suits him and he funked nothing in the Drakensbergs."

"This drink is delicious."

"Neither did Jasper."

"Oh. You mean 'funk anything', as you put it. No, neither did his brother judging by the papers, which is more than can be said for Kinsley. Why can't all brothers be the same?"

"They might all have turned out like Kinsley."

"Yes. Yes, I suppose so. This drink really is delicious. I think I might just have another one."

"Of course. I forget it is so warm at this time of the year."

"Yes, it is."

"I'll make you one in another glass."

"Thank you. Maybe a little more gin."

"Yes. I forgot. The story."

He turned to the drinks trolley.

"I sometimes wonder whether gin is all I have left."

The tone of her voice was so startling that James looked up from making the drink, but she was looking out over the garden. He did not think she was seeing very much of the flowers.

"In case of your memory being bad, I had better start at the beginning. Thank you. That new drink will help. Telling someone what a flop you have made of your life is never very easy. I met Rhys when he was at Liverpool University. It was one of those charity theatres and the students were making and moving the scenery. I had sold a volume of tickets and was rewarded by seeing the show. Not that I wanted to, but it was the done thing. I met Rhys at the small reception backstage. I suppose, looking back, that we must have been desperately in love at the time, but life afterwards has spoilt any memory that might have lingered.

"We were indiscreet and Gavin was conceived. My father, being a peer of long standing, was not interested in having the son of a Welsh sheep farmer as his son-in-law, and so the child was born without knowing his father and was given away. Rhys found out before me where the child had been sent and gave the foster parents money to give him an education. And then, before Rhys was killed, you came to England and told us both the details, except that you never told Gavin my name. Well, I don't think it matters any more. After Gavin was born I was made to marry Edgar Crichton, as he was the only one who disregarded the shame that I was meant to feel. It was two years after you left England in '93 that I discovered the reason why he had married me. Up till then he had been a good husband and I loved him in a way. But there is always a reason for everything. You never get anything for nothing.

"My father should have seen it clearer than me, since he'd always said that Rhys had only seduced me for my money. We lived in part of my father's house, and, in his will, he asked the present baron to allow us to remain in the lodge. Apart from a comparatively small amount, my father left his money to his first cousin, who inherited the title. You see, the power comes from the money and not the title. My father was only interested in preserving the name. Up till then we had received an allowance from my father, which he didn't think to continue after he died. Either it was his last piece of vengeance or he thought that Edgar had money of his own. I told Father once that I could live without him. That was just after Gavin had been forcibly taken away from me. You wouldn't mind pouring me another drink before I go on. Thank you.

"It was all right for two years, until the capital ran out and then the bills weren't paid and when I tackled Edgar he laughed at me and said it was my job to pay the bills. It was soon after this that I learnt the truth about Gavin. The foster parents were so proud of the boy, and once he had gone to South Africa they just had to tell me about him despite what they'd promised my father. Or maybe it was what my father had bound them to say. Even when he was dead, it seems, he wanted to make me unhappy. So after that I was able to follow his career and yours – they seem to be linked together. The simple truth is that I have come to ask Gavin for money. Not a very proper way of introducing myself, but there is nothing else for me to do. Jasper's father left me after the money ran out and Kinsley will end up in jail for fraud, the way he lives off other people's money. If it wasn't for Gilham sponsoring Jasper into the army I don't know what I would have done. But now he is dead. Do you think Gavin will help me?"

"If he doesn't, I will. On behalf of Rhys. I owe Rhys a lot of what I have."

"It is very kind of you."

"No, not at all. Where is your baggage?"

"At the docks. I'm afraid it is only one small case."

"Some clothes and a hairstyle, I think, before you meet Gavin. You will be the first of his parents that he will have met. Do you intend living here or in England?"

"I could never live anywhere but England. All my friends are there."

"Do you have any left?"

"Oh, yes. I kept up appearances to the very last moment. Then I came straight out here. No one in England has any idea of my financial difficulties. They merely think Edgar an absolute cad, which he is."

"I see."

"You really are most kind."

"I'll ring for Kosa. He will send a trap to the harbour. We can dine together tonight and then tomorrow we'll see what we can do and maybe take a drive out to Morgan's Bay in the evening."

"Where is that?"

"Morgan's Bay? Yes. You must be one of the very few arriving in wartime who haven't heard of it. It's the place where your son entertains."

"I see."

"No. On this one, I very much doubt if you do."

4

1901

"Wars," said Gavin Morgan to no one in particular, "are things that are best left behind. To have gone for so long without once getting thoroughly drunk is a crime. Do you agree, lieutenant?"

"Most indubitably," said Colin Tenant.

Colin Tenant was also drunk, as was, for once in his life, Colonel Gilham. Surprisingly, Oswald Grantham was sober, but it had nothing to do with the amount he had drunk; it was just a night when his liver was working particularly well. There were only men in the party and seven of them were trying to play one game of snooker. As a result, the table was being churned as much as the balls. Gavin had announced every time the green was torn that it didn't bloody matter as he would get a bloody 'nother one.

The reunion party, three weeks after they had returned from the Transvaal, had been a great success so far. Gavin, in his drunkenness, had said it was a pity Koos was not with them, and they had all agreed. Van der Walt had already landed in Ceylon, having been sent to the same prisoner of war camp as Carel Viljoen. Gavin had discovered that evening where Koos had been sent and it was this that was the main reason for his drunkenness. He had a premonition or, more rightly, a guilt complex.

"Thought we'd finished the damn war," said Gilham as he missed the ball with the cue. "By the way, which one of you put a damn bend in this cue? Had it aimed dead centre of that red. Must have missed it by a couple of inches."

"The war should be over soon," said Grantham, "but a pity the Queen didn't live long enough to see a victory. Seems odd to be drinking the toast to the King at dinner."

"If they want to finish the damn thing," said Gilham tetchily as he reluctantly allowed Roger Quinn to take his cue, "they'd send back the Charlottes."

"What about Morgan's Mercenaries?" slurred Tenant as put his hands on his hips.

"We'll find a place for both of you in the regiment," answered Gilham.

"Not for me, thanks," said Gavin. "One campaign in a lifetime is enough for me."

"You're not drinking too well," slurred Quinn to Lagrange.

"Don't like the stuff anymore."

"That must please your sisters," said Gavin. "How are they?"

"I saw them yesterday. Fine. They've rented a small house near the harbour with our mother."

"She's arrived?"

"'Fraid so."

"Can't please Louise," said Gavin.

"No."

"We'd better throw a party and get them out of their cage."

"Yes, I think they'd both like that. Pity James isn't here."

"He's tired. He had more of the war than us."

"They say the old sea captain is dying," said Lagrange.

"He's had a good life," answered Gavin.

"I wonder who will get his money. With two fifths of Carregan Shipping, it could give James control."

"It won't. He's left it between me, James and Willie."

"That's generous of him."

"Without each other, we wouldn't have made the money in the first place."

"I hear that Mrs Dalton has been invited to visit Rhodesia."

"I heard it too," said Gavin. "Sent her a ticket to Beira. She goes up on the train from there to Salisbury. When she sees the solitude of Morgandale she'll come straight back."

"Maybe not. Life never works out as you expect it to do. Take her daughter, Lillian. Who would have thought she'd end up with such a reputation? It's even worse than Louise's."

"Thank you, Phil. I understand your meaning. But don't worry. Roger Quinn will make an honest woman out of Louise yet, eh, Roger?"

"If she'll let me," he slurred. "Doesn't want to be hurried."

"Do you think James will marry Sonny?" asked Lagrange.

"No," said Gavin. "He's very disillusioned with women. Despite what he says, he's looking for a utopia. He may just go on looking for that perfect woman for the rest of his life. If he marries, it will be to someone he knows nothing about. Someone he can fit into the image that he has created for his wife. He knows too much about Sonny, though she's probably the best he could marry. She's over the stage of novelties. She knows by now that there should be more in a man than just being different to the ones before. She would settle for James, but I don't think he'll settle for her. At thirty-four, however, he hasn't got long to make up his mind or he'll be too old to enjoy his children. I rather doubt if you can keep up with a woman if you are too much older. Ten years, maybe, but not more."

"And you, Gavin? When are you getting married?" asked Lagrange.

"I'm young. Twenty-four. A lot can happen to a man when he's young. Despite his wealth, he's not secure. To marry, a man must be secure. There are great responsibilities."

"But you have security in Carregan Shipping."

"A different type, Phil. If it crashes, there's only me to face the consequences. Alone, I don't have to worry. With a family it would be different. You can't draw someone else into your own problems."

"But you don't have any problems."

"Maybe not. But maybe I would be too inexperienced to recognise them if they were there."

They drank for a while, watching the snooker balls crash around the table and onto the floor.

"No one seems much good at snooker," said Tenant and leant himself against the end of the table for support.

"When is Ester arriving?" said Phil, taking the cue and hitting the green into the pocket. Everyone clapped.

"James said next week," said Gavin. "It will keep Oswald in his place."

"He's not that bad."

"He's not that good either. She'll be staying with James since she can't very well stay in the mess with Oswald. Maybe he'll move into Ship Corner as well."

"How about some more champagne, Gavin?" said Gilham. "To celebrate our deliverance we must do it properly. When next you come to the mess you can drink on my card."

"Very kind of you, Colonel. Let's have the champagne on board the *Cape of Good Hope*," suggested Gavin.

"Good idea," they choroused, all except Lagrange.

"You'll drown getting out there," said Lagrange.

"You'll have to guide us. Two of the crew are on board. A bit of rowing will sober us up."

"One drink for the dinghy," someone suggested, and it was an hour later before the dinghy pulled away from the jetty to the sound of army drinking songs. The boat rocked and the oars caught crabs. Gavin was accidentally slapped across the face with the wet oar by Gilham as he fell back off his bench. The oar made a sharp crack and they all stopped rowing to applaud.

"ARE you Captain Morgan of the Drakensberg campaign?"

"Yes," replied Gavin. There was a tight constriction in his throat. The man in the hall was short, dressed in civilian clothes and wore a pair of rimless glasses. A hat sat on his head at an angle. Gavin was certain the man was a detective. "My name is Anders, Owen Anders. I'm the war correspondent for the *Daily Herald*."

"Come in and have a drink," said Gavin with relief. "But don't talk too loudly, as I'm suffering from a hangover."

"I hear you nearly drowned the Charlottes's colonel last night. Though that's not why I'm here. Must have been quite some party?"

"How about a pink gin? They say that at eleven o'clock in the morning it's the only thing to drink. It might just help my head."

"Sounds fine. Mind if I leave my hat?"

"No. Not at all. We'll go out onto the veranda. There's an awning to keep off the sun, and the sea breeze is cooling."

"Nice place you've got here."

"Built it myself."

"Made the money yourself, too, so I hear, and you're only twenty-four?"

"Yes. That's it. That's about all of it."

"The whole thing is going to make a better story than I thought."

"You want to write a story?"

"About you. And this. And the Drakensberg. Back home, they're sick of VCs. They want a little colour. Any women in your life?"

"Not one."

"Pity. A few photographs. All makes up the story. That your boat?"

"Yes."

"Make a nice photograph. Now if you'd like to start at the beginning, we can begin to put together a story of your life. Who was your father?"

"Rhys Morgan. He was killed with Alan Wilson in '93 on the Shangani Patrol. The Matabele War. That was when Lobengula was finally deposed."

"Is your mother still alive?"

"I don't know. I never met her."

"But you know who she was?"

"No. I know her Christian name was Annabel."

"Who brought you up?"

"Foster parents in Liverpool. My partner, James Carregan, knows the name of my mother, but he was bound by her not to tell me. Doesn't really make much difference any more. They all know I'm a bastard, but they tend to ignore the fact these days."

"Money does many things. Do you mind a little publicity?"

"Not about the Drakensberg. At one time I was criticised for making money out of the war and doing none of the fighting."

"It would make it more interesting to give them some of your background."

"If it will help clear my name of not wanting to fight. The reports in the newspapers were good after the Drakensberg but they were short and to the point. Quite rightly, Gilham took the main story. It was his regiment that took the worst losses. I only lost six men."

"But they say you stopped over three thousand from leaving the pass, and you yourself killed De Jong and made five hundred of his men surrender to you."

"They saw Gilham's charge. They knew Farrow was close and they had seen Carregan was aiming to come up behind me. They had lost heart. It wasn't only me and my mercenaries."

"That's the caption. Morgan's Mercenaries. I think we'll even have this one syndicated in America. We'll make you a household name, Mr. Morgan, if that is acceptable to you?"

"As I have said, I don't want people only to remember Carregan Shipping during the war. Things have a habit of being distorted. It would not be so good for business in the future. Now, let me go and mix us that gin. It just may help my head."

Gavin brought back the drinks and gave one to the newspaper man. They both drank hard but did not continue the conversation. Gavin walked away from the shade of the awning and leant on the railing which prevented him from falling to the rocks below. He looked out across Morgan's Bay, the name it had now been given officially, and a picture of Colonel Gilham falling over the rail of the schooner came back to him clearly. They had all dived into the water clothed. The water was bitterly cold, but when they had climbed back onto the boat they had still been drunk. With towels wrapped round their bareness they had continued drinking until the sun from afar had shown the sea and the sky in grey and then in colour. Then they had rowed back to shore. Gavin could not remember how he had got into bed, but he was there and undressed when a servant had woken him and said there was someone to see him downstairs. Now, there was his world in front of him. His yacht looked perfect, returned to its rightful harbour.

Without his hangover, the world would have looked everything he wanted it to be. He looked round at the tall mountains and the peaks were shown to him so clearly that he felt he could reach out and touch them. He licked his dry lips and took another sip. He was still slightly drunk from the previous night, despite his sleep.

He felt shaky, but not only from the drink. He had been convinced at first that the little man had come to tell him that Carel Viljoen and Koos van der Walt had accused their captors of selling ammunition to the Boers. The last consignment had gone in with Kevin Grant some weeks before the fight that had ended in the Drakensberg, but there was still the history. Bitter men could find their proof.

If he did not like so much what he was looking at then he would have gone someplace else. They would never have found him in America. But there was too much to run away from. Too many people and too many good memories. What he had built with his luck was his own. Maybe the luck would last him a little longer. He had nearly paid for his gold in full, and so had Willie. Jasper had died as easily as any death; a bullet through the stomach and friendly hooves tearing his head to pieces. But Gavin knew now that it was better to have done nothing in the past for which there could still be a future reckoning. It was not worth the perpetual niggling of the worry.

"She makes a pretty picture," said the newsman.

"Yes. A yacht makes a line of true grace as she gently rides to anchor."

"Must have cost you a lot."

"It did."

"Did you buy it for any purpose?"

"Pleasure. We've had some good parties on board."

"And some good women."

"How am I meant to take that?"

"Virginia Webb. Louise Lagrange. Sonny Fentan, so they say. Emily Hargreaves. Lillian Dalton. Others. You are well known in this town. No offence, but it was my job to find out. A good story, like a good diamond, must have all its facets. You said there were no women in your life. This is the part that doesn't seem right. Not from the stories that I've heard them tell about Gavin Morgan."

"There are no women in my life. The ones you mentioned came and went. Like the next few dozen. I am like that with women. I enjoy them intensely for a while, then, for me, they lose their interest. It is not their fault. It is mine."

"We should present you as the gay, reckless bachelor."

"As you see fit, but don't mention anyone's names. Some of them still have something of a reputation to maintain."

"So we are agreed that I can write up your story."

"Yes, Mr Anders. You can do that, but I want to sign the proofs before they are printed. The press have a habit of making the facts suit the story. It is not the words that you leave in that tell the lie, it's the words that you leave out."

"Hell, we all have to make a living."

"I would prefer that you did not make yours at my expense."

"Yet you must have made yours at the expense of others."

"What do you mean?"

"Your competitors, for instance. The British government and their war effort. Anyone, in fact, from whom you can make a profit."

"You make business sound as if it is not honest."

"Is it?"

"No. No it isn't, really, but maybe the laws are wrong and not the businessmen. If you give a man an opportunity, he would be a fool not to take it, don't you agree?"

"Of course. That's why I'm here. I sense the opportunity of a well-rounded story."

"I wish you luck in its writing. Your health." They raised their glasses.

"Cheers, Mr Morgan."

"You do remember my mother?" said Phillip Lagrange.

"Of course," said Gavin. "I'm sure your mother is a person one finds it difficult to forget. Hello, Mrs Lagrange. How nice to see you again. And Louise, Sarah, how nice to see you both as well. Having arrived, won't you have some lunch? I presume that you've come out from town to collect Phillip? The party went on rather long last night, otherwise I'm sure you would have found Phillip at his home this morning. People usually stay the night when they come to my parties."

"So I have gathered, Mr Morgan," answered Mrs Lagrange with her chin thrust forward and up. "If your male guests wish to sodden themselves with alcohol, and find it necessary to sink where they drink, then that is their particular problem. But when it refers to my daughters, then I find it necessary to travel six thousand miles."

Gavin smiled at her weakly and looked around at the others for support. Sarah shrugged her shoulders and raised her eyebrows in disapproval. Phillip refused to catch his eye, and Louise was watching him with the curiosity of someone who had never before seen him at a loss for words.

"Well, Mr Morgan? Do you have anything to say for yourself? It seems that I allowed a viper to come into their midst when they were children."

"Oh, Mrs Lagrange," said Gavin with relief as Gilham and Grantham came down the stairs. "Some of my other guests. Good morning, Colonel. Morning, Oswald. May I introduce you? Mrs

Lagrange, I'd like you to meet Colonel the Honourable John Gilham. And this is Oswald, Viscount Grantham."

"Pleased to meet you, madam," said the colonel. "Morning, ladies. Is it true, Gavin, that I fell off that confounded yacht of yours last night?"

"We all did, sir. All of us. He went for a swim. We only found out that it was very cold when we joined him in the water. Are you feeling all right this morning?"

"No, I'm damn well not. You'll excuse me, madam. Confounded head. Celebration, you know. Remains of me regiment. Left the others in the Drakensberg. You got anything for breakfast, Gavin?"

"Lunch, Colonel. It's one o'clock."

"Lunch, then. Don't mind what it is. Always hungry the day following a men's party. You all staying for lunch? Damn good food here if you'll pardon me again, madam. Damn good food."

"How about a drink," said Oswald shakily.

"Do you think it will help?" asked Gavin, moving a little further away from the glare he was still receiving from Mrs Lagrange.

"Two, or maybe three. I find it the only way. Have you any idea why I might have cramps in my stomach?"

"The cold water."

"Ah. Yes. The cold water."

"Ah, what have we here," said the Colonel, lifting the silver tops from the dishes that were set out on the sideboard. "Looks like a damn good cold buffet. Crab. Lobster. Ah, oysters. Smoked Fish. Eel. Salads. And over here the chilled white wine. You must admit, Mrs Lagrange, that your son and daughters have chosen wisely the company that they keep?"

"I'm not so sure that I approve of any of the company they keep in South Africa."

"Oh," said the Colonel, putting the bottle of Hock back into the chilled water, having read its label with approval. "And why not? Is a full colonel, the heir to a barony, and Colonel of the Sixth and Ninth Queen Charlottes not sufficient for your daughters and son? They must be rare birds if he is not."

"It is not you, sir, with whom I quarrel. It is him," she said, and pointed nastily at Gavin.

"But you can't blame him, madam. He is only the master of ceremonies."

"Do you mean to tell me that you attend this man's parties?"

"I certainly attended the one last night by the feel of my head."

"This house is disgusting. We'll leave immediately. Come Louise, Sarah."

"Yes, Mother," they chorused.

"And you, Phillip, will drive the buggy."

"But Mother, I was invited to lunch."

"I don't mind if you were invited to dinner. You will come with us."

"Yes, Mother."

Gavin watched them leave and managed to wink at Sarah as she turned to take a last look back.

"Extraordinary creatures, women," said the Colonel. "Never quite know why I married one of 'em. Confounded thing is you've got to have heirs. I think a glass of that German Hock, Gavin, would clear my palate for the crab. Very fond of crab."

"You stay in the cab," said James to Mrs Crichton. "I just want to make sure that last night's guests have gone. It was going to be quite a celebration, but I didn't feel up to it myself. And right now I don't like leaving my grandfather for more than a few hours. I don't wish to come back and find that he has gone. It will be better when Ester arrives so she can look after him. Nurses are very good, but when you know you are dying I think it's your family you want to have around you. There is comfort in the knowledge that you've left something behind and that the whole of your life has not been wasted."

The cab came to a halt and James stepped out into the afternoon sun. He walked across to the main entrance, which was at the back of the house, away from the sea, and knocked. The door was almost immediately opened by Gavin.

"Oh, it's you. Thought one of them had come back."

"Well, that's a fine welcome."

"Not meant. It's just that I may have had enough of people for today. First the party and then Louise's mother descends. Real old battle-axe. Tangled with the Colonel. Bloody funny, really, but don't let's stand here talking. Come in and have some tea. I've had enough of alcohol for one weekend."

"I've brought someone out to meet you."

"Who?"

"Your mother."

"My what?" said Gavin, craning his neck to see who was in the cab.

"Annabel. Mrs Annabel Crichton. You and Jasper were half-brothers. I'll go and fetch her."

"No you damn well won't. I've waited twenty-four years for this. I'll fetch her myself."

When he reached the cab, she was crying and it took him some time to comfort her before they could move into the coolness of the house. When they settled, just looking at each other, she insisted on having a small gin to celebrate and so the two of them had to drink to keep her company.

"How extraordinary. You have the colouring of your father but the face is like that of my own father, Lord Levenhurst. What irony. The one grandson he ignored turned out to look like him. And you have outshone them all. This is quite a house for a boy of twenty-four to have earned for himself. And that lovely boat is yours as well? You must have worked hard to achieve all this. Not now, but later, we can talk together about ourselves. There is a lot to tell you. A lot to explain. James knows the history. He has been part of it for many years, but I would prefer to tell it to you myself. Maybe tomorrow. There have already been twenty-four years. Maybe another small gin for the moment. In fact, under the circumstances, couldn't we make it a large gin? It is not often that a woman doesn't see her son for nearly twenty-four years. They took you away from me when you were six months old, Gavin. I weaned you and then my father had you taken away. Yes, a large gin is the least a mother can have under circumstances like these. Stand up again and turn round so that I can have a proper look at you."

James watched him stand up and slowly turn around for his mother and Gavin's eyes were bright, but as the afternoon went and the sun began to dip into the sea, James could see bitter disappointment and pain in the same eyes as Gavin saw the mother he had never met before become drunk. Eventually they helped her up to a room in the big house, where she began to cry. They left her crying. They left her fully clothed, face down on the bed, sobbing for the son she had lost and not even remembering the one she had found. The gin was in full control.

"Now I really need a drink," said Gavin as they wound round the stairs. "You can say that that was a big image broken in a short time."

"She wants money, Gav. She's broke."

"Thought it must be something like that, since she hasn't come to look into my bright eyes."

"You'll give it to her?"

"Of course. Provided she goes back to England."

"That's what she wants. From you she only wants the money."

"How can the man you've told me about have seen anything in that woman?"

"She's changed. If you pour us both a good drink, we can sit on the veranda and I'll tell you the story from the start. There's always a reason for everything. It's just that people never turn out to be what you want them to be."

5

The articles appeared weekly in the *Daily Herald*. There were five of them. They told the full story of Gavin Morgan, and he became the small man of England's ideal: from a hidden birth rising at twenty-four to great wealth and charm. The women were depicted as women of the world caught up in the power of war, which was what they were, but by the time Owen Anders had finished with them they were good women to be envied, who had been part of making a new type of Englishman and had helped them all win the war. The fact that Morgan's father was Welsh was not brought into the story. Half of England saw pictures of the *Good Hope* at sunset, and at dawn with the mist and shades of grey, and Morgan's Bay became an idyll in many readers' imaginations. The photographs of Gavin were good and brought him, unknowingly, a new list of women for his parties. He was invited, at last, to Government House.

"WITH THAT BEHIND YOU," said James in his office at Carregan Shipping, "nothing, not even Viljoen and Koos in the same witness box, can bring you down. The public would ridicule anyone who suggested it."

"I hope you're right," said Gavin. "It still worries me. I can tell you now that the whole thing wasn't worth it. And we've still got to sell the gold."

"Wait a few years, now that the war has finished, and you won't have any trouble. Everything is in the London Office?"

"More than five hundred thousand pounds of it. The price of gold has gone up."

"And will do again. You're not losing anything by leaving it where it is. I presume you'll sell it in India or Hong Kong?"

"Hong Kong. It's easier. But we'll need that bullion company to cover the shipment. Licences. You need licences to sell gold."

"We can start looking now. What do you think of Roger Quinn?"

"He'll be good. Phil is back better than he was before he went on the bottle."

"I'm glad you diversified out of South African waters. The freight rates have dropped by half already."

"They'll go on down."

"But we'll still make money if we maintain efficiency. Are you going up for Willie's wedding? We should."

"How about taking the *Good Hope* round to Beira and then catching the train up country? It will take a few weeks, but the weather is perfect for sailing. We all need a holiday. They must all come. Everyone. It'll be such a surprise for Willie, and Morgandale needs to breathe a little life. That'll be me, you, Roger, Phil, Lillian, Sonny, Louise and Sarah. Thank God that mother of theirs has gone back."

"That, Gav, is a good idea. To hell with business. For once we'll all enjoy ourselves together. It is always necessary to take the opportunities in life that are given to us."

"I would have preferred not to have taken the one with the gold. We'll need a crew of two. Kevin Grant can skipper. He's stupid, but a good sailor. One other crew to do the cooking and keep the boat clean. It will take us a good ten days even with the wind in the right place. With the war over, Sarah and Louise wish to return to England. Their father is being forced to cut their allowances unless they go back. Phillip is supporting them at the moment. The trip will give Roger a chance to make up Louise's mind."

"And give you a chance to catch Sarah on the wrong foot. I'd be careful, Gavin. A woman scorned, you know. Louise just might scratch your eyes out."

"But it's all over between Louise and me. We haven't been alone together for months."

"True, but a woman never likes losing anything. They like to discard people in their own good time. They do not like being dropped. Especially for a sister."

"I will, for once, be discreet."

"There is not much room on a yacht to be discreet."

They fell silent for a moment.

"I'm glad that your grandfather has recovered," said Gavin.

"It was seeing Ester and her two children. He never believed he'd see his great-grandchildren. He wanted to get up so that he could dandle them on his knee. So much in life centres around the strength of the mind. I have the feeling that he'll live a good few more years. Hal Fincham was a shock to him. They'd done too much together for too many years. I'll stay in Cape Town for as long as he's alive and then I want to go back to Morgandale. You'll want to run the line by yourself, and I prefer farming anyway. I prefer watching crops grow up than freight rates go down."

"Yes. Yes, I suppose you do." Gavin remained thoughtful for a moment. "You know. I wonder if I should not have made my mother stay in South Africa," he said. "She's gone back to a world that is completely false. They don't give tuppence about one another; secretly, they probably loathe one another. They think they achieve an element of success by appearing better than someone else. She knows this, or at least she says she does. But she's so much part of them, so much like them herself, that she says she cannot live any differently. What an existence. The babble of forked tongues. She will never remarry and no one will care for her again."

"Maybe the husband will go back when he sees she has money."

"That would be irony. The seed of my father's money paying to keep up the appearances of my mother's husband. But it would be better. Left on her own, she'll drink and, in the end, the appearances will show and when her friends discard her as an embarrassment it will be the very end. Maybe some of us are not born to be happy. She started off well. That grandfather of mine sounds a right sod. Ruining his daughter because she had damaged his name. Pity her mother hadn't lived. The old man was left with one daughter and no sons. Cut him up, the thought of having to give his wealth and title to a cousin instead of some seed of his own. The thought to him must have been like dying forever. I suppose I could bribe the husband to go back to her. Pity Jasper was killed or we could have worked out something together. Damn queer, finding out afterwards that he was my brother."

"You should first see what happens when your mother returns," said James. "You can always go over yourself on one of our boats. Now, I think we had better begin organising our trip. The thought of seeing Morgandale again is exciting. I hope Willie is looking after Garret properly."

"Hope so too," said Gavin. "I must take that horse back from you. Brought him all the way from England."

"He's yours when you're on Morgandale. He could never settle down in Cape Town. That is a big-hearted horse who needs plenty of space."

"Will you contact Sonny or shall I?"

"No. I'll do it. She may not want to come. She's grown into herself recently. Changed completely. Doesn't even go to the parties."

"Old age. Suppose I'll have the same problem one day."

"Not you, Gavin. You'll go on forever."

A LIGHT BREEZE pushed the *Cape of Good Hope* through the clear blue water of the Indian Ocean. They were out of Natal waters and running gently between the islands off the coast of Mozambique. They had been on the water for eight days, crammed into the limited space of a sailing boat. The weather had been perfect; blue skies all the way, and they were all brown, well-tanned, full of sun.

Kevin Grant had taken exception to having been brought down from a large ship powered by steam to a small sailing boat. He had taken a liking to Sarah Lagrange, however, and, much to Gavin's amazement and annoyance, she was reciprocating. There was nothing that Gavin could do about the man, as they were stuck with him until the schooner returned to Cape Town.

Lillian Dalton had set herself directly at James Carregan, having tried Gavin and found that he was more interested in Sarah. For her, Phillip Lagrange and Roger Quinn did not have sufficient money. So far, however, she'd found that while James might have had sufficient money for her, he seemed to have little interest in her.

The other crew member hired on for the voyage had been unable to cook but they had only found this out when they were two days out of Cape Town. They had changed cooks in Durban, but the new man, Amin, was an Indian, and though his cooking was good, it was a little hot for their liking. Lagrange had taken to fishing and cooking his own catch and had become very popular as a result. The alcohol ran smoothly for most of the day and Gavin agreed with himself that there would be much else if the cabins were not so small.

After ten days, two of which were spent in Cape Town through his own volition, he was feeling uncomfortable, especially with so much flesh around the decks of the *Good Hope*. Once away from the eyes of society, they had discarded a large amount of their parent-taught morality and lain on the deck with a good deal of flesh to the sun. Louise had retired after the first day, red in places she had never imagined before, but after a week, taking the sun little by little, she had become brown and comfortable. Sonny had lost weight and was looking particularly well. After the first day, she had given up trying to be with James. He had made it quite clear that he was not interested. He was moody and not himself and Gavin hoped he would improve when they reached the farm.

The wedding was one week ahead, to be held in the new house

they had built themselves before war broke out. It would take them a day to reach Salisbury from Beira by train. They were within a day's sailing of Beira, so Gavin had decided they would put into one of the small islands where he knew they could obtain fresh water. The small dot that was the island grew larger and became a half-moon in shape, with tall palms running almost to the water. The island was uninhabited, but a hundred years earlier it had been visited by Portuguese traders who had dug a well and planted lemon and palm trees. There were crabs and crayfish to be found among the coral rocks.

They came into the bay formed by the crescent shape of the island and pulled down all of the sails except for one, creeping as near to the shore as possible before they dropped anchor and the schooner lost way. Everyone hung on the rails and looked at the perfection of the first coral island that any of them had ever seen.

"The war seems a long way from this," said Quinn.

"I thought my bay was something," said Gavin, "but this is equally beautiful in its own tropical way. The sand is quite white and the sea quite blue. We shall camp ashore. There will not be mosquitoes at this time of year and if there are we can hang the mosquito nets from the trees. Let's get the dinghies down, Kevin, and run a little closer to this paradise. Maybe we'll all get along a little better once we're onshore. We'll have space to walk and breathe in our own air."

"We must make an open fire and cook fish in the ashes," said James. "Bring your rod, Phillip. Bring two, in fact. Fresh baked fish with salt and no curry powder. We'll make Amin try a little cultured food. He probably won't taste anything, but it will do him good. Give his stomach a surprise."

"And mine," said Quinn, and they all laughed rather weakly. They lowered the boats and went ashore in two parties. Sonny trailed her finger in the water from the first boat.

"The water's warm," she said.

"Mind the sharks," said James, and she looked at him for a sparkle of life but there was none there.

"A few days on this island is everything we need," said Quinn. "I think it should be big enough for all of us.

"THE FISHING SHOULD BE GOOD," said Kevin Grant in the next boat, and they all knew that he meant nothing that was to do with the fish. "We should split up and get out of each other's hair. You should have brought one more girl, don't you think, Phil? An island like this could be a lonely place without company."

"Why don't you shut up," answered Lagrange.

"That's not very polite in front of the ladies," said Grant.

"It wasn't meant to be. And we are not in the salons of Mayfair just at the moment."

"I was always told that gentlemen behaved like gentlemen even when they were alone."

"What do you know about gentlemen?"

"About as much as you, judging by the tone of your conversation in front of the ladies."

Louise gave Grant a hard, derisive stare but said nothing. Sarah gave no appearance of having seen or heard anything untoward. She was looking out across the water at the island that was drawing closer.

"I don't think you would behave as you are," said Quinn to Grant, "if James or Gavin were within earshot."

"You want a bet?"

"Yes. Any money you like."

"Look, you've got me until we get back to Cape Town."

"That depends on Gavin. He might just leave you in Rhodesia. You're the one who's created the bad feeling on this voyage. If you kept to what you are, the paid skipper, we would all enjoy ourselves."

"I'll be just what I want to be, as I know something about Morgan. He thinks I'm stupid, but I'm not. It's foolish to underestimate people, to make an open fool of them, to despise anyone, Mr Quinn. You'll find out. All of you. You all make your money from the same source. If I were you lot, I'd be a little bit nicer to Kevin Grant, and if you don't know what I'm talking about then just ask Morgan. He won't tell you, but he'll go very quiet for a while.

"WE'LL JUST MAKE HIM SWEAT," said Grant to Sarah when they were alone and out of earshot of the others. "Someone will talk to him. Even without real proof I can make him pay, but even when he pays me he'll never be able to rest. Does it make you happy?"

"Yes. But I'd like to know what you can hold over him. He's very powerful; whatever you think you can do to him, he'll be able to brush it aside."

"Not this, Sarah."

"Why won't you tell me what it is?"

"Because then I would have nothing over you. You might try to use the information by yourself. You dislike him sufficiently to destroy him without reaping any benefit for me. But it's you, Sarah, who will be my real benefit."

"How do you mean?" she said sharply.

"I want to have you before I do anything about Morgan. I want to have you on this island."

She looked at him and, slowly, she understood exactly what he meant.

"You're worse than he is."

"Yes. I'm probably that."

"But how do I know until you've told the press?"

"Mention to Carregan that I know something about Morgan. Ask him what it could be and then see his reaction. This island is very romantic, don't you think?"

"Yes. Yes it would be, in the right company."

"YOU MUST MAKE up your mind by the end of this trip," said Quinn.

"I'm not sure, Roger, whether I can change my way of life," said

Louise. "You become something because you need something and maybe I need men in the plural sense. I don't know whether I would be faithful, and faithfulness is the essence of marriage. Without it you can never live at peace with each other. Undercurrent, deception, lies are no foundation for happiness. Maybe I'll change as I grow older. What I want now, in this setting, the warm sea air, the gentle sound of rustling palm leaves, the soft sucking sound of gentle sea upon sand, what I want is you as a man, not you as a husband. You see, I'm different to other women. My need is everything back to front. Back to front for you, that is. Come. Let's sit down on the sand. I can feel with my feet that it is still warm from the sun, despite the night being half way done."

"Why are opposites always attracted to each other?"

"Because we judge other people by ourselves. Often we don't want what we are. We imagine the very opposite to be the better. The moon from here is right behind the schooner. Perfect. Very few things are perfect. Hold my hand at least. Come on, come and sit down with me. We can't have all this setting for romance and leave it all to itself. We must join in just a little. Ah. That's better. You see, the sand is warm and dry. James says it's made of crushed seashells and coral. That's why it squeaks when it's walked upon. The wine tasted so special tonight. Phillip's fish were delicious. Oh. Yes. These must be all the ingredients of life for it to be perfect. The sea, warm air, palms, tropical scents, a moon like that, a yacht, good food and wine and a male that you want, want right inside you, deep and warm like the setting, to bring it all to the stars and a final, overwhelming climax. Total satisfaction. And then waking to the dawn and finding that you are ready, ready to start again, and you do. Don't you want me, Roger?"

"Yes. Yes of course I do," he croaked.

"Hell, then take me, now, here on the sand."

"I would never, never be able to face myself again."

"Why?"

"Because I love you, Louise."

.   .   .

"Did you ever have an affair with Louise?" asked Sonny Fentan.

"Not quite the question to ask," said James. "But yes, I did. Very brief but very exciting. It was during that year before the war. It was your idea for me to let down my hair."

"Did you enjoy it, James?"

"In a way, yes. I would not be a normal male if I had not. The body is always weak. You just need a strong mind to keep it under control."

"Being always under control can be boring. Like now. Do you know, James, after all these years of knowing each other, we have never come closer than a kiss? It may be the problem. Once the finality of sex is out of the way, the barriers will have gone. We can both be natural. No more pretence. As a good Victorian girl, I should not be talking like this, but people do not change inside just because they are told to behave in a certain way. You have had many women and, being honest, which women never are on such a subject, I've had many men. But we have never had each other. Why, James?"

"Because we know each other too well. Because we'd both, most probably, be embarrassed."

"Only if we didn't like what we found together. Are you frightened that you wouldn't satisfy me, or shouldn't I be talking like this?"

"Does it matter? One way or the other?"

"You're just not a romantic, James. You're too much of the practical man. You don't' show your feelings."

"No. It is just that I don't like making a fool of myself."

"Do you think you would be making a fool of yourself by making love to me?"

"Yes."

"Come here. Come here and I'll prove just how wrong you are."

"Lillian," said Gavin Morgan as he lay on his back naked and exhausted, "when it comes to expertise you have everything."

"But it can only be like that," she said beside him, "when you both know exactly what you are doing. This island must be a total aphrodisiac. I've never climaxed so many times in my life."

"The island, yes, but I think the waiting had something to do with it too. We saw too much and did too little on the schooner."

"Maybe we should take that boat on our own for the next trip. Let's walk down to the sand like this."

"And leave our clothes where they are?"

"Why not?"

"Why not," said Gavin. "But we'll run."

"Wait for me. I'm coming."

"Not again. That's impossible."

"You just have one of those minds. Slow down. We need to conserve our energy."

"You're right. I still have things to show you that even your imagination won't have thought of."

"Don't be too sure about that, Gavin. That's better. Walking's better."

"You're right. Running was uncomfortable."

"See. There you go again. It's your mind. Dirty. Filthy. Lovely. That Sarah is too frigid. You'll do much better with me. Didn't you see what I was after at the beginning of the voyage?"

"Yes. But I hadn't been out of Morgan's Bay for so long."

"I like you. You're honest. You're basic. And you take what you want, when you want it."

"They're not much fun any other way."

"Let's go back to the clothes, Gavin. I think I'm ready again."

"Don't you ever grow tired?"

"Not very often."

"Good," he said and pulled her back by the hand.

"WHEN ARE we going to set sail?" asked Sarah the next day.

"You had better ask Gavin," said James.

"You don't mind going for this walk?"

"It's a little mysterious. If you have something to ask me, why can't you do so in front of everyone?"

"Because, if it's true, it would be embarrassing. My brother began drinking again last night. Did you see? He'll be back where he was before he went to the war. And as for the way that everyone disappeared around the island last night, well, I think it's disgusting. And you as well. I thought you were different to Gavin but I can see that you're not."

"Is this what you wanted to tell me?"

"No, it wasn't that. It's Grant. He says he knows something about Gavin that would see him hanged."

"And by the tone of your voice, you'd like to see him hanged. Is that what you wanted to say?"

"No. Grant says that you know what it is. Do you?"

"No, Sarah. I can't help you. But be careful what you do. Your sister is what she is because she was made that way. She likes men, always has done. She would have been the same, with or without Gavin. And without Gavin, Phillip would be nothing. He needs a hand behind him, a push, he needs to be forced into making something out of his life. And he is. He drank again last night because he felt out of it. He was the only one with no one to walk round the island with. Oh, and you were seen with Grant despite what you said about going to bed. Be a little more natural, more honest, Sarah, and you'll begin to enjoy your life. If you carry on the way you are, you'll end up just like your mother."

"And what's wrong with that? What's wrong with my mother?"

"She's an old bitch."

"How dare you!"

"Easily. I've done it. Now, if you'll excuse me, I'll continue this walk on my own."

"You may regret what you've just said."

"May I? Well, you seem to know more about our friend Grant than me."

. . .

"D<small>ID YOU SEE WHAT</small> I <small>MEANT</small>," said Grant while they watched a large parrot fish being roasted over the fire. It was lunchtime and the sea air had made them all hungry.

"I'm not sure," said Sarah. "He frightens me. He's so sure of himself."

"He won't be when I've finished. He won't be sure of anything. He'll go with Morgan, as I see it. Now, is it worth my while?"

"I don't know. I don't know which is worse. You touching me or my not doing to Gavin what he has done to my brother and sister."

"You won't feel a thing. You might enjoy yourself. There's something exciting about doing what you know you shouldn't. You always want what you think you can't have. That's why I want you. For once, I might get myself really excited."

"You're disgusting."

"Perverted is the word. I've had too much of the ordinary stuff. In or out of the brothels of Cape Town. You excite me because you don't want it so much."

"You frighten me now."

"There is a price for everything. You make up your mind by tonight. We're leaving tomorrow. Morgan thinks the winds might change and he's right. You do what I want tonight and I'll do for you what you want when we get to Morgandale."

"How do I know that you'll do it?"

"You know what I'll do if you don't. Nothing. But I'll do it then. I hate the little arrogant bastard nearly as much as you. He's been too successful, has Morgan. And he despises anyone who doesn't have his brain and his charm. But if you want to, you'll be able to watch his charm coming to an abrupt end. Now, we'd better join the others. I was told it was rude to talk when others were unable to hear."

"G<small>RANT KNOWS ABOUT</small> V<small>ILJOEN</small>," said James at the first moment he could find Gavin on his own.

"Tell me."

"Sarah is using him. She really hates you, Gav. She's just like her mother."

"Someone should lay her on her back and get rid of some of the frustration."

"It doesn't work for everyone."

"It would for her if I know my women. Grant may think we were doing something with the Boers but he has no details and certainly no proof."

"Unless he opened a case on the boat. He came in on his own for two trips."

"But he'd still have to prove that we sold it to the Boers."

"Mauser ammunition? If we hadn't sold it we'd have to show them we still have it in the warehouse."

"We'll replace it. Put it back as it was when the war began," said Gavin.

"Funny place to store Mauser ammunition."

"We can admit that we were trading with them before the war. It's our northern-most warehouse outside of the trading posts."

"You're not frightened of him?"

"No. I'm only scared of Viljoen and Koos."

"Don't worry about Koos. I know him well."

"We killed his wife. It was in the papers. I didn't know at the time. She was killed in that last bombardment from the heights. And she was also Carel Viljoen's daughter."

"They really have reason to hate us," agreed James.

"There's nothing we can do about Grant. I may have misjudged him. I've obviously rubbed him up the wrong way. On his own, he hasn't enough guts to go through with it and put his suspicions into action. And he certainly won't know that we had anything to do with Koos or Viljoen, so he can't go to them for verification. Grant's a little man with ideas of power and Sarah is just plain frustrated and envies her sister."

"YOU WERE RIGHT, KEVIN," said Sarah as she pulled on her drawers.

"That was not nearly so frightening as I had expected. I just hope I won't have a baby. Now, will you tell me?"

"Morgan sold Mauser ammunition to the Boers during the war. A full investigation will draw out the details. They'll have him shot for treason. Von Brand was in on it too. I'm not sure about Carregan, but they certainly used his ships. I was captain of one of them."

"Thank you, Kevin. That is better than anything I expected. Much better."

"First we prolong it for him. Make him pay me money. The waiting will be worse than the firing squad."

"Yes. I like that idea too. Now we must get some sleep. Not to worry about waking the others. They're dotted around the island. Funny. But you were right. I rather enjoyed myself tonight. We might even try it again when I am a little less sore."

"Oh, we'll be doing it again," said Grant, and patted her bottom.

Her brain told her to shudder, but she didn't.

6

"It's good to be home," said James as the buggy turned in at the sign reading 'Morgandale'.

"Hey, it's crooked," shouted Gavin from the trap behind him.

"What is?" asked von Brand, who was driving the horse and sitting next to James. Behind them were Mrs Dalton, her daughter and Sonny.

"The sign. It was crooked the first day I arrived. Stop the horse," he said.

Lagrange pulled in the reins and Gavin got down and put the sign up straight. He stood back and brushed the palms of his hands together.

"That's better," he said. "That's much better. Now I feel at home."

They all laughed and Gavin got into his seat and they drove for a mile with the lands of Morgandale spread out on either side of them.

"Tonight, we'll have a real farm party," said von Brand to James. "Nothing is being served, except the alcohol, that hasn't come off of Morgandale. All the neighbours are coming. Colin Tenant, Jack Hall. I even met Jimmy Thorpe in Salisbury when I came in to meet you from the train. He was going back to Inyanga, but now he's coming over. We've put up a number of rondavels to sleep you all. We started building when we received your wire. I asked Koos, James. They gave him back his farm, thank goodness. He said he would come eventually, but it was too soon now. Carel Viljoen is staying with him. Viljoen is talking of settling in Rhodesia, so I hear."

"Soon they'll say there are more Boer commandants in Rhodesia than there are in the Transvaal. He's not bitter, Koos?"

"No. He says it was as much their damn arrogance as our greed. He says they'll win the place back again in the end and I believe him. They live hard and breed a lot of children. You should go over by yourself. I don't think the old man will shoot you. He didn't shoot me."

"You didn't capture him."

"I don't think he'll shoot."

"Neither do I. Are you nervous about the wedding?"

"No. The problem was finding my first wife. We hadn't written for years. Apparently we'd been divorced for twenty years. She'd told a court I'd gone to Africa and had never come back. They didn't even bother to find out what I thought. They waited for five years and when I didn't turn up they gave her a divorce. Polly has settled down well on the farm. Haven't you, my dear?" he asked, turning to her as the new homestead came into sight.

"Yes, I like it. We're both too old for gallivanting. What we need is companionship, which we have now both found."

No one spoke and the clip-clop of the horses came back to their ears.

"That house is three times the size of the one that was burnt," said James.

"You wait till you see what a woman's touch can do to a house," answered von Brand. "Within months it'll rival Ship Corner and Morgan's Bay."

"You think there'll be room for me?"

"When you come back, we're going to build ourselves another

home. Polly has started to draw the plans. Bit of an artist. There's much more to Mrs Dalton than meets the eye."

'I'll bet there is,' thought Sonny to herself with a chuckle. 'Yes,' she thought, 'I like the house. I can live on a farm. I hope I'm pregnant this time and then he'll have to marry me. Funny to think that I own a fifth of all this land. James is right. It is like coming home.'

A HUNDRED YARDS from the house, the dogs came bounding down the road and milled, barking, around the horses. It happened every time to the same horses, so they took no notice. Three African servants came out of the house with smiles which showed the brilliant whiteness of their teeth. The horses slowed, then stopped in front of the house. The entrance was in the centre, with the two bedroom wings falling back parallel on either side. The eleven new rondavels had been built over on the left of the high ground. The men got out and helped down the women, while the servants rummaged in the last buggy for the baggage. James, von Brand and Gavin greeted the servants and James's dog tried successfully to get his front paws up on James's shoulders. It licked his face.

"Come on, you mad dog," said James, wrestling with the animal and tickling it hard behind the ears. "It may be nearly three years, but you don't have to get hungry at my expense. Come here. Come here and we'll have a proper fight. Do you know," he said to the others, "I think this damn great Bull Mastiff has missed me. Haven't you, Shaka? You're just like a Zulu. Always wanting a fight." The dog stood back and looked at him and James was certain it winked. He looked back at the others.

"Welcome to Morgandale. You've seen my Ship Corner and Gavin's Morgan's Bay, but this is the jewel of my life."

"WEDDINGS," said Louise to no one in particular, "make me feel very nostalgic. They're so final. Oh, you know what I mean."

"Indubitably, you are right," said Colin Tenant. He was a little drunk like everyone else, and was very proud of that word.

"This is such a lovely setting for a wedding," said Sarah, who had also had alcohol for the first time in her life. "I mean, everything just runs away from the house. All those funny trees. You know, Willie, you really must cut the lawns."

"Those are not lawns, my dear. That is bush. Virgin bush."

"Oh. Is it? Well, I would have called it trees interspersed with long, uncut grass. And why is the grass so long and brown? It would come up to my waist." She wafted out onto the vast veranda without waiting for an answer.

"See," said Gavin into James's ear. "Prick a fine lady and that's what you find."

"You're malicious," chuckled James.

"No. Just a realist. Everyone wants to pretend that they're not what they are. By the way, Grant has a smirk on his face every time he looks at her. The smirk reads filth."

"I'm not sure that we haven't underestimated Kevin Grant."

"I took him on because I thought he was stupid. I didn't want him to think."

"The people with small brains are often more dangerous. They're capable of seeing what they want but not the consequences. Where did he come from?"

"I don't know. He never says anything about his background. I needed a good skipper for the *Good Hope* and his previous employer said he was the best sailor in Cape Town."

"You can't pry into everyone's private life before you employ them. It would take too long and you wouldn't necessarily get the right answers. We'll check on him when we return to Cape Town. Let's go and pour ourselves another drink. There's no point in worrying about a problem before it's happened."

"You're right," said Gavin.

They walked towards the long bar that had been set up at the back of the living room, which ran the length of the front of the house with the kitchens and dining room behind. There was no ceiling to the roof and the bush timber poles rose high up into the rafters and up to the thatch. The room was cool and full of space and led out onto the veranda, which was as large as the room itself.

"Willie looks happy," said Gavin as they stood at the bar.

"Yes. He does. Never thought I'd see Willie von Brand with a wife."

"He treats her like a pet cub. No one is allowed to get close. You seem to be getting on better with Sonny."

"Yes," he said, and looked at Gavin with an impish smile. "We're going to get married. I haven't asked her yet, but I will before we leave Morgandale."

"About time. What made you make up your mind?"

"A few things."

"In other words, mind my own business?"

"Something like that," answered James. "Something like that."

"Michael would be pleased."

"Yes. Strange how things happen. When he died, we didn't even know that he had a sister."

"What are you two talking about?" said Sonny, coming up to them.

"You," said Gavin.

"Now, isn't that nice."

"I think so," agreed Gavin.

"But you're not going to tell me?"

"I wouldn't dream of it," said Gavin and shrank away in mock despair.

"Are you enjoying the reception?" said James, putting his arm around her shoulders.

"Yes," she said, drawing close to him. "I like weddings."

"Excuse me," said Gavin and left them alone.

"Now what made him run away?" asked Sonny.

"He thinks it's time I proposed to you."

"Does he?"

"Yes."

"Will you?"

"Will I what?"

"Marry me?"

"Yes."

"Good. Let's have another drink and then we'll make the announcement."

"Now isn't that nice," said Lillian Dalton when everyone had finished kissing and shaking hands. "You start one wedding and everyone gets the same idea. Don't you want to get married, Gavin?"

"No. I'm too young. Servitude should be given to those who've reached an age where there's nothing better for them to do. I'm far too young."

"Suppose so. Pity. I could have helped you spend all that lovely money."

"I like you, Lillian. You're honest. You admit you like me only for my money."

She looked at him deliciously and leant towards him, gently touching his knee with her fingers. "When do you think this reception will be over?" she said huskily.

"Whenever you're ready," said Gavin.

"I'm ready."

"Come on then. Let's go."

"They're sneaking out in the middle of the reception," said Louise to Quinn as she watched Gavin lead Lillian through the main entrance that led out between the kitchens and the dining room. "If I was the jealous type, I'd throw something. Fortunately, the only jealousy it creates in me is the fact that in only a few moments' time she'll be reaching the heights of enjoyment while I will be still standing here with a gentleman."

"Sometimes you are quite disgusting," said Quinn.

"Sometimes you are right."

· · ·

"WHEN ARE you going to do something?" said Sarah to Grant, away from the others.

"Not now. He's had too much drink to be serious. The first opportunity. Did you enjoy last night?"

"Yes, I did. It is not at all what I was told it would be like."

"Tonight again?"

"Yes."

"Will you come across to me this time?"

"All right."

"YOU DON'T REALLY THINK you can frighten me into giving you money?" said Gavin. Grant had caught him alone at last, saddling Garret up for an early morning inspection of Morgandale's crops, and had wasted no time in threatening him with blackmail.

"By saying that," said Grant, "you're admitting that you sold the Boers ammunition."

"I did before the war started."

"Then what about your stocks in Oudekraal? The ones I brought in."

"What about them?"

"They're not there anymore. Chris O'Connor checked again last month. We both agreed there'd be money in it for both of us, and he's on the spot. He didn't have very much chance of making money as a mine captain. Where did the Mauser ammunition go?"

"Back to Cape Town."

"Who shipped it?"

"I did."

"But only my ships called at Oudekraal."

"You, Grant, were merely a minor employee. Are you trying to tell me what happens to my own ships and that I should tell every petty little captain everything I do?"

"You're lying."

"Am I? And if I was, which I am not and can prove it, which is worse: a liar or a blackmailer? A blackmailer is a frightened, rather pathetic little man who has no strength to do anything for himself. It is the weak man's way to crime. The pettiest of petty thieves. A man with no guts is a blackmailer. He's failed at everything and his jealousy forces him to try and get his own back on the people who've succeeded. He's a man I pity but above all despise. You will now ask a servant to drive you to Salisbury. Where you go is no longer any concern of mine. You're fired."

"You'll regret this."

"Oh, go and drink your mother's slops."

Gavin pulled Garret's head round, spurred him on and cantered out to look at the new tobacco they had recently begun to grow on Morgandale. Grant watched him. If he had had a gun he would have shot him in the back.

"WHAT HAPPENED?" asked Sarah.

"He told me to go and drink my mother's slops."

"And are you?"

"Don't you laugh at me."

"I'm not. What are you going to do?"

"I'm going to bring him down whether or not I make any money."

"Good. Now we really understand each other. I gave up my pride to ruin that man and I don't want to come out of all this with nothing. How are you going to do it?"

"I'm going to tell the story to Owen Anders. He wrote the articles on Gavin. Those people always like a story and this could end up the biggest scandal of the war. I'm certain now of one thing that I wasn't certain of before. Gavin Morgan did sell Mauser ammunition to the Boers, and right up until the last months of the war."

7

"No. It's all over," Koos van der Walt told James. "You had your job to do and so did I. We live in the same country but we have our responsibilities of birth. Come in and see Carel Viljoen, James. You'll have to talk in the *Taal*, as he knows little English. But that you will remember. Now tell me, man. They say you are growing this tobacco. You must tell me about it. I would grow it myself. We all need a good cash crop, especially after the war. My house was still standing, but after three years of neglect everything else will have to be started again from scratch. But it's good soil. I'll have the crops again and the cattle."

"I'll lend you some cattle to breed from. You did it for me when I started. I'll also send you some of the seedlings for the tobacco. We're not sure how best it grows, but we'll find out. Willie says the Portuguese first grew it here hundreds of years ago when they came up from Mozambique. He believes the wild tobacco you find by the rivers was once cultivated. He's read the old books. It would be an easy crop to export, since when it's dry it's light and fetches a good price in relation to its weight. With our transport problems, tobacco could be what we're all looking for. Oh, and I'm sorry about Hanneli, Koos."

Koos turned on him as they were walking into the small

construction he referred to as his house. All the friendliness had drained from his face.

"As long as we remain neighbours and friends," he said, "I'll ask you not to mention her name again."

James dropped his eyes away from the frustration and pain that showed so clearly in van der Walt's eyes. As they entered the house, he made a mental note never to bring up the subject of the war himself. It was too close to the nerves around people's hearts.

"It seems," said Viljoen in the *Taal* when they laid eyes on one another, "that we are to be neighbours."

James held out his hand and the Boer put it between both of his and shook it hard. Viljoen looked younger by ten years than when they had last met. His beard was well trimmed and his clothes were clean.

"There was no chance of my carrying out my threat," he went on, "but if I had been in your position I would have let the prisoner go and shot him in the back. When I met Koos again, we laughed together because he knew you better than I did. You once said we would look at each other's farms. I am looking forward to seeing Morgandale. Here you have us. Give us time and we'll make it right. How are Morgan and von Brand? We thought it best not to come to the wedding. Later, when we are all used to each other again, then it will be all right. Come in, man. We'll sit on the *stoep* and drink some coffee together."

"Do you think we should have a big wedding?" said Sonny Fentan to James as she went down the gangplank of the *Cape of Good Hope* and stepped onto the quay at Skipley Wharf in Cape Town.

"It's well your mother isn't alive, otherwise we'd have had to face up to the question of religion."

"I've not been to Shul in years. I'll leave it up to you to decide which church."

"The cathedral. We'll have a big wedding. It'll be the only one we're going to have so we might as well do it all properly. We'll need a month for reading the banns, making clothes, cakes and all the other trimmings."

They stood waiting for the others, lightly holding hands as they looked at the other ships in the harbour.

"Well, we all look healthy," said Gavin as he stepped ashore. "The return voyage without Grant was a pleasure. Amazing how one person can poison everyone around him. In future I'll sail my own boat despite the hard work. Sarah didn't look so happy on the way back, but then you cannot please everyone in life. The trouble with a holiday is that when you get back you have twice as much work to catch up on. I'll be driving Lillian home and then I'll be going to the office. Can you join me there in an hour, James? Afraid there will be a lot to discuss. Wilkins can brief us both on the last month's happenings. Roger and Phil will be taking Louise and Sarah home. We must make another trip like that next year. There are so many more islands to visit off the coast of Mozambique."

"Give me two hours," said James. "I cannot bring my mind onto business quite as quickly as you."

"Two hours then. Can I stay at Ship Corner tonight? I've never met your sister and I don't much like the idea of the hour-and-a-half drive to my house."

"Of course. You'll be welcome."

Their luggage was brought ashore and they saw it being loaded before waving goodbye to each other. James had never felt so happy in his life. For a brief, almost imperceptible moment, Gavin, watching him, envied him his future married life. Then he thought again and realised that he had never, and probably never would, meet the girl who would hold his attention for that length of time. A whole life. The only life he would have.

"I'LL READ it to you, James. Wilkins says this is not the first report on the subject. It's my old friend Owen Anders. Sit down."

They were alone in Gavin's office at Carregan Shipping. It was large and spacious, with framed photographs of Carregan

Shipping's first twelve ships on the walls. The carpet was red and thick and the chairs and desk were covered in a heavy, light-grained leather. It was the type of office where rich men worked.

"I think for the first time that we must take our Mr Grant seriously," continued Gavin. "There's no mention of names for fear of libel, but Anders is calling for an inquiry and some of the other papers are taking up his cause. Wilkins says we should sue the paper for libel immediately, as even he can see that they're referring to Carregan Shipping." He shook the paper out and began to read the report aloud:

> *Further information has come to light in our relentless search for the truth. For two weeks we have been drawing the government's attention to the need for a public inquiry and the naming of people involved in what must be the greatest scandal of the Boer War. We have our proof but there is nothing we can do to bring such foul guilt, such abysmal depths of human greed, such murder, to justice without our government's help. They are the ones who must draw out the Judas and put him and his accomplices on trial for their lives.*
>
> *This is treason, the very foulest treason. It was Englishman killing Englishman in exchange for gold. They were not satisfied with their millions, their youth, their fame, their honours. They needed more gold and threw back into your faces the adulation, the praise, the very hero worship. They used this to kill your father, your husband, to prolong the very agony of war. How can the Boers even praise them for this work? Who do they think they are? A God? A tin God? No God, I say the devil himself.*
>
> *These are not men. These are cowards, so low, so bad, that no good man or woman would waste an ounce of their own dry spittle upon their names. We now know the Boer commanders with whom they negotiated, against*

*whom they fought if irony can play its part. Carel Viljoen
and Koos van der Walt. All our Government has got to do
is ask them. They will be proof enough. How long must it
be before this Government takes action! The public
demands this. It is their right. Selling arms to the enemy
in time of war! Can any reader tell us a crime more foul
than this?*

"Maybe your paper man," said James when Gavin had put down
the sheet, "can do harm as well as good. He knows how to make
inquiries and he is careful to name no one who can harm him. He
must be pretty certain that he has stumbled upon the truth. What
do the other articles say?"

"That the culprits own a shipping line, are young, famous and
lead lives that many good living Edwardians would find it difficult
to stomach. What do we do?"

"Sue the paper or call an inquiry ourselves into the affairs of
Carregan Shipping. I'll think tonight. The two people who will help
us most are the two you feared most."

"Who are they?"

"Viljoen and Koos. I think they would perjure themselves for us.
They know what it was like to face our own bullets and have to kill
people with whom we had no personal quarrel. The Grants and
Anders of this world would foul themselves at the sight of a Boer
with a gun pointed at them."

"What do we do, James?"

"We find out everything we can about Grant and Anders. We're
rich. Now we'll need some of that money. We must show our
accusers up for what they are. Forget about the crime. We'll go for
Grant and Anders. If we can find some real filth on either of them,
even Anders' paper will fail to back him. They'll drop him as fast as
they've dropped you. Irrespective of what action we take, public or
private, I'm going straight away to confront the GOC. He'll think it
strange that I've not done so already until he hears that we've been
away for a month. We must certainly attack. Our silence, in their

eyes, could be the proof of our guilt. Now, Gavin, we'll find out who our real friends are."

"You don't have to be involved. It had nothing to do with you, James."

"Yes it had. I didn't watch you closely enough. And Viljoen was right. No one would believe that I knew nothing about the most lucrative side of Carregan Shipping. Anyway, I'm certainly an accessory after the fact."

"Do you know something? I'm going to enjoy this. We've achieved too much. We need a challenge."

"You may do, Gavin. I'm not so sure about myself. Now, if there's nothing else to report, I'm going up to see General Thackeray."

"I'll begin on Grant. I'll cable the London office for information about Anders. You're right. We'll rake up every piece of filth we can find."

"I'm sorry, Colonel Carregan," said the adjutant, looking at him queerly, "but General Thackeray asks that you apply for an interview in the normal way. The informal days of wartime have been replaced by the strict code of military command. You will have to apply to the GOC in Rhodesia, who would then pass your application through to the usual channels."

"You might mention to the General that I've been away for a month," said James. "Otherwise I would have been in this office the moment these extraordinary articles appeared in the local newspapers. We will, of course, sue everyone concerned. They did not have to put my name to their articles. My lawyers, both here and in London, will be attending to the matter. By the way, how far north did you get during the war?"

"I remained in Cape Town."

"I thought as much. You might also, Captain, remember your rank when you address a colonel."

"Yes, sir."

"Good. That sounds a little better. You should not believe everything you read in the newspaper. Good day to you."

"I'M SORRY, Colonel Carregan, but General Farrow is not accepting calls at the moment. If you wish to see him in his office, then of course you know the channels through which to apply for..."

"Yes. You have no need to go any further."

"COME IN, JAMES," said Colonel Gilham. "This is damn serious. Pity you weren't here when it started. I called on you immediately the first article was brought to my attention."

"Farrow and Thackeray won't even open their doors to me. They believe this slander."

"No. That's not quite it. They just don't necessarily believe that it's all false. If instructed to, they will convene a court of inquiry. Only then will they give an opinion. Until then, and until your name and that of your company has been cleared, they will treat you as if you have the measles. It's the way of men who have reached positions by never being wrong. The fact that they have never been particularly right is immaterial. I would not normally talk against my fellow officers but this press business is damn serious. The governor is talking openly of an inquiry. In the ultimate, this is what you must want. What I fear is your case being swept away by public opinion in England. The army will ride whichever direction appears to be in the best interest of the GOC and any other person who finds himself concerned. This regiment is behind you, James. Every one of them. They respect a soldier and despise the people who only talk. Now, tell me, what is it all about?"

"Gavin fired a man. Kevin Grant. The man stumbled on some Mauser ammunition we've held at Oudekraal since before the war. Before that, as traders, we were entitled to trade with whoever wished to do business. Once hostilities commenced, we stopped. Over a period of time the ammunition was brought back to Cape

Town, and since it was too old for use it was destroyed. Grant tried to blackmail Gavin to stop the nonsense with which we are now faced."

"What about Viljoen and van der Walt?"

"They will tell the truth."

"Are you sure? After killing the one's daughter who was also the other's wife?"

"Yes. They are honourable men. Men both you and I respect."

"Yes. You are probably right. Men like that would not take their vengeance in such a way. But this man Anders is clever. He knows what the public want. He gave them Gavin and now he's brought them to the point where they wish him to take Gavin away. Two sensational stories. The armchair soldiers like to destroy people who've fought the battles they've only ever read about. It salves their consciences. Let's go down to the mess. Everyone will be glad to see you. It'll make a change, you drinking on my card."

"THE WHOLE OF Cape Town is talking about these articles," said Sonny to James as she sat on the edge of the sofa in the drawing room at Ship Corner. "I'm worried stiff."

"One of the problems of possessing anything," said James, "is preventing someone else from taking it away from you. We have faced up to problems before."

"But not this serious."

"It depends upon whether you consider the story to be true."

"Knowing Gavin, it probably is. It's the type of thing which would amuse him. Basically, he dislikes the establishment. But that's not the point. Right or wrong, how do we overcome the problem?"

"To begin with," said James, "we must be logical. We must analyse the aspects and their consequences. At the moment, it's paper talk. There have been many such instances in the past that have been blown up by the press and then killed by responsible editors or just fizzled out. We must decide which fate ours will be.

We must determine our strengths and weaknesses, the fair-weather friends.

"What we see at the moment is a mammoth problem, but if it is looked at piece by piece, what do we find? A man who has been discharged for attempted blackmail, a mine captain in need of money, and a newspaper man who will do anything to increase his own renown, his feeling of power and his self-importance. They have the foundation of a story and the medium to place this before the public in such a way that the public know to whom they are referring, but a court could be shown that many people have shipping lines, youth, fame and honour. And again, guilty or not guilty, how does one define an insinuation? By establishing your line, fame, honour and youth, you might be trying too hard to wear the cap that fits. Each man to his profession. Owen Anders is a professional. He has been doing such things for twenty years. He knows exactly how far he can go and still be able to do a somersault on Grant if it suits his cause. He has no interest in right or wrong. His only interest is in sensation."

"How can you sit there talking like a professor when your lives are at stake? Just when I've got what I want, they're talking of putting you on trial for treason. They'll shoot you. Why now? In a month we're being married. Why do these things happen to me?"

"More correctly, my love, they are happening to me. Panic, which is what you are showing now, could well see the three of us facing a firing squad, guilty or not, as it is the public, now, here and in England, who are judging the case. Right now, no jury, military or civil, would be impartial. As you have found out, Cape Town is already referring to the firing squad. They believe what is printed."

They both turned as Gavin came into the room. He was smiling and completely relaxed. Sonny even thought he looked like he was enjoying himself, which he was.

"I overheard the last bit. Hello, Sonny. You're right, James. They do believe the printed word, which is why I've spent all this afternoon buying the *Cape Sentinel*. It's bigger than Anders' local paper and we'll be able to syndicate the articles in England. It was expensive, but if I can streamline its management and printing works it will be a good investment. For the moment I've bought it in the name of a nominee. Rhodes owned the paper, but after his death the estate had no real use for the investment. Rhodes had used it for his politics. We'll use it for ours.

"My nominee will be appointed the new editor. The staff will be led to believe that he is the new owner. His price was twenty-five per cent of the equity, but from my brief but thorough investigation I'm sure he'll make an excellent editor. It seems that wealth needs a mouthpiece. Now, may I have a drink? This afternoon and this evening have found me thinking harder than at any time in my life. Oh, and the shares will ultimately go to Carregan Shipping. The money has been channelled to Frobisher through four channels, three of which are banks. And banks, bless them, keep their clients' business completely to themselves. How does it feel, James, to be chairman designate of the largest newspaper in Southern Africa?"

"How much did you have to pay?"

"Fifty thousand pounds. And then I gave a quarter to Frobisher."

"A lot of money."

"A lot at stake. Now, how is your grandfather?"

"Not good," said James, still thinking of what Gavin had done. "Not good. He's gone back to bed. His mind is wandering, but then he is old. Yes... yes, you're right, Gavin. It's exactly what we want. We'll not fight this in a court of inquiry or in a libel suit. We'll fight them in the papers, where everyone can see. Do you know, I really believe that you deserve what you've achieved at the age of twenty-four."

"How about that drink?"

"Oh. Yes. The drink. I think I'll go and get them myself. A drink, Sonny?"

"Thank you, darling. I would love a small whisky."

"I'll ask Ester to come down so you can meet her. She sits with grandfather for a lot of the time. Oswald preferred to stay at the Mount Nelson. Thinks it important to remain with his fellow officers. He's hoping for the colonelcy when Gilham retires next year. The two children are asleep upstairs. Maybe Oswald does not relish the idea of living with his brother- in-law. I think Ester is a little lonely. No, Gavin, we'll have no looks like that. Anyway, she's thirty-two."

"Go and talk to him," said Ester as she carefully closed the door to her grandfather's bedroom. She and James were standing in the corridor. "He's lucid at the moment, though his mind is rambling. He was active for too long. Once the driving motor stops they don't take long to stop altogether. He's enjoyed the children, seen what he wanted. I'm glad I came out to look after him."

"Gavin is downstairs with Sonny."

"I'll go downstairs and introduce myself. You go in and see grandfather."

Ester smiled rather forlornly, squeezed his arm and left him outside the door. She had changed so much from the girl he had grown up with. Their lives had grown a great distance apart, but to his surprise their old closeness was still there. James had been ten and his sister eight when their mother had died, and after that they had seen very little of their father until he had mellowed in his later years. Ernest Carregan had only been interested in the Liverpool and Maritime Insurance Company. There was no room for children, or so he had let it appear. More likely, James thought, he had not known how to approach them. How to bring himself down to ten and eight. 'Well, he's dead now,' James thought sadly, 'and grandfather is about to go as well.' He would grow old and go too, if the pattern of his ancestry was to see him die of age. He opened the door and went inside.

"Hear ye've got yerself a spot of bother," said his grandfather as James sat down in the armchair next to the bed.

"Nothing more than usual."

"Had a few me'self. Never look so bad when they're over. Prop up me pillow, lad. Like to see the sea through that big window. Sun's almost down. Good day for sailing. Can see it. Make seven knots in that wind. Your grandmother used to watch me go out in a wind like that. First house we had overlooked the Mersey. Didn't give her much of a life. Never there, I was. Never there. A good woman. Gave me a son, she did, but in the end she couldn't take the loneliness. Poor Emma. Loved her in me own way. Should have done more. But ye couldn't have a wife on the old *Mirtle*. Wasn't enough room for the crew. That was sailing, lad. Pity ye never met yer grandmother. I think I'll go and join her soon. A lot to make up for. Good woman. Gave me Ernest. And you and Ester. Not many men have a grandson like you. Fair looked after yer old grandfather, you 'ave.

"Oh, I know ye built this place for me and Hal. So we could look out at the ships. Don't think we didn't notice. Hope it's daytime when I go and I can think like I'm thinking now. Me mind's been wandering lately. Would like to die looking at the sea, knowing it was there. Me life, it was. Too much me life. But a good one. Life's been good to me. Right to the end. A boy it was, and a girl. New generation. The new ones come and the old 'uns go. Always has been. No. Got no regrets. What for? What for, I say to me'self? Ye work yer life and ye build a bit and if ye can die in yer family happy that's all ye need. Look after Sonny. Ye should have married her years ago. Couldn't tell ye. Not me business. She did a few bad things but so did I when I was young. We all do. None of us can be good all of the time. Shouldn't 'ave seen but I've got me eyes.

"Ester. Glad she came. Sad, she is. Ye'll have to look after her, James. Keep an eye on her, like. She's yer sister. Family. Never thought ye'd turn out like you are. Twenty-one when I first set eyes on ye as ye came up the plank of the *Dolphin*. Yer father was being the snob in those days. Didn't want to recognise an old seaman for a father. Never mind, we made it up in the end. Poor Ernest. Missed the boat, he did. I got the best of his son and thank ye, lad. Old age can be bad without friends. Ye made me young all over again. But I'm going now. Ye'll be all right on yer own. Gave ye help when ye needed it. Remember when Hal slapped that wharf when he came in on the *Annabel*? Or was it the *Ester Carregan*? Carregan Shipping and me old *Dolphin* sitting up on sixty funnels. Never thought I'd see a day like that. But I did. Thanks, my James. Give me yer hand while I'm thinking right."

"HE'S GOING, ISN'T HE?" said Ester when she met him in the hall. James nodded. "Yes, he's going. I'll be out for a while. Look after the others. I want to walk by myself. Something in me is dying up there with him."

8

"I would call it," said Gavin Morgan as he threw a small piece of rock far out into the sea, "the in-between time. Tomorrow, the first, very small element of doubt will be sown regarding the *Mercury* and its handling of the 'unknown traitors'. We'll build up from there. Must make the public believe that they're drawing the truth out of us."

They were standing on the headland to the far left of Morgan's Bay, he and Lillian. Gavin still found Morgan's Bay dull without a woman or other people. He enjoyed company.

"Have you heard from your mother?" he asked.

"Yes. They're very happy. Never thought I'd see my dear old mother settle down on a farm."

He threw another rock out to sea and it went a little further than the last, a fact he noted with satisfaction.

"Are you not worried?" asked Lillian.

"No. Not a bit. It's a problem that I can see and do something about. Our first article questions the right of a newspaper to build up public opinion against an individual on hearsay. 'Is the *Mercury*,' we ask, 'interested in the truth, or in sensation and circulation? If they are unable to answer this in logical as opposed to mass hysteria words, then it will be the job of the *Sentinel* to warn the public by example not to believe the words they read in the *Mercury*.'

"Much of this is true, as Anders' style of writing may as well have originated on a soap box in Hyde Park Corner. If you follow what he says and believe it, you can only end up in a state of righteous indignation. From this it is a matter of time before the man in the street will demand and get blood, every drop of which he is demanding because of what he's read and taken as fact in the popular press. People like to be swept along on a tide of common feeling. So we must take them off at a tangent and then lead them back onto a new path of righteousness. The public do not like to find their trust misplaced.

"Firstly, we'll state where Anders received his information. We will then give the public a certain fact, together with copies of the published reports in England. A double newsprint they could never disbelieve. They will read that Grant lost a ship and two members of his crew through drunkenness. To run a ship aground and kill two people, is this not murder, by neglect if not intent? And must we the public believe the word of a man who is directly responsible for the deaths of two men, and who lost his master's ticket as a result of the accident? Even the court of inquiry found him guilty! And now we find him in Cape Town with false papers, claiming the right to captain a ship."

Gavin threw another rock out to sea and saw it fall short of the last. He did not feel as brave as he sounded. He knew that he was dealing with a man who knew more about newspapers than he and Frobisher. But Gavin also knew that unless he displayed the correct attitude, he would be unable to build up to the point where everyone would brush the situation aside as another piece of newspaper sensationalism. He knew perfectly well that he was on the defensive.

"TAKE THE PAPER TO COURT," said Sarah to Grant in frustration. "Sue them. They're calling you a murderer. Sue them for everything they've got. I know it's Gavin behind this. His money, of course. Well, don't just stand there. Do something. Get a lawyer. Sue them."

"What for?" said Grant. "For stating facts? The court of inquiry were all for putting me on trial for manslaughter and I don't want to spend two years in jail. I was blind drunk and had been for three days, and so were the two Chinese girls who were doing the round trip to Hong Kong. But the real fact was that my number one found himself in such thick fog with a heavy sea running and his engine not working. I could have done nothing, sober or drunk, but it's the captain's job to be on the bridge in an emergency and they couldn't even stand me on my feet. I was still drunk when I came off the lifeboat. A sympathetic cameraman took a shot of the weary sailor, only to ask my name for publication and hear me ramble on in my cups about being the captain. He had a story. He printed it. Within days they wanted me damned. But the facts are right. So are those Anders has printed. No, I can't sue Gavin. But if I know from experience, Anders will have a simple but lethal answer."

"Why do you always have to leave everything to somebody else?"

"Because in this case he knows more about it than me."

"WE HAVE YET TO WIN A ROUND," said James to Gavin as they sat in James's office at Carregan Shipping. "His reply about Grant was perfect; that newspapers in unscrupulous hands could so often mislead the public. And then he showed that Grant had lost his ship through bad luck and a little improper behaviour, something that every sea captain had done in his time. He has used it to show the public that the *Mercury* would never be unscrupulous. They believe him even more than before."

"Well, then," said Gavin. "We'll print an article on Grant the blackmailer."

"That is the next step. Are the articles being printed in England?"

"All the more irresponsible papers are quoting us word for word."

"Have you found anything on Anders?"

"Not a thing. He's holier than the Pope. A man like that would be, of course. He revels in everyone else's filth."

"A pity. I learnt from Gilham today that the authorities are at last taking the matter seriously. I think it may come to an inquiry."

"It can't, James, we'd never stand up. When is Willie arriving?"

"This afternoon. He's left his new wife to look after Morgandale."

"Good. He must use his brain as well."

"Don't you think it better for you both to get out of the country? They will have no proof that I knew what you were doing. I can run the line for a few years until the matter has been forgotten."

"No thanks, James. I may be a lot of things but I am not a coward. I put you all into this little lot. If I run, they'll tear whatever is left of the line to pieces. And they won't let you off, James. They'll want something to show for their troubles."

"Maybe you're right."

"What Willie is bringing with him is maybe the answer."

"What is that?"

"A sworn affidavit from Viljoen and Koos to the effect that they did not buy ammunition from me, you, or Carregan Shipping."

"But we can't use that until Anders puts our names into print."

"I know. But he will. Very soon he must state his case in detail. He has been threatening to do so for long enough."

"Thank goodness there are some men in this world. I was beginning to wonder. Apart from Gilham and his officers, all my old compatriots are cutting me dead."

"Me too. Especially the ones who spent the most amount of time at Morgan's Bay. Their careers, you know."

"I DON'T like doing this to you and James, Gavin," said Quinn, "but I don't enjoy living in Cape Town now that Louise has finally decided she has no wish to marry me. You probably need me more now than at any other time, but even when I am here my mind is not on the job. You do see what I mean?"

"Hell," said Gavin. "Yes and no. If you have this problem, running away from Cape Town will not remove the knots from your stomach. Oh, and none of this out of sight, out of mind business. And, Roger, don't look so forlorn. You obviously played a few cards the wrong way. It's not a case of the whole female race rejecting one Roger Quinn. Please, sit down. You make me nervous standing in front of my desk."

Reluctantly, Quinn sat down. Gavin looked at him. Quinn looked a mess, not even his hair was brushed. "The immediate remedy is to find a woman and take her to bed. Your manhood will feel better."

"But I'm not like that."

"Well, it's about time that you were. Grown men, older than me, fought brilliantly in a war, and you sit there as if someone had hit you on the head with a sack of mealies. You're not dead, Roger. You are merely slightly wounded. Now, be a good lad and find yourself a nice woman and put her firmly upon her back. Get a little drunk first if it helps. Afterwards, you look for a nice girl to have an affair with. There's nothing like another woman to cure the one before. And Roger, if you put your whole heart into the subject, it always works."

"I don't think I'd know where to start."

"Hell I do. We'll meet tonight at the Mount Nelson. There'll be me and Lillian and another girl I've yet to choose. I'll cure your ills and at the same time show the public that we're not afraid to be seen in the army's den. It will be pleasant to dine there again when only half the place belongs to the army. Shall we say nine o'clock?"

"Yes. You amaze me. All your problems and you want to sort out mine."

"Have you ever considered that I might enjoy an evening out?"

"No. Not really. But then I'm not like you."

"Probably just as well, for your own sake," said Gavin.

. . .

"WELL," said James. "He's named us and suggested we own the *Sentinel*, having found out that it changed hands two weeks ago. He's ignored the blackmail charge by bringing out a bigger sensation."

"Well then," said Gavin, "in three days' time, the time it would have taken to obtain it from Rhodesia, we'll publish the affidavit."

"If he's not managed to have us arrested by then. He's calling for it openly enough. Come on. Let's go up to my house for a drink. We've done enough work. If the truth is going to catch up with us, then catch up it will. Let's hope we have enough time to bury my grandfather tomorrow. I wouldn't like to be arrested at his funeral. I've not announced the time or the place, since I have no wish for the press to use him for morbid curiosity."

"Did he know we were in trouble?"

"I told him it was all over and kept him away from the papers. He had very few rational moments towards the end, anyway. No, I'm not sorry he went when he did. He died happy, on top of everything that he wanted to be. It would have made his last moments sad to see us being destroyed."

"We're not destroyed yet."

"No. Maybe not."

"Come on then. You mentioned a drink."

"I'M NOT SURE, Sarah, whether you have come out here to gloat or to give me a lecture," said Gavin as he stood with Sarah on the veranda of Morgan's Bay. "The spring is definitely here. A few more weeks and we'll be able to swim."

"If you're not in jail," she said venomously. "What, tell me, is worse than selling an item that kills people?"

"Manufacturing it," he said, turning to her. "Being a government and allowing the guns, the bombs, the bullets to be exported freely, caring nothing of whose guts they destroy. Being part of society that allows a war to begin. If I have done what I'm told I've done, then I've merely made another profit along the line of destruction. If my guilt is so bad, if I've killed so many people because I've no scruples, then let me see the others in that dock. Let me see everyone who assisted those bullets into that final belly. You know what you'd see? Not just Gavin Morgan, the factory workers, the management of the munitions factory, the shareholders, the crew of the ship who transported the ammunition, the dockers, stevedores, railways, and everyone else who touched that cargo. You would find the whole of humanity on trial. It's the balance of nature, the need for strength to be wrought in adversity, the whole complex creation of life, that creates wars. Not me, Sarah."

"AND WHAT CAN we do that we haven't already?" said von Brand as he eased his bulk into an armchair. His hair was silver grey and the thickness around his stomach was larger than it had ever been before.

"Nothing," said James wearily. "Nothing. They say the governor is considering issuing a warrant for our arrest. But first he requires permission from the army. The country is still under military law."

"So Thackeray has the final say," said Gavin.

"Yes. He and his staff. Most probably they would make a joint decision."

"Well. They left us to bury your grandfather by ourselves yesterday," said Gavin.

"Maybe we did need him and his advice around a little longer."

"Well," said von Brand, getting up cheerfully. "If there's nothing to be done, we may as well have a drink. I presume Morgan's Bay still has a stack of alcohol?"

"Yes. Yes, that hasn't run out," said Gavin.

"When they come and get us, we may as well be drunk," said von Brand on his way to the bar.

He came back with the whisky bottle and poured each of them

a glass. They drank in silence. James stood looking out of the back window of the morning room. He could see the mountain.

"We came a long way," he said.

No one answered.

"That was a good holiday," said Gavin, looking out the other direction across the bay at the schooner. There was silence again.

"Do you remember, James, when you first found gold with Rhys?" asked von Brand.

"Yes."

"Michael died looking for the stuff," said von Brand.

"Don't be morbid," said Gavin. "Have another drink."

"How can you be frivolous?" asked James.

"Because this whole damn business has become so serious," said Gavin, "that all there is left to us is to be frivolous. We tried and failed. Now we drink and crack jokes."

They lapsed into silence.

"Here they come," said James. "It's a military carriage. I suppose treason is more in the province of the military."

They heard the carriage stop in the courtyard behind the house. Gavin stayed looking out to sea and Willie remained in his chair. He drank slowly, as did Gavin.

"Well, that does it," said James. "They've sent Gilham."

"The servants will let him in," said Gavin.

They waited. A few minutes later, the servant opened the door and let Gilham into the room. He was in full uniform with his hat cradled in his arm. He looked to them and they smiled at him weakly.

"Now, what's the damn matter with you lot?" he said without coming further into the room.

"That depends upon you," said James.

"Aren't you going to offer me a drink? You've all got glasses in your hands."

"Whisky?" asked Willie.

"Definitely. Now, I'll tell you something. I don't care a damn whether one of you sold Mauser ammunition to the Boers. I can show you incompetence in the British High Command that has done more permanent harm to England than any bullets could ever have done. What I like are men. Men with guts, courage and ability. What I like to see is a man ten years older than me going up a vertical cliff when I thought my own lungs were going to burst. I like to see a man without experience face a whole bloody army and not run away. I like farmers who win the Victoria Cross. And I like men who are men in the eyes of the enemy so the enemy will perjure themselves for their sake. So does Farrow. He saw you fight. He didn't have to believe a newspaper. There will be no arrest, no inquiries. Thackeray has quashed the whole damn thing. That's what I've come to tell you."

a beam of sunlight played directly onto the back of James Carregan's head through the sliver of stained glass window half way up the great wall of the cathedral. Red bricks, the walls, fluted on the pillars, taller than the eye could see without craning the head. And high up there was the dome and its world of morning sunlight, above them all, a definition of purity, a dome of goodness.

The cathedral was as silent as a tomb. Not even the well-dressed children scuffed their feet. Little Bertie Grantham, pageboy, watched his sister and bit his lip for fear of noise. In the aisles behind stood many people, a full cathedral, uniforms, morning suits, dresses with hats. Emily Hargreaves was crying, but then she always did at weddings, soundlessly. The Dean of Cape Town watched them waiting. He held the only key to movement. In the front pew, General Farrow watched without expression. Little Mary Grantham, bridesmaid, wanted to giggle, but was too overawed to open her mouth. The choir – small boys and big ones, ties frilled with black tickling their chins, white surplices down to their dirty shoes that were not meant to show, the big brass cross away on their right – waited in the gallery above, well-trained and ready to give their souls in song.

"Who giveth this woman?"

"I do," said Gilham.

"Will you, Sonja, take this man James to be your lawful wedded husband?"

"I will."

"Will you, James, take this woman Sonja to be your lawful wedded wife?"

"I will."

The dean held out his hand for the ring and Gavin stepped forward and held it out resting gently upon its cushion of plush red velvet. The dean took the ring and gave it to James, who placed it on Sonny's finger.

"With this ring I thee wed."

"In the name of the Father, the Son and the Holy Ghost, I pronounce you man and wife."

James and Sonny stood up together and mounted the three carpeted steps and walked towards the two cushions set below the altar, with the great, brass cross high above and watching, the dome of light above still further. They kneeled, his left hand holding her right, apart except for this, him praying, her wondering whether she should pray in a Christian church and then deciding it didn't matter and giving her heartfelt thanks for man's humanity, the integrity of a few and their power to do good as well as bad. Dressed in white, her black hair, parted in the middle, just sweeping the top of her brow on both sides and framing the olive skin and the long, graceful and slightly tilted nose that was truly Semitic. James in morning dress, great red carnation, hair just thinning slightly, face beaten hard by the sun, but chiselled. Shoulders square and tight fitting with the cloth, showing the shape of shoulder blades and a strong, tough back.

The power of sound came back to the organ. Soft, so soft at first, not wishing to break that one held moment in time, and then swelling. Johann Sebastian Bach. Swelling to the fluted pillars that drew it up to the heights of grace, ran the notes around the dome and then sent them back again to wash the people, embalm their souls for a fleeting moment and let them feel the purity of goodness.

Gavin drew in this feeling and understood a little more of life. The relief at deliverance was still very much part of everything he did, and so this new feeling was made part of this as well. He glanced at Gilham next to him, who nodded, and they turned and marched back towards their pew, where the bridesmaid and pageboy were sitting fidgeting either side of their mother. Gilham, his sandy hair and drooping moustache immaculately groomed, the medals making a slight jingle on his chest, the sword held firmly at the hilt by his left hand, acting the part he knew best of all as Colonel of the Sixth, Ninth Queen Charlottes. Every officer in his regiment watched him carefully from their pews, but none of them could find a fault in his scarlet dress or the measured step which took him back to his pew.

The choir sang and the music rose and with it the people, who watched the bride and groom, his relations and their friends, as they moved slowly towards the small show of light at the end of the one great aisle. The dean smiled as was his custom and the press used cameras as much on Gavin Morgan and Willie von Brand as they did on the groom. Then the sunlight of a new summer came into their eyes and the bells were pealing, tumbling over themselves, and the four great carriages were waiting, horses' hooves clicking at the cobbled street. The carriage springs gave as James helped Sonny into the first carriage and faced the horses. Gilham and Gavin got in and sat opposite, smiling now, and the rice began to fall around their heads. The coachman, splendid in his livery, took up his tall whip, cracked it gently at the leading horse and the wheels went round, drawn by the four black horses with tails trimmed and rhythm in their feet. Everyone smiled. Ester, Oswald, their two children and Farrow came next, drawn by two horses. Then von Brand, his wife, Louise and Sarah, with Lagrange on the dicky seat. Finally, in the last coach, Roger Quinn, Lillian, Commodore Wilkins and the Dean of Cape Town.

The carriages turned down St George's Street and made their

way towards the harbour, the *Cape of Good Hope* and the reception at Morgan's Bay. The morning sky was blue, quite perfectly blue.

THE SAILS CRACKED and took in the wind. Sonny stood at the bow with James and watched the prow push out into the sea, the froth of its own wake going out behind. "With this wind behind us we'll reach the house before the other guests," said James.

"Our luck has changed."

"Yes. I think it has. Are you cold?"

"No, James, and I don't want ever to be again."

"I'M damn sure it's not etiquette," said Gilham, who had hung his sword on the rope hook next to the centre mast, "but if we're on this confounded piece of equipment that is more suited to the navy for an hour, we should at least be allowed to drink."

"I think, Colonel," said von Brand, "that I have the answer. I've stowed away two dozen bottles. Heidsieck Dry Monopole, '93. Gavin, be kind enough to ask the skipper to lower some of that sail. The longer we take to get there, the more time we'll have to drink."

Von Brand collected four of the bottles and Gavin and Lagrange brought out the glasses. The corks were fired over the stern, well away, as Gavin said, from the bride and groom so as not to disturb them.

"Just as well there's only a steady breeze," said Gavin as he handed round the drinks.

Finally, he had given everyone a glass. "To the bride and groom," said General Farrow and they all raised their glasses and drank.

"I definitely like these receptions before receptions," said von Brand as he poured himself another glass of champagne, drank it quizzically and topped it up again for good measure.

. . .

THE FIRST GUESTS had arrived and the house at Morgan's Bay was beginning to fill. The string section of the Cape Town Symphony Orchestra was playing Mozart and waiters were offering the first glasses of champagne. The eleven o'clock sun of the late spring was warm but not too hot. A fresh but gentle breeze came up to them from the sea and the washing of the waves could be heard above the quieter moments of the music. The conductor, immaculate in tails, faced the musicians, who were spread in a semi-circle on the right hand side of the vast veranda. An awning flapped softly above them and their sheet music was pegged to their stands. The woodwind sat silently, as did the brass and percussion. The conductor kept looking over his shoulder, out to sea. As he looked back, his eyes caressed the slopes of the mountains and the great cliffs. Guests gathered at the other end of the veranda and the music held them silent. A murmur broke out behind him and he looked again out to sea. Rounding the head under full sail, the *Cape of Good Hope* made a picture to rival the music. In the prow of the boat he could see the bride's white dress. Gently, he fluttered the Mozart into silence, held them for a moment and then drew them into Wagner. The music went out towards the schooner, washing the sea with its soul. The guests waited, spellbound, as the schooner and the music drew closer together.

"WHAT IS THAT MUSIC?" asked Sonny.

"Wagner," said James. "*Lohengrin*. The wedding music. Gavin managed to engage the string section of the Cape Town Symphony Orchestra."

Sonny looked up at the white sails and back at Morgan's Bay, the house, the people waiting and the orchestra playing music that wrung the very sinews of her feeling.

"I'm going to cry," she said.

"Cry into my shoulder."

James stood there with the woman he had known for eight years and who now was his wife, the future of his name and people, and the music drew them across the water. Behind him, no one spoke. The music of Wagner wrapped itself round the very sails as they came into anchor and lowered the dinghies and the bride was handed down and rowed ashore. As they came to land, the music faded to its finish and the guests clapped. As the bride set foot upon the wooden jetty, the conductor brought out the first bars of the overture to *Tannhäuser*.

"Damn funny way of getting to a reception," said Gilham in the second boat, and the guests within hearing laughed and the waiters began to circulate on shore.

"THEY SAY that that man Grant has left the country," said Gilham. "No one would employ him. Do you know where he went, Sarah?"

"I have no idea, colonel."

"Oh well. No matter. Can't know everyone's plans. Thought you might. Now, Anders? What happened to him? Don't like the type, meself."

"After seeing pictures of Farrow at the wedding," said Gavin, "he may go back to England."

"Damn good of the General. Underestimated him, meself. No accounting. Well, Oswald," he said, turning to Grantham, who was also in full dress uniform, "are you looking forward to going back to England? We'll have missed the hunting and shooting seasons but we'll still be in time for the Derby and Ascot. You going to live in Cheshire?"

"Yes. James has made Halmeston over to me. Damn good of him. Should be able to keep up the tone of the regiment from a place like that."

"Heard the damn place was full of artificial battlements?"

"James says those can come down."

"Good show. Your wife like the idea? Damn fine woman."

"Yes. She likes it.

"Damn fine reception, what? Like the music. Prefer a brass band."

"You can't have everything," said von Brand.

"Damn right, you can't."

"Ah. There's that man Lagrange. Fine job in the Drakensberg. Now that took courage. Shot through the arm. No damn fun with a ball through your arm. Happened to me on the North West frontier. One of those damn skirmishes. Hear he's looking after Morgan's Bay, Gavin, while you're away. Now, what takes you from the Cape?"

"Firstly, I have to sort out my mother's affairs."

"Didn't know you had one."

"Yes. James found her for me."

"Damn considerate of him."

"And then there's all that gold we're supposed to have collected," he said with a laugh. "I thought I'd find a buyer in England."

"On which boat are you sailing?" asked Louise.

"*The Annabel*," said James.

"Sarah's travelling on that one, too. How strange."

"Yes. Isn't it," answered Gavin Morgan.

~

PRINCIPAL CHARACTERS

∼

The Carregans

James — Joint owner of Carregan Shipping
Captain Carregan — James Carregan's grandfather
Ester — James's sister
Ernest — James's father

Other Characters

Annabel Crichton — Rhys Morgan's lover and wife to Edgar Crichton
Bertie Grantham — Ester and Oswald's son
Bethany Dalton — A forty-nine-year-old English woman visiting Cape Town
Captain Hugo Dalton — Bethany's husband who died in a motor car accident
Captain Jack Hall — A member of James's commando
Carel Viljoen — A guerrilla Boer commander
Chris O'Connor — An Irish mine captain
Christiaan De Jong — A Boer commander

Emily Hargreaves — Virginia Webb's best friend

Gavin Morgan — Rhys Morgan's natural son and joint owner of Carregan Shipping

General Farrow — A British commander

Hanneli — Koos van der Walt's wife

Johanna — Christiaan De Jong's wife held in a concentration camp

Kevin Grant — The skipper of the *Cape of Good Hope*

Kinsley Crichton — Annabel and Edgar's son

Koos van der Walt — A Boer solider in the Pioneer Corps and friend of James

Lieutenant Colonel the Honourable John Gilham — Colonel of the Sixth, Ninth Queen Charlottes

Lieutenant Jasper Crichton — Annabel and Edgar's son

Lieutenant Roger Quinn — An officer in the Sixth Queen Charlottes and a member of James's Mashonaland Horse

Lillian Dalton — Bethany and Hugo's Daughter

Louise Lagrange — Phillip's seventeen-year-old sister

Michael Fentan — James Carregan and von Brand's late partner an brother to Sonny

Owen Anders — War correspondent for the *Daily Herald*

Phillip Lagrange — Gavin Morgan's school friend

Sonny (Sonja) Fentan — Michael Fentan's sister

The Honourable Oswald Grantham — Ester's husband

Virginia Webb — An English nurse who travelled to Cape Town

Wilkins — Commodore of Carregan Shipping

Willie von Brand — Pioneer Corps's scout and James Carregan's business partner

HISTORICAL FIGURES

∼

il *John Rhodes* — co-founder of the southern African territory of
ɔdesia (now Zimbabwe and Zambia), which the British South
rica Company named after him in 1895

Dr Leander Starr Jameson — was for a time an inDuna of one
Lobengula's regiments as well the leader of the infamous *Jameson Raid* in South Africa

Frederick Courteney Selous — was a British explorer who agreed to
be a guide for the Pioneer Column

King Lobengula — king of the Matabele people and son of Mzilikazi

Major Allan Wilson — an officer in the Pioneer Corps and leader of
the Shangani Patrol

DEAR READER

~

views are the most powerful tools in our kitty when it comes to
.ing attention for Peter's books. This is where you can come in, as
by providing an honest review you will help bring them to the
attention of other readers.

If you enjoyed reading *Carregan's Catch,* and have five minutes to
spare, we would really appreciate a review (it can be as short as you
like). Your help in spreading the word and keeping Peter's work
alive is gratefully received.

Please post your review on the retailer site where you purchased
this book.

Thank you so much.
Heather Stretch (Peter's daughter)

PS. We look forward to you joining Peter's growing band of avid
readers.

ACKNOWLEDGEMENTS

~

With grateful thanks to our *VIP First Readers* for reading *Carregan's Catch* prior to its official launch date. They have been fabulous in picking up errors and typos helping us to ensure that your own reading experience of *Carregan's Catch* has been the best possible. Their time and commitment is particularly appreciated.

Agnes Mihalyfy (United Kingdom)
Andy Gentle (United Kingdom)
Daphne Rieck (Australia)
Hilary Jenkins (South Africa)

Thank you.

Kamba Publishing

Printed in Great Britain
by Amazon